Bad Luck Good Luck

🌴

Roy Paul Shields

Copyright © 2017 Roy Paul Shields.

All rights reserved. No part of this book may be used or reproduced by any means, graphic, electronic, or mechanical, including photocopying, recording, taping or by any information storage retrieval system without the written permission of the author except in the case of brief quotations embodied in critical articles and reviews.

Archway Publishing books may be ordered through booksellers or by contacting:

Archway Publishing
1663 Liberty Drive
Bloomington, IN 47403
www.archwaypublishing.com
1 (888) 242-5904

Because of the dynamic nature of the Internet, any web addresses or links contained in this book may have changed since publication and may no longer be valid. The views expressed in this work are solely those of the author and do not necessarily reflect the views of the publisher, and the publisher hereby disclaims any responsibility for them.

Any people depicted in stock imagery provided by Thinkstock are models, and such images are being used for illustrative purposes only. Certain stock imagery © Thinkstock.

This is a work of fiction. All of the characters, names, incidents, organizations, and dialogue in this novel are either the products of the author's imagination or are used fictitiously.

ISBN: 978-1-4808-5484-0 (sc)
ISBN: 978-1-4808-5482-6 (hc)
ISBN: 978-1-4808-5483-3 (e)

Library of Congress Control Number: 2017918537

Print information available on the last page.

Archway Publishing rev. date: 1/8/2018

Contents

Prologue v
Chapter One 1
Chapter Two 9
Chapter Three 14
Chapter Four 18
Chapter Five 23
Chapter Six 28
Chapter Seven 35
Chapter Eight 42
Chapter Nine 50
Chapter Ten 57
Chapter Eleven 63
Chapter Twelve 70
Chapter Thirteen 78
Chapter Fourteen 86
Chapter Fifteen 93
Chapter Sixteen 98
Chapter Seventeen 106
Chapter Eighteen 113
Chapter Nineteen 121
Chapter Twenty 128
Chapter Twenty-One 133
Chapter Twenty-Two 138

Chapter Twenty-Three 145
Chapter Twenty-Four 151
Chapter Twenty-Five 158
Chapter Twenty-Six 167
Chapter Twenty-Seven 172
Chapter Twenty-Eight 179
Chapter Twenty-Nine 186
Chapter Thirty 195
Chapter Thirty-One 202
Chapter Thirty-Two 208
Chapter Thirty-Three 214
Chapter Twenty-Two 219
Chapter Thirty-Four 221
Chapter Thirty-Five 225
About the Author 231

Prologue

Stephen Christian and his six-year-old son Scott pulled up and parked in their driveway. Shirley, Scott's mom, and ten-year-old sister Stacey came running out of the house for welcome home hugs. Stephen was a survival instructor for the USMC. He had been taking Scott out for survival training since he was four years old. They had shared many weekends in hot and cold climates. At six years old, Scott could handle just about any survival situation.

Shirley told Stephen the unexpected good news. Their house had been on the market less than a week and buyers put earnest money in escrow Friday. Stephen let out a hip- hip hooray! They had been planning an ocean adventure in their forty foot Jeanneau Sun Odyssey 409 sailboat for the past year. They had been accumulating all of the essentials it may take to be on the ocean for up to four months.

Their plans were to sail to Hawaii to resupply for a long journey. From Hawaii, they planned to explore and visit islands in the south pacific. From there they would sail to Australia. They would sell their boat in Australia and go exploring until they were ready to return to the states. They had shipped supplies to Hawaii for the possibly four months at sea. Stephen figured up to sixty days to sail to Hawaii and from there up to four months to make it to the south pacific.

Their forty footer had been custom built to accommodate such an adventure. Food and water were the two most important essentials. Their boat, the Gigo-Gigo was equipped with fiberglass water tanks that would hold enough drinking water only to last four people six months. They had a food supply from Mountain House that had a life span of twenty-five years and would feed four people for six months. They had two sets of extra sails and Stephen had survival gear for almost any situation.

They set sail from Glorietta Bay Marina in San Diego, California the last week of April. They had taken the Gigo-Gigo for many shake down cruises in all kinds of weather. Stephen even had a small Honda generator with enough fuel to make sure they would always have charged up batteries. Shirley was a registered nurse and ex schoolteacher, Stacey, and Scott would have classes every day, weather permitting. They had been out to sea a month when they encountered the first bad weather. A two day squall gave them a rough ride; Stephen had put a sea anchor out which kept them heading into the waves.

When the weather broke, there was no damage to their boat but it took them a couple days longer to reach Hawaii. They docked in a pre-determined area and had supplies that they had previously shipped there quickly loaded. They had been to Hawaii on vacation so more sightseeing wasn't necessary. Stephen checked every square inch of their boat and they were ready to head for the open sea.

Stephen entertained them singing "Sailing-Sailing" and "Barnacle Bill the Sailor" as they cleared the harbor and headed for the open sea. They hit bad weather about a month at sea. It was a scary storm with lightning lighting the sky and huge waves. Their boat was made to take on rough seas but it was a bouncy ride. By morning the sea had calmed down a hard rain began to fall.

It was Stephen's first chance to hook up the rain catcher and show his family how simple it was to use. They captured enough rain to refill their water tanks and take an open-air fresh shower thanks to the heavy rainfall. Day after day on a forty foot boat could get very boring; But not on the Gigo-Gigo. Between on board school classes five days a week and everyone taking care of assigned chores, card games and taking turns at the helm, boredom was not allowed. They were going on their third month at sea and the only sight of human life was they saw a couple of merchant ships off in the distance. The weather had been near perfect and they were about two weeks out from reaching the first island on their adventure. They had a dreaded three days for anyone on a sailing ship, as there was absolutely no wind. Stephen made sure everything was absolutely secure and he seemed a bit nervous. They had been out of radio contact for several days now.

Scott's Story

Chapter One

The calm became a light wind that increased through the night. It was a strong wind but nothing dangerous as we cut through the water for the next few days. That night Dad stayed up as the wind increased. He pulled the sails down and we all knew it was getting serious when he got us up and put our life jackets on. Waves were beginning to not just break over our boat, but were crashing down on us. Dad herded us into the cabin, as we had to hold on for dear life. It seemed like our boat was lifted clear of the water and we seemed to roll a couple of times. I somehow managed to grab the light fixture on the cabin roof and the noise was deafening. It seemed like I was rolled and tossed and I held on to the light fixture for dear life.

    I am not sure if I lost consciousness or fell asleep but when I opened my eyes the sea had calmed down and it was turning daylight. I was lying on top of part of the cabin roof. I was alone. I didn't see our boat, my mom and dad or sister. Fortunately, the section of roof I was on was foam sandwiched between fiberglass panels. It began to rain; I mean pour! I took my shoes off to catch rain and lay on my back with my mouth open. I must have been totally exhausted as I fell asleep. I thought I was dreaming when I woke up; I had washed up on a beach, a very deserted beach. I wanted to cry but remembered dad telling me when one cries they are wasting energy they may need. I scanned the ocean and that is all I saw; Ocean and a lot of it.

I had no idea of the time but knew I was very hungry. I dragged the roof section farther up on the beach to keep it out of high tide. I was definitely on an island that was heavy in vegetation. As I looked around I saw a treasure; Coconuts. I used one to crack another but It been on the ground too long and was no good. The fourth one I cracked was good, I will always remember how wonderful the milk tasted, and I ate every bit of the meat. As I walked up the beach, I found various things from our boat but nothing that would help me. Just up ahead the beach ended and rocks jutted out into the ocean. As I got closer to the rocks my childish prayers were somewhat answered. Lodged in the rocks was the ice chest from our boat. I dragged it up on the beach and opened it. Everything was salvageable but wouldn't be in another day except the canned meat mom had put in there. I ate as much as I could of the perishables. There was enough salvageable food to last me ten days if rationed it. It was beginning to get dark and there was no way I was going to try to sleep in the jungle. I was about out of steam and it was getting darker. There was a place in the rocks where it was sandy, and that is where I decided to spend the night. The only comfort I had was knowing I had food to keep me going while I explored to see if there were people on this island. I did sleep through the night and woke up to a good sign, I was hungry.

I climbed to the top of the rock pile and it looked like a rocky shoreline as far as I could see. I did think I saw some possible wreckage from our boat. It would take me forever climbing up and down the rocky shoreline. I had made up my mind, I was going to have to try to explore the jungle coast line. I took a can of canned meat out of the cooler and luckily, it had a key to open it. A lesson learned can be a lifesaver for sure. Thanks to my dad I walked along the edge of the jungle when sure enough, I found what must be a game trail into the jungle. It had to be small animals using this trail, as the trail was very small. It was hot and humid and so far, all I found was more jungle. I was about ready to head back when I thought I heard and smelled water. About seventy-five more feet and I found a treasure for sure. A small stream bubbled across a mossy gravel bed. I lay on my belly and drank until I couldn't drink any more.

I had eaten the canned meat several hours ago and knew I had better beat feet back to the safety of the rocks. I ate what I could of the perishable food in the chest, as it was getting dark. The humidity and struggling along the game trail was the perfect sleep remedy. I was sound asleep until the sun woke me up. I had to get a game plan. So much of what my dad had taught me raced through my head. Of course, I hoped humans would discover me and get me out of here. But, what if there were no humans here? Then I had better think about what I must do to survive until I was rescued. I remembered that we had only seen two big ships off in the distance our entire journey so far. There was no way I could make it through the jungle without chopping my way through; that meant I needed a machete or something similar. Sure, let's see, I will run over to the hardware store and get one. Dream on!

My only choice of survival was to find a safe place to build a shelter and figure out a food source. I knew where fresh water was and I had coconuts, but it would take more than that to survive. If I didn't try to hurry, I would have a lot of rocks to climb over but it was my safest way to head up the island. I knew by the rising and setting of the sun that would take me south. I could carry four cans of food from the cooler in my pockets and two bottles of Gatorade. I would have to rely on coconuts and their milk. By the time I needed to call it a day, I had made about a hundred yards of hard scrambling through the rocks. There was a tall rock outcropping about a quarter mile up the beach. I didn't set any land speed records, but three days of tedious picking my way and I finally made it to the base of the highest rock elevation. I was scratched up and tired. I found a sandy spot and had a coconut and milk for dinner. I had been lucky so far; the days were hot and muggy; but the nights were cool. I wondered what the seasons were here.

I woke up early, which was good as I had some climbing to do. It seemed to take forever to finally get to the top and it was beginning to get dark. I was going to have to sleep sitting up, as there were no flat places in the rocks. The only good thing about exertion was I could sleep in almost any position. It was getting light and a light sprinkle was actually welcomed. I found a place where the fresh water was trickling down the rocks and filled an empty Gatorade bottle. The morning sun broke through and I thought here we go. As I gazed towards the south I thought I saw something white. I had water and one can of food left. It looked like very rough going to get to where I thought I saw something white. Well I wasn't getting anyplace just thinking about it. Two days later and I had to make a decision; I was out of food and almost out of water. It was hard to tell, I thought I was maybe a day away from what I thought I saw. Do I gamble? I had lost track of time; I was a long way from my meager food supply.

I could head for the jungle and coconuts; or gamble that I could get to whatever the white was I thought I saw. My dad's words rang in my ears; the coconuts were a sure thing. No matter what, survival was first. It took over a half a day but it was worth it. I drank the milk from three coconuts and ate one. There were all kinds of sandy places to sleep in the rocks. Unreal! The bright sun woke me up. I filled my pockets with coconut meat and drank the milk until I was full. I took a coconut with me for the milk and headed out across the rock pile. As I climbed the last pile of rocks, I heard a funny noise and as I climbed to the top of the rocks, I just sat there and cried. Wedged in the rocks was a battered Gigo-Gigo. It was low tide and it was almost entirely out of the water. One thing for sure; It would never sail again. As I climbed down towards it I was almost afraid of what I would find; or wouldn't find. What would I do if I found my mom or dad or my sisters body? I sat and cried until I had no cry left.

The aft of the boat was under water; Three fourths of the boat was out of the water because it was low tide. I checked to make sure the boat was secure in the rocks before I attempted to climb aboard; it rocked slightly but seemed securely wedged. As I climbed over the side of the boat I almost cried again; everything seemed damaged. I had to be careful, as everything seemed slippery. The main cabin door was gone. My mom and sister had been in the cabin with me when I was washed out of the boat through the roof that was torn off. All three members of my family were gone. I gazed out at the ocean and thought maybe they were lucky and had made it to shore and were on the island somewhere. Food, water and weapons were my first concern. Both fresh water tanks were intact and were about a fourth full. I made it to the front of the cabin to the storage area; there were four full cartons of survival food plus two full sets of extra sails, extra rope and a small Honda generator with five gallons of gas. It had all been securely fastened and survived. Wrong! As I moved the generator, one side was destroyed.

My dad's AK47 and .40 caliber Glock and hunting knife were wet but salvageable along with an abundance of ammunition. It took me the rest of the day to get the weapons and two cartons of food ashore. I made it back to the boat just before dark. I had laid blankets out on the rocks and they were thankfully dry as the air was too cool to be comfortable without the blankets. I woke up to a windy much cooler day. It was a good thing I found a place near the top of the rocks to sleep; High tide and come in and receded and the boat had slipped back maybe three feet. It was not as stable as it was yesterday. I was able to get the remaining cartons of food ashore, along with the extra sails and rope. I had worked much longer that I realized and the tide had been coming in and the boat was rocking more than it had before. I found a backpack and filled it with cooking utensils and a box of candles. I found a framed picture of my family and me; I wanted to cry but the boat was rocking and I had to hold on until I was able to get off. The tide seemed higher and I had to be extremely careful until I made it back to shore.

Fortunately, I had grabbed the blankets on my way to the beach; there was no way I could make it back to where I had slept the night before. A wind driven rain came in suddenly; I unrolled one of the sails, covered everything and tied it securely. I opened one of the boxes of food and ate a much welcomed dinner of cold beef stew. It tasted like the best meal I could ever remember. It was a good thing I had dragged everything up the beach as far as I did as the wind and storm had the surf within ten feet of where I spent the night. I finished off the can of stew for breakfast and headed back for the Gigo-Gigo. The storm had turned the boat around and it was two thirds submerged with the aft sticking out of the water. The rudder had broken loose and was barely hanging. I needed the metal from the rudder. I made it back to shore and got the hacksaw, hammer and chisel in my dad's toolbox I had salvaged.

As I began to saw the three brackets holding the rudder, the boat shifted slightly. There was no doubt the Gigo-Gigo was heading for Davey Jones locker. I was sawing on the third bracket when the hacksaw blade broke. The boat had shifted again and it was slowly disappearing into the water. I had to chance it and used the hammer and chisel, and finally broke the last bracket. I dragged the rudder higher up on the rocks and began tediously making my way to shore. It was tough going as it took both of my hands to carry the rudder. By the time I made it back to my temporary camp I was hurting and wanted to lay down and cry. It was as if I could hear my dad tell me to get up and not be a wimp. My entire desire was always to have my dad proud of me. I had thrown a bunch of clothes up on the rocks to dry. I actually found myself smiling as I thought if I wasn't found I would wind up wearing a skirt made out of palm fronds. I had a can of cold chicken noodle soup as a stormy night made it difficult to fall sleep. I woke up in the morning as I was too warm under the canvas; I peeked out and It was a bright sunny morning. I had a coconut and milk for breakfast and headed back for the boat.

The clothes I had laid out on the rocks were there but the Gigo-Gigo was gone. There were still things I wanted to salvage; but I had the most important things safely on shore. I gathered up the clothes and headed back for shore. It was difficult to get the lay of the land standing on the beach. I had no choice; I was going to have to go inland and explore. I made sure all of my salvaged items were safe and secure. I put several days' supplies in the backpack, picked up my weapons and headed back to the game trail where I found the fresh water. Once again, my dad's words rang in my ears. Preparedness was the first essential for survival. It took all day but I had rearranged what supplies I had closer to the game trail. I looked at the picture of my family; it had been water damaged but once dried was my greatest treasure. The next morning I had cold chicken and dumplings for breakfast. It was a struggle but I finally got the rudder, hacksaw with extra blades, file, hammer, and chisel back to the little fresh water stream.

It took most of the day but I finally cut a piece off of the rudder about thirty inches long and about three inches wide and only broke one blade. Once back to my supply area I decided, I wanted a warm meal. I used a shoelace and made a bow; there was a tree that must have been hit by lightning as it was dead and full of powder-like, fine sawdust. I cut a wood, top and bottom, block. It didn't take long and a little smoke began to show. I added more of the powder, a little twigs, and there we go; I had fire. I had warm spaghetti and meatball for dinner sitting beside a nice warm fire. I stoked the fire and got the first comfortable night's sleep since being washed up on the shore. I even had a warm breakfast of vegetable soup and crackers. I spent the day by the little stream filing on the metal I had cut from the rudder. By the end of the next day, I had a homemade machete complete with a comfortable bamboo handle.

Chapter Two

The next morning I found a tall tree I was sure that I could climb and maybe get an idea if the island was flat or what. I was winded and pooped by the time I had climbed as high as I thought safe. There was some hills maybe a half mile to the northeast. That was a good sign except it was dense jungle all of the way. I thought I could probably make it to the highest spot in four to five days. It would be quicker getting back as I was sure I would have to cut my way through the jungle to get to the high ground but I would have a somewhat clear path to get back. I would go for it tomorrow. My heart raced as I thought I heard an airplane; I found an area to where I could see the sky and saw a jet that was just barely a speck. Just the sound of the jet brought a smile. That was the first sound related to human beings I had heard since "arriving" on the island. I stocked the backpack with what I figured was at least eight days of supplies in case my exploring took longer.

    I was up early the next morning and got an early start. I wouldn't have made it a hundred feet without my machete. It was hot slow going but I was making headway. I had made a hammock out of a piece of one of the sails. Dad's tool chest had produced just what the doctor ordered; A grommet kit. There was no way I was sleeping on the ground. I had seen two snakes since stranded on the island. One not large but looked menacing; the other was a big rascal, probably a boa constrictor. By the end of the third day if I hadn't made it this far I would have turned around and went back. On the fifth day, I stood on top of the highest hill. I went one step farther and climbed a tree. The island was pear shaped and I guessed maybe four miles long and two mile wide at the widest. The entire island was covered with what looked like a sea of green.

It was going to be a chore but I decided to build my camp on top of this hill. I could see the sea that surrounded the island. I would build a big fire pit that was ready to light in case a ship came close enough to maybe see the smoke. As I was cutting my way through the jungle, I had seen three different things that looked like maybe it was some kind of fruit. I even saw what looked to be a small deer like animal that scared me as I must have scared it as it crashed through the jungle. I would gather samples on the way back to the beach and experiment to, first and foremost, see if they were poisonous. My precious food supply wasn't going to last forever; I almost cried as I thought I may spend my entire life on this island alone. My dad's words were ringing in my ears again; be prepared! It was a lot easier going getting back to the beach. Two of the three samples I brought back to the beach were somewhat sweet and tasted all right. The third one was tart and no doubt not something to eat. Just to be safe, it took all of the next day nibbling on the two I gambled on to find they were safe to eat.

As I looked out across the ocean, I had to laugh; I had an ocean full of seafood; I wasn't going to starve. I walked a way down the beach and in the process dug up six clams. No problem gathering seaweed. I wrapped the clams in the seaweed and set it them around the edge of the fire. I warmed a package of dried mixed vegetables and had a warm gourmet meal of steamed clams and vegetables. I had a game plan; I would begin packing my supplies up to the hill where I decided to build a more permanent camp. I realized that since I washed up on the beach it was almost like my mom and dad were with me. Dad had thankfully taught me so much about survival and mom had taught me a lot about cooking. I knew for a fact, I was only six years old but there was no doubt I could give lessons in survival thanks to dad. Crabs were in abundance on the beach. I was going to steam one and see if it was edible. I had all of the fishing gear off of the boat but had a lot of work to do before I would take time to fish. I sharpened my machete and packed for tomorrow.

I awoke to a heavy downpour; it was raining so hard I couldn't see ten feet. About the time I wondered what I would do today it stopped raining as quickly as it had started. That took care of my day of rest. I had found a water soaked calendar on the boat of which I had dried. I had lost track of how long I had been on the island and took a researching guess. I was sure it was about forty-five or fifty days. I had salvaged three packages of computer copy paper and a box of pencils and several ballpoint pens that belonged to my mom. I would use the calendar to keep track of time and write a daily ledger. In the meantime, head to what I would call "my home on the hill". It took most of the day to get to the hill. It is almost unreal how fast things grow in the tropics; I had to use my machete to keep the path clear. I found a neat place to hang my hammock and began searching for the perfect place to build a one-room structure. I had to laugh when I climbed in the hammock for the night; this was my first night in my new home away from my beach home.

My mom had schooled me in many important things that we used or needed throughout our lives. I knew how to measure with the tape measure from my dad's tool assortment. I found four trees that would give me a twelve by sixteen one room ten feet off the ground. Yes, I guess you could call it a tree house. It took almost a week to clear the area under where I would build my one roomer. Nothing I cut would go to waste; I used the three and four inch diameter trees for cross struts that would eventually support the floor. I built a ladder of which I would raise every night when I called it a night. Getting my beach supplies to my home on the hill took a lot longer than I figured; but I did have to laugh as every couple of days I put the machete to good use. There is no doubt that if I didn't keep the trail opened it would be completely overgrown in two weeks.

Almost everything on my house had to be notched and tied. The spool of nylon rope I salvaged had two hundred and fifty feet of rope on it. I unraveled it for what I needed for tying my house together. I got four strands of eighth inch rope out of the half-inch rope. All work and no play don't get it. I decided to catch a couple of crabs, boil them, and hope. Mixed vegetables and crab for dinner made me smile. I was glad there were a lot of crabs running around the beach; between the crabs and clams, I was in as my dad would say, "Hog heaven". It was taking a lot longer to build my tree house than I had figured on. I celebrated with a seafood dinner and a drink made from the edible fruit that was in abundance. I was one thankful guy when I put the last of the palm fronds on the roof. Next, I built a bed frame, a table, and two chairs. Why two chairs? Wishful thinking I suppose. I had been on the island about six months when I had my official house warming.

I had salvaged six packages of vegetable seeds mom had packed in the ice chest; There were a lot more packages but they had gotten wet and weren't salvageable. There were three squash, two broccolis and one turnip. The four potatoes that hadn't rotted had sprouts and were questionable. It seemed like everything else grew here; Why not vegetables? Once again, I had no idea of the seasons in this neck of the woods but so far, I couldn't foresee a frost or deep freeze. I was rationing the survival food that I had salvaged off of the boat. How many people get crab for dinner once a week? I do! Between the coconuts, seafood and fruit whatever it was I could survive on just that. I had been thinking of the deer or whatever it was; maybe one of the days I would have venison for dinner. Thinking a garden and making a garden were miles apart. It took over a month to clear an area big enough to plant the garden. I didn't have to worry about irrigation as it rained at least twice a week. Through it all, my roof only had one leak, which was easy to fix. The garden would require a fence. That was almost another month to cut what was needed to finish a security fence around the garden area. I was a happy young man when I sowed the seeds.

Chapter Three

It was almost a year since I washed up on the beach here. It had been a busy year. I was getting close to my seventh birthday. I looked around at my tree house, which was a major accomplishment, and my garden and lawn chairs I had made. I knew there weren't a lot of people who could accomplish what this six year old had accomplished let alone even survived what I had been through. I was proud of my accomplishments. I grew sad as I thought how proud my parents would have been; especially my dad as he had taught me so much about survival. I was probably the luckiest unluckiest six year old in the world, and the loneliest. It had taken a while but I had learned how to rid myself of the loneliness shortcoming; I would start another project or find something to get busy. I even made a couple of flutes out of bamboo, it took trial and error, but I was finally able to get the sounds I was looking for. I did have visitors, there seemed to be two breeds of monkeys.

I learned the hard way to make window closures and keep the door closed when I wasn't there. I had gone to the beach for crabs and when I got home, about five monkeys came bailing out of my house. They had basically turned my place upside down. The bowl of fruit on the table was gone and various things were scattered all over the place. Now that is what I would call mischievous monkey business. I had used dry seaweed to make a mattress which was quite comfortable, that was scattered all over the floor. Luckily, they hadn't torn the cover I had made out of the sail material. I woke up one morning to a strange sound and discovered two of the deer like animals trying to get into my garden. I got the AK, sighted in, and decided against it. I wouldn't kill an animal unless it was badly crippled. The animals were, as was I, only trying to survive. I lucked out as I had planted about thirty potato sprouts and had at least half that were like the rest of the garden, growing rapidly.

    I noticed a large amount of bats every evening when it wasn't raining. They seem to be coming from the north. I decided it was time I began exploring my island home. I had become quite adapt at gauging distance and time it would take to do round trips. The north end of the island seemed to gradually climb and was evidently a lot higher than the hill I was on. I could get to the beach, which would be easy walking until I was across from the higher ground and a lot less jungle to cut my way through. But that wouldn't be near as much exploring as if I headed straight for that area through the jungle. It would be about an eight day round trip, if I took the beach route. It would probably be twelve days or more going through the jungle. I decided on the beach the first time. If I found it interesting enough, I would do the jungle route the next time.

    I woke up the next morning to a funny noise right outside my door. I opened the door carefully and there was a large what I thought was a parrot. I closed the door carefully and got a piece of fruit. I opened the door carefully and it tipped its head and seemed to be jibber jabbering to me. I held the fruit out and it snatched it out of my hand with a set of claws I wouldn't want to tangle with. I talked to it as it quickly put the fruit away. I got another one and same thing; It snatched it out of my hand. It kept tipping its head but never took its eyes off of me. That day as I did some weeding in my garden it flew back a couple of times like it was checking on me. Just for the heck of it I walked towards where I would gather the fruit and it flew around following me. I picked one of the fruit it seemed to like. It flew down to get it and perched in the tree while it ate it. I'll be darned it didn't fly down and perch on a branch and pick another one with those dangerous looking claws. As I turned to head back to my place another smaller one, and not as brightly colored, flew in and perched on the same branch and plucked a piece of fruit. It looked to me like maybe it was a mom and pop

I finally loaded up my backpack and headed up the beach. I had walked and gradually climbed for a few hours. As I topped a little hill I was in for a shock; there was like a large creek flowing into the ocean. That was worth exploring. I worked my way through the jungle for a hundred yards or so trying to stay close to the water. I could barely see what looked like a large pond or lagoon. The ground was getting a little muddy of which I didn't like. As I cut the last bit of green blocking my view, I almost turned and ran. There were at least ten large alligators lying around the perimeter of the lagoon. I found a rock and threw it in the lagoon and almost all of them quickly disappeared under water. Well one thing for sure; I wouldn't be trying to wade across that water even if it were possible. It was dark by the time I got home and I was really glad to get home. My day was the kind of day nightmares are made of. Well how about that, Mr. and Mrs. Polly were sitting on the rail in front of my place! I only had one piece of fruit that they liked so I cut it and gave them each half, which they quickly devoured and flew off in the direction of the fruit trees.

I got a brainstorm. It was just a little farther east to reach the beach on that side of the island. There was no way, nor a good reason to go back on the northwest side of the island. Those gators didn't have to show me that running water and lagoon was theirs. I'll do a scouting trip when I head east through the jungle. I found myself being a lot more watchful even around my place. I figured two or three days to get to the easterly beach as I was probably going to have to machete my way over there. I made it to the beach in two days but my arms were worn out from swinging the machete. I probably made the path wider than was necessary; but I couldn't get those gators out of my mind. Somewhere I had read that there were salt-water gators. I was probably over doing it, but I had brought my hammock along. There was no way I was sleeping on the ground. I did some scouting up the beach the next morning. The ground was much higher on this side of the island. I would rather climb than even think of trying to get across the water on the west side of the mountain. I would head back to my place in the morning and get ready for my next exploratory adventure.

Hiking back was a lot easier as I had little machete work to do. By guess and by golly I was making a map of the island. It was larger than I first imagined. It was beginning to look like it was up to five miles north to south; Probably three and a half miles wide at the widest. I would scout out the high ground to the north. Vegetation was sparser on the high ground; I had to laugh as I thought; I never heard of alligators climbing. This time it would be an easy two-day hike to get to where I would begin exploring. I would take a week's worth of supplies; that would give me three days to explore. I made a fruit run before it got dark as I was out of my and the parrots favorite fruit. I was awakened the next morning by two parrots making more noise than I deserved. I decided to call them Molly and Polly. I gave them each a half piece of the fruit; they gulped it and flew off towards the fruit trees. I was going to have to harvest my garden when I got back. I was going to try drying the crop for future use. I had prepared what I was going to take; I loaded up and sang Hi Ho exploring we will go. It was a great day for hiking as there was a light breeze and a beautiful blue sky.

Chapter Four

I made it to where I had turned around and headed back to my dwelling. I was anxious to begin exploring; I wasn't sure but there seemed to be a very old unused path. I awoke early to what sounded like some shrill screeching noises in the distance. I chuckled and thought, "As long as it wasn't alligators". Coconut meat, milk, and fruit for breakfast and Tally Ho and away I go. I had to roll boulders of all sizes to stay on what seemed to be a path. I was about to stop for a break when I saw what looked to be a small opening to a possible cave. I had salvaged a flashlight and extra batteries from our boat of which I had never used but checked it every so often to make sure the batteries were still up. I got close enough to the opening and turned the flashlight on. Oh boy, it was a cave about the size of a medium sized house. There had to be another opening as there was a constant draft. The smoother parts of the walls were covered in very crude drawings of people and animals. There were bones scattered about including human bones. It had a heavy musty smell and I needed fresh air.

As I stepped out of the cave I heard that shrill screeching a lot closer, As I began to head north again there was a large clear tall grassy area down below. There was a herd of maybe twenty of the animals that looked like deer except they had vertical stripes on their flanks. They were feeding on the tall grass. It looked like there were about a dozen young ones in the herd. All of a sudden, there was that screeching again. I'll call them deer; as whatever it was that screeched all of their heads popped up and I could tell they were skittish. Off to my right was another cave opening; this one was very large compared to the first one I explored. I had only taken a few steps towards it when this thing came running out of the forest. I couldn't believe my eyes; It looked like a miniature tyrannosaurus rex; It ran on its hind legs and caught a young deer in its mouth and ran back into the jungle. We had two digital cameras on our boat but I guess they weren't "digitating" on the bottom of the ocean. I'll call them, what I believe prehistoric animals, T Rexes. The one I saw looked to be about five feet tall. I patted the stock of my dad's AK and thought T Rex, don't try me.

I made it to the opening of the large cave and that solved the bat mystery. It was a huge cave. I shined the flashlight in and it seems the entire cave moved as it was covered with bats. I'd had all of the exploring I wanted for one day and headed back to where my hammock was. I was one hungry young man and splurged as I ate a much-rationed can of stew. I looked the area over for tracks where I was going to sleep and was happy to find no tracks. I loved all wildlife, well almost; alligators and T Rexes weren't on my list to bring home for a pet. I may be young but I am not stupid and slept snuggled up with the AK in my hammock. By sunrise, I was ready to head back home. Yes, I said home. My house in the trees on a deserted island was the only home I had now.

On the way back, I began thinking of the little crystal clear stream that ran over a bed of moss covered rocks. When I had knelt down to get a sample drink I was surprised how cold the water was. Well it was too small for alligators and I had never seen or heard anything that resembled the T Rexes on this side of the high country. I would not hurt or kill anything unless I was in danger. I would explore the stream in hopes of possibly using it for food storage, especially potatoes. As I climbed the ladder to my home,

I remembered my mom would always say as we pulled up in our driveway, "There is no place like home". As I opened my door and looked around, I thought a porch would be really neat. Aha; a new project; the creek and my garden were my top priorities.

I didn't have a clock; so when I was hungry I ate; when I was sleepy I slept. A growling stomach and Polly and Molly let me know that I had slept in. I split a piece of fruit for them and had coconut meat and milk for breakfast. I packed up whatever I thought I might need for my day of exploring and headed for the little stream. I had to do a couple of hours of machete work to get to the stream. I knelt down and took a drink; it was even colder that I remembered. It took about three more hours of machete work and the landscape had turned to mostly lava. The little stream was being fed by two springs that were bubbling up through the lava. I thought that is really strange; cold water coming from a defunct lava bed. But, this was perfect, there was an abundance of various sized lava rocks and I would build like a big box about twenty feet below the springs. I would dig an area about four feet square and about a foot and a half deep of which the box of lava rocks would cover. Then I would make a pipe out of a piece of dried bamboo and use it for a pipe to run some of the spring water over the top of the lava box which would absorb the water and allow it to drain into the box and flow back into the little stream.

Piece of cake huh? It took me five days to dig the pit in the lava that would be covered with the rock box. By the time the project, which I was mighty proud of, was ready to be used I had put two hard weeks building it. But it looked good and worked perfect. I was putting the first load of potatoes in it when I heard a strange loud grunting noise; I looked up just in time to grab the AK and put five rounds into what looked like a big hairy pig with two large teeth on the outside of its mouth. That did unnerve me. Its feet looked like pig's feet so it must be some kind of a pig and it must weigh close to three hundred pounds. My mind began to spin and I had to smile; Hmmm? Pork chops and ham. I hurried back to my place and got my knife and hack saw. I didn't want to butcher it where it lay. I would cut it into two pieces and drag it back to my place on palm fronds. It was dark by the time I got it back to my place. I was one worn out young man; but I couldn't let it lay on the ground until morning. I cut the head off and hoisted the two halves up in the trees in my "front yard". I dragged the head down one of my trails and rolled it down a slight incline. Between this pig, the alligators and the T Rex, I wasn't sure what was on the island that might like meat.

My mental alarm clock worked and I was up very early; I was one young feller that had a lot to take care of. The pig was the most important thing. I could only eat so much; it wouldn't keep very long in my homemade refrigerator. The only chance I had of saving the meat was in a smoker. Thanks to my dad again, we had built a smoker in our back yard out of mostly junk and scrap we had laying around. About half way back to the beach, I had to walk around an area that looked like slabs of flagstone or slate. I didn't have a lot of time to waste; I loaded up my backpack with a hammer, chisel and food and hurried off to the rock pile. I would need five pieces no more than one inch thick and two foot square. Trial and error but I had the five pieces cut and ready to head back. I carried two pieces at a time but had to stop for a breather and water a couple of times. It was late afternoon when I got the pieces back to the area I would build the smoker. I had to have it in operation by tomorrow or lose my pork chops and ham. There was a dead fruit tree where I gathered my fruit. I would get up very early tomorrow and hopefully have the pig in the smoker tomorrow. I sure could use a helper. The thought of ham and pork chops had my mouth watering. I was up before sun up and had the smoker ready for a screen before lunch. I wove a screen out of green bamboo. I dragged enough of the fruitwood back for a couple of days. I built a trial fire but had to lift the screen a few inches higher.

Having watched and helped my dad dress out a couple of deer helped me butcher the pig. I kind of mangled the first half making me wish I had a grinder to make sausage; the second half dressed out much better and went in the smoker. I did get ham, pork chops and pork ribs out of the first half. What a treat. I had ribs, baked potato and squash for dinner. I cooked what I couldn't eat well done and took it to my cooler. I would eat pork for the next few days until it was gone. I stoked the smoker before going to bed. The meat was looking good; I was sure I had something. I disposed of what I wouldn't keep where I disposed of the head which was gone. Hmmm! It seemed weird that I was alone on this big island but seemed like there was never enough time in the day to get done with one of my projects. I built a drying rack out of bamboo to dry some of my vegetables. I had recovered more than enough seed for the next crop. I had to work fast as the smoker had done its job and the meat turned out great. I hung it from the ceiling in my humble home. The eight foot by eight foot drying rack was almost too small for the end of the vegetables from my garden.

Chapter Five

I was putting the last of the potatoes in the cooler when I thought I heard what sounded like a baby in distress crying very loudly. It was coming from the southeast to an area I had never been to. It would stop and then seemed to almost sound frantic. I knew I should probably let well enough alone; how could there be a baby on the island. I started back for my place the crying sounded more frantic. That means I was going to have to do a lot of machete work to try to find where it was coming from. I filled my Gatorade bottle with cold water and began swinging the machete. About an hour of almost frantic arm breaking cutting my way through the jungle and I knew I was close. The crying stopped when I was using the machete; when I quit cutting the crying began. I knew I was close and I began just spreading the underbrush and pushing my way through; And then I couldn't believe my eyes. There was a large gorilla lying on its back and a tiny baby gorilla sitting beside it crying.

As I carefully walked towards the gorillas I talked very softly; the poor little guy was crying just like any baby would. Then I saw the problem. Evidently, the mama had climbed a fruit tree about ten feet off the ground when the branch she had a hold of broke and she fell backwards. There was a fallen dead tree with a large jagged branch that had gone through her and protruded from her chest. She was dead. Now what? I gathered a couple of coconuts, broke one, and held it towards the little guy. It took some coaxing and it moved closer to me, and I moved closer to it. It had quit crying and it finally got close enough to smell and taste the coconut milk. Well the little guy was hungry as it drank the milk from three coconuts. Now what? I couldn't just leave it here. I didn't want to keep calling it "it"! I picked him up; yes, he was a boy. He put his arms around my neck and it looked like I was the father of an adopted baby gorilla. How do I get myself into these things? I had no choice; He was going home with me. I gathered half dozen coconuts to take with me. He hugged me all of the way home and even kind of dozed. I had no idea what gorillas ate; actually the only thing I knew about gorillas was they got big and were very strong. What was I getting myself into?

Get ready for this. Once we were in my house, I sat him on my lap and he wiped out the milk of two more coconuts. He climbed out of my lap, picked up a piece of fruit off of the table and began eating it. He was a regular baby; when he sat the fruit down, he had fruit and fruit juice all over the front of him. I took him over to my water source and washed him just like a baby. He even wanted to play in the water. I took him outside for a walk and lucky for me he did his duty twice. The second time he kind of jumped around and chattered like, "Look what I did daddy" We started back for my place and he sat down and held his arms out and made some strange sounds. I picked him up and once again, he hugged me like any baby would. By the time we got back to my place, he was ready to call it a night. I put him at the foot of my bed and said "Good night little buddy". The sun was just coming up when I heard a noise; there was Buddy on the table working on a piece of fruit. Yes, he needed a bath.

He liked to splash and play in the water when I washed him. I had to laugh because he was ticklish. I began putting what I would call my sun deck together. I had the outer framework together when I quit to go gather fruit and coconuts for Buddy. He was a kick. He had quickly gotten used to me. He would run and play, but never getting more than ten feet from me; then he would stand up, make a funny noise and hold his arms out to be picked up. He had to be very young as he was a little guy and acted very much like a baby. I found myself calling him Buddy, so that is what I named him, Buddy, my little Buddy. It took longer to build the sun deck then I figured because I had to haul the bamboo I built it out of so far. I thought why not? I had no idea if a gorilla could be trained. So, I built Buddy like a high chair so he could sit at the table. I found that food can be a great training tool. Good conduct got special rewards. My cold-water refrigerator worked out as well as I had hoped for. I was fixing the fence around my garden area and glanced towards my home, I had to laugh; Molly and Polly liked the new sun deck. I had built a little pond and that was Buddy's favorite place.

    As I looked towards my place I had to chuckle. Here I was, going on an eight years old single guy and my family was growing. As I looked towards my place, if my family continued to grow I could build a room on the north side of my place, as the trees would be perfect if I groomed it a tad. I thought "Dear Lord, don't let there be elephants or giraffes on the island". Then there was Buddy, he was a kick. I had put a couple half-coconut shells in his pond; He would fill them and pour the water on his head and I swear he was laughing. If only he could talk. I would talk out loud sometimes just to feel like I heard someone talking. In the civilized world, I would be called a "Loony tune". I had a taste for seafood and told Buddy "Let's go for a walk". We had gone about half way to the beach when he held his arms up for me to carry him. As I picked him up, I realized it was time that he was not going to be picked up and carried. He had grown more than double what he was when we found each other. I did pick him up and carried him a short distance.

    I sat him down and I sat down; I took a drink of water and held the bottle for him and he drank. Then I had a talk with him that of course only I understood. (I think.) I told him from now on when he held his arms up to be picked we were going to sit down and have a drink of water. We had gone about a half mile when he began making his pickup noise holding his arms up. I found a place to sit down and took a drink. I held the bottle of which he held and he took a big drink. I put the bottle away and told him "OK big guy, let's go". I took his hand and he held it all of the way to the beach. I dug up a dozen clams and got four crabs. He had a blast playing in the surf; He got the stuff scared out of him when a wave rolled him on his butt. There was no doubt he did not like the taste of the salt water. By the time we headed for home Buddy was one pooped little guy. I did carry him the last half mile. I carried him right to his pond and rinsed the salt water off of him. This guy was a kick. He pretty well let me know when it was dinnertime, as he would climb up and get in his chair.

One problem; He needed a bigger chair. Not only that, but I realized if he was going to live here with me I would have to strengthen my floor. I'm not sure how heavy he would get. Buddy was making my young life more complicated. Time can become an immaterial thing; what difference did it make what day it was? Life here was like a wheel that never stops; every day is constantly rolling along. Every day is doing something to insure Buddy and my existence. I am planting, harvesting or heading for the beach for seafood. Buddy is a big boy. I made him his own bed and had to enlarge his pond. He never lets me out of his sight and is scrounging food when we are getting materials or enlarging and clearing our "yard". I was enlarging the lava refrigerator and noticed Buddy was nowhere to be seen. He had been just south of me the last time I saw him. I had only gone a couple hundred yards when I saw him sitting amongst a bunch of vines and bushes. He was picking something and eating it. As I got close, it looked like he was eating big red grapes. I thought "Why not?" I picked one and took a small bite. It was delicious. I told him good going Buddy; Another food source.

According to my calendar I had been on the island six years; Buddy was a big boy He didn't worry me much if I didn't see him for a few hours. He turned me on to another food source; it looked like a banana and tasted much like one. They were Buddy's favorite and it dawned on me; He was doing all of the exploring. I was always doing what had to be done right down to repairing things when a bad storm would come through. I had done a neat thing. I planted grape seeds around the perimeter of my place; in three years, I had like beautiful green vines surrounding my place with more grapes than Buddy and I could eat. Polly and Molly liked them and evidently turned their relatives on to them, as we would have as many as ten parrots wolfing down grapes. No problem; we weren't going to run out of grapes.

Chapter Six

I was cleaning my place one afternoon and noticed the fishing gear standing in the corner. I had been here going on ten years and never been fishing. A little ocean fishing sounded like a good idea one of these days. Just like for whatever reason, I had never explored the south end of the island. I had things well under control here on the home front; it was past time I explored the south end of this island.

Buddy had been staying away from home more and more these past six months; the first night he didn't come home he had me worried. I had never seen any big cats but had seen their prints. I had no idea if it were lions, tigers or what. Buddy would stay away as much as three nights now and I did worry about him; but he was a big boy and didn't need "Daddy" any more. The sky had been a strange color all day and it was deathly still; there was not so much as a breeze. The surf was a lot more ferocious than I had seen it in a long time and along towards evening the wind picked up and grew stronger with each passing hour. It was going from bad to worse; I wasn't even sure if my house would survive as it was swaying and lurching. All the years I had been on the island, I had never put an alternative survival plan together. My dad would not have appreciated that. It began to rain like I had never seen before.

The roof on my house began to peel away and rain began pouring inside my house. I wrapped some things in canvas and put them under the house. I had to get out and away from my house right now as it was beginning to come apart. I took a piece of canvas to wrap myself in and found a spot in the jungle that seemed somewhat sheltered. I wondered about Buddy. Then I thought, I had better be wondering about me. This storm was like a worst nightmare. The rain eased up and I finally, mercifully, fell asleep. I woke up to a much calmer morning. My first concern was my home. I made it back to my clearing and could have cried. My home and even the fence around the garden were basically destroyed. My cleared area looked like a war zone. My first concern was my house. I had a major replace and repair job on my hands. This was the first time since I was on the island I felt like throwing the towel in. Then I thought, it could be worse, at least I have the tools needed to do the work I had facing me.

It took me ten days to clean the area before I could begin putting my house back together. Fortunately, I was able to salvage a majority of the materials. It took another week just to get things cleaned up that I was able to salvage. I had just sat down to take a break when Buddy showed up. If only he could talk. He made it evident he was as glad to see me as I was to see him. It had become evident these past months that this was his home away from home. It made me wonder what he was up to. He was one big boy now, and no doubt, he could take care of himself. We shared a bowl of grapes and I got back to work. Tomorrow I would begin putting my house back together. One thing for sure! A lesson well learned. Three weeks of hard work and I had my house ready to move back in. It would be much stronger this time as I realized where the weak spots were and double reinforced those areas. I had lucked out and had not lost anything of importance. Fixing my garden fence went a lot faster. I had to replace most of the vertical poles as the original ones had snapped off at ground level. Buddy seemed to have a routine as he visited me every two or three days.

I spent the next two weeks cleaning and pruning my general

area. The Island was full of a variety of multi colored flowers. I spent another week gathering and transplanting my favorite ones. I hadn't seen Buddy in over three weeks. I had built a neat gazebo patio creation in my front yard that I enjoyed when I worked on my ledger and had fruit snacks. I was about to clean up and head upstairs when I almost cried with excitement. Buddy came towards me and stopped; another gorilla and a baby gorilla stepped out of the jungle. Buddy came up and we gave each other a hug. He had about broken my ribs when he was growing up; He knew he had hurt me and never squeezed me that hard again. How about that? Buddy looked to be a married gorilla. He had to coax the female to get closer and the little guy wasn't letting go of mama. I held the bowl of grapes out for Buddy and he took a few. I held the bowl out to the female; She backed up a little bit and finally took some grapes out of the bowl. She gave the little guy one and he knew what to do with it.

It took some coaxing but the little guy began taking the grapes from the bowl. Some more coaxing and I had him sitting in my lap. Mama was paying close attention but I could see she was more relaxed. I decided to call the female Becky. Buddy and Becky had a good sound to it. It is too bad I didn't have a camera. Buddy went over and got in his pond. Becky was quick to follow and get in. Becky had to get out and get the little guy who I decided to call Skipper. Once Skipper was in the water you would think he was a human child as he was having a blast. It was close to sundown when Buddy and Becky got out. Becky had to pick a crying Skipper up and hold him as he wanted to get back in. Buddy herded them back to where they had exited the jungle. He turned and grunted something at me and I laughed and grunted something back. I stood looking at where they had disappeared and missed them already.

I had just enough light to make an entry in my ledger. The pencils and pens had given out a while ago so I had made a quill pen from one of Polly's feathers and made a red ink out of berries

I squeezed and strained. I had developed a short hand to save on paper of which I had two sheets left. I went upstairs and lit one of the candles, which I used sparingly and only had three left. I had decided to stay on the east perimeter of the island. I would go to the south most point of the island. I packed supplies for eight days. I would go as far as I could go for five days and take three days to get back home. I would see how that went before I made any future plans. I got up early as the first day would be a test to see what the lay of the land was and how thick or bad the jungle was. I thought about the meat I had enjoyed from the pig I shot. I hadn't seen another one since that first one attacked me. I decided if I saw another one, I would shoot it. The thought of pork chops and ribs had my mouth watering. I would have settled for one can of the survival food but that was long gone.

I had discovered a plant that had grew something that looked like a large gourd, I found it by accident. When it was dry I could use a flat stone and a round stone and grind it into something that resembled flour or corn. I could bake it in the oven; Of course I had an oven that I made out of the slate like flagstone. It had a taste all of its own but was a good enough substitute for something like pita. Drying fruit and vegetables was a trial and error thing; the fruit dried easily; but the vegetables took more TLC. I made a jerky out of crab and clams. It was actually pretty good. I had made a tent out of the sail material and of course, had my hammock and it was a good thing. It began to sprinkle late that afternoon; by the time I had my hammock up and the canvas tent stretched from four trees for a roof it began to seemingly drain heaven of all the rain it had stored.

If there was a good and bad thing about the tropical rain, it would be like a cloud burst for a while, then suddenly quit. That was better for keeping a heavily foliaged jungle. It was a very gradual climb as I headed out in the morning. It was so humid I was soaking wet a half hour into my hike. I made a headband to keep the sweat out of my eyes. By the time I decided to call it a day the jungle didn't seem as dense and I made pretty good time. I did make it to what I considered the south most point of the island the fifth day. I estimated the land was a hundred and fifty feet above sea level. I was tempted to head back through the jungle but I was low on supplies and my body needed a break. I did get a good look at the lay of the land. I think I could make it from here through the jungle in six days. That meant six days to get here and four days to return. I was anxious to give it a try, which meant get back home and get rested.

I was two days away from home and decided to gamble and head diagonally through the jungle and cut the corner off. I was a half day into the jungle and heard animal activity not too far ahead. As I got closer it sounded like pigs; the wind was in my favor and luck was in my favor. There were five of my pork chops playing in a small pond of mud. I sighted in on a medium sized one and fired; it ran about ten feet and fell over. The other four were long gone. The one I dropped was about two hundred fifty pounds. I dragged it to where I could put it on a piece of my canvas and dragged it to the edge of the jungle. I cut its head off, gutted, and skinned it of which I dragged out into the ocean. It was getting dark so I hung my hammock. My butt was dragging and I had no problem falling asleep. I woke up to what sounded like a low growling noise. There was no sense taking a chance so I fired a round towards the ocean and heard something crashing through jungle.

I slept until the rising sun woke me up. By the time I dragged my pork chops to my clearing my legs were wobbly. It was dark by the time I had put Mr. Piggy in the smoker, which I had enlarged. I kept chops and ham out for tomorrow. I didn't remember going to bed or sleep. When the sun woke me up it was one of those mornings when I wasn't raring to go. A fried slab of ham for breakfast and I did feel better. I worked on the map of the island I had started a long time ago. I had one more section on the west side and I would have a decent map completed. I knew part of the west beach side; I decided my next adventure would be to take the beach to the very point and come back through the heart of the jungle. So probably four days up the beach side because I would have to do some hiking through the jungle as doing the majority of the hike would have been tough going as it was so rocky. I figured eight days through the jungle to get home. I would wait a few days before that adventure as I had some garden work to do.

I had just started working on the garden when Buddy, Becky and Skipper showed up. Skipper headed straight for the pond and was a regular child at play in the water. He brought back memories of Buddy when he was a little guy; I had to be careful as my emotions were going wild on me. I wanted to scream and cry and laugh; I walked towards the pond, and Buddy and Becky both got in. Enlarging the pond was my next project. When my "Company" got out of the pond I sat a bowl of grapes on the table. Skipper was about twice the size he was the first time I saw him. I sat the bowl of grapes on the table and the little rascal quickly ate about half of them. Then he proceeded to run around the yard showing off. They headed back into the jungle about the time my stomach began growling. Knowing I was having pork chops for dinner probably induced my stomach to begin growling.

I had been alone on the island going on eleven years. Today when Buddy and family were here is the first time my emotions about got away on me. I can't let that happen again. If I did, I would begin doing hard time alone on this island and that would not be a good thing. Keeping busy is what had kept me going so far. I had noticed on my southerly hike an area where it almost looked like humans had been excavating rocks or stones. That was worth looking into. I could only carry so much in my backpack. Of course the longer I was gone the less my backpack weighed; the majority in the pack was food. I would include the flashlight and batteries and a couple of candles. The more I thought of the adventure the more excited I got. I entertained myself by thinking about pirates and hidden pirates treasures. If you are going to dream, they may as well be good ones. In the years I had been here I heard an airplane go over four times and saw one freighter off in the distance. I talked out loud every so often to make sure I could still talk. Mom's dictionary that I had rescued was a treasure as I used it to educate myself with whatever I could gain in knowledge. I wouldn't allow myself to think any farther than the next day. It had to be one day at a time.

The sun awoke me; I was packed and ready to go. I laughed as I climbed down my ladder; my dad always used to say "And don't forget to turn the lights out". I wasn't old enough to have a good picture of what it took to live in a house in a city. I knew you had to pay for electrical and water use. I remembered mom and dad talking about the house and car payments. I know mom and dad both worked to pay for what we had. Life here is so simple. I had no payments, food and water was in abundance and basically there for the taking. I got up when I wanted and I went to bed when I wanted to. I would like to have someone here if for no other reason, someone to talk with. But I know I have so much to be thankful for. I remember going to Sunday school; I know there is God. I know that he watches over me.

Chapter Seven

Camping the first night on the west beach had my mind swirling with memories. I was just a little boy when I washed up on the shore here. Not that I needed proof. But as I lay there I was almost too exhausted to get up. I had never been separated from my parents. Because my dad was a tough guy and a survivor trainer and I was the only son, he taught me survival since I was four years old. My survival mind being as young as it was ready to do what I could do. And here I am on the same beach in my comfortable hammock and I am tired, good night.

I woke up to my hammock rocking in a strong breeze. I sang "Rock a bye baby" and got a laugh out of that. When I ran out of beach I decided to cut my way through the jungle. Going the rock route was just too dangerous. It was a hard fought five days when I reached the spot I had been at previously. It was higher ground here. I was able to find a spot to get a compass reading to my return spot. Not just me, but anyone could get totally lost in the jungle. It is unforgiving

I spent the night there; the sound of the surf lulled me to sleep; the sound of the surf woke me up. A fruit and biscuit breakfast and" look out jungle, here I come". I decided to take the northerly route half the day and then go due east. That stone area still had my curiosity. I wonder how man ever made it without a compass. I had found the juice from what looked to be a berry, but was not edible, to get bugs away. I could understand why it kept bugs at a distance; when I put it on it would take me several minutes to find it acceptable. I had been heading east for about two hours when I saw something that stopped me in my tracks. It was so covered with vegetation it took some research to realize it was a long single story building with an attached at least two story building behind it. It was rougher built than Mayan or Aztec. My mom had been a history teacher, Roman, Grecian, Mayan and Aztec were her favorites, and she would read to me and show me pictures. Unless I almost bumped into it I never would have found it. The jungle growth had totally hidden it

I figured there must be an entrance somewhere. I spent the rest of the day clearing an area where I thought an entrance or door should be. There was a spring fed little stream beside the structure where I took a sponge bath as I was totally soaked with sweat. As I hung my hammock, I noticed several very large birds that looked like pheasants. Hmm! The thought of fried chicken made my mouth water. I was tempted to shoot one and have fried pheasant, or whatever they were, for dinner. Darkness comes quickly in the jungle; I had been swinging my machete all day and I did not need Brahms Lullaby to put me to sleep. I had all kinds of weird dreams about this place. I woke up anxious to continue my exploration. Almost a half day of swinging my machete and I found the opening. The overgrowth had totally sealed what seemed to be the entrance.

As I cut through and opened up what had to be the entrance an over powering musty smell made me back up. I would hold my breath and cut the over growth away. I finally had cleared to the opening and the smell had become more bearable. I was dripping wet with sweat, hungry and tired; but I had the opening exposed and the smell was bearable now. I would look inside tomorrow. I had visions of piles of golden treasures. Several of the large birds had moved in closer. I really wanted to shoot one but only shot my

AK when it was important enough to pull the trigger. It was too late today as it was getting dark; I would make a snare out of the nylon string I had and put a piece of bun I had made in the center of it and see if I couldn't snare one of them. That was a tomorrow project; I was one worn out guy. I guess I was too tired to dream and even slept in a bit as a bright sun woke me up. After a bun and fruit breakfast I was excited as I headed for the entrance I had uncovered. The smell was still bad but tolerable.

As I flashed my light inside it was a large empty room except for what looked to be a narrow stone table in the middle of the room. There was a tall doorway that opened up in to a larger room. There was a large stone chair against the far wall and then what I saw almost caused me to drop the flashlight and run. Both walls next to the chair were covered with skulls. I estimated over five hundred skulls. The whole scenario was a strange deal. I sat down in the big stone chair and the stone table in the low room was clearly visible. I could easily imaging that table was probably like a sacrificial alter where unfortunate individuals were beheaded while someone of importance sat in this throne or chair and watched the beheading process. I needed fresh air like right now. The area was so heavily overgrown it would take more than one person to clear the jungle away for further exploration. This would be a treasure for archeologists as there were all kinds of pottery and weapons in the small area I cleared. The crumbs I had put down for my finely feathered friends were gone. Before I called it a night I put some more crumbs out with my string snare ready to try.

A strong breeze woke me up early the next morning; I put some more crumbs out around the snare. Within a few minutes, here they came; there were five of them going after the crumbs. I yanked the string and bingo I had one. He was flopping so bad I had a difficulty getting a hold of it. I finally got it under control enough that I slit its throat. It was a big bird that probably weighed five pounds. I was hoping I could skin it and save trying to pluck the feathers. Skin it I did and had an awesome brunch. I cooked the entire bird so it wouldn't spoil before dinner. There wasn't much else I could do here as I wasn't up on archeology. I got back on my northerly course and headed for home. It was tough going as the jungle was a tangled mass that I had to cut my way through every foot of the way. I did see a large cat; it looked like a smaller version of a tiger. I checked its tracks and it was the same tracks I had seen near my place. He seemed more afraid of me than I was of him. I was OK with that.

It took the better part of seven days to make it back to my place. As I entered my clearing I began undressing and headed straight for the pond. This was the first time I had ever gone in it; but it wouldn't be the last. Vegetation grows unbelievably fast in the jungle, as did the vegetables I had planted; but weeds and such grow just as fast. I was just finishing up the second day of weeding when Buddy and family showed up. Skipper seemed to have doubled in size in the last few weeks. He was getting to be a big boy. He recognized me and wanted to be picked up, which I did but this would probably be the last time as I had to strain to pick him up. I sat him down and he ran and jumped in the pond. I thought why not? I walked over and got in with him. You would swear he was a human child as he splashed water on me and laughed a toothy laugh. Buddy got in and as Becky got in I sat on the edge of the pond which if this "family gathering" were to continue, I would have to enlarge the pond.

Buddy was the first one to get out and go to the edge of the forest. Becky had to give Skipper a couple of swats as he didn't want to go. If only they could talk. I had some potatoes to put in the stone cooler. Just as I turned to leave I heard a strange animal cry; if you live in the jungle long enough you begin to recognize animal sounds. This sounded like a smaller animal that was hurt. It let out a mournful cry of which I headed for. It didn't cry again until I had just turned to head home and it let out a mournful cry. I knew it wasn't too far away; it cried again and I knew it was close and I found it. It looked like a baby fox that had its left front leg stuck in a hole in the lava. As hurt as it was, it didn't want me near it and snarled at me. I got it from behind to where it couldn't bite me and carefully freed its leg.

There was no doubt its leg was broken, probably from its frantic effort to get loose. Now what? I decided to chance it and carried it carefully so it couldn't bite me. Once I got it home I made a loop out of string and closed its mouth with it. I made a little splint and tied it so it couldn't get it loose. It was a little female. I put it in a cage I had built for a parrot I never caught, with a coconut bowl of coconut milk, which the little gal drank and watched me. I put a bowl of water in the cage and sat on the floor and talked to the little gal. I decided I would call her Sadie. By the end of the week I could put little pieces of pork on my finger and she didn't hesitate to take it and munch it up. I had a lot of pruning to do around the perimeter of my place; I kept the cage close to me as I worked. I would stop every so often and sit on the ground, and talk to Sadie and give her little pieces of pork treats. I had to redo the splint twice in the next few weeks; I thought I remembered hearing human bones with proper care healed in six weeks.

I wanted to get back on another southern exploration and decided to chance it? I took the cage and Sadie outside, took the splint off and sat her on the ground. She walked around sniffing but didn't run off. I walked about ten feet away and had to laugh; she followed me. I sat on the ground and had two little pieces of pork left of which she took. I walked back by her cage and she got in on her own. It was beginning to look like I had added on to my family. I didn't close the cage anymore and it was like her own little dwelling. I had to make the opening bigger and enlarged the cage for her. I also made her a bed beside the cage and she quit going in the cage. Between Sadie and the garden and pruning on my place, time was getting away. Buddy and family showed up for a visit and a dip in the pond. Sadie was afraid of them at first. Before the day was over Skipper and Sadie kind of chased each other back and forth and kept me laughing until Buddy took his family home.

I really wanted to go exploring again; Sadie didn't eat much, but I was almost out of pork. I had scouted out the muddy area where the pigs hung out; there were as many as ten at a time there. I didn't want to shoot one there as they may never come back. It took another day and I shot one a couple of hundred yards from the mud hole. The shot scared Sadie and I had to go home without her. I had been prepared and dragged my catch a couple hundred yards and cleaned it there. I figured what I cleaned and left there would be gone in a day or two. I was putting porky in the smoker when Sadie came gingerly out of the forest. A nice treat of raw pork and she was my buddy again. I had spent almost two months doctoring Sadie, harvesting, and taking care of my bountiful garden crop. Buddy and family showed up; Skipper had become a big boy. I did take the time to add another ten feet to the pond of which Sadie was having no part of. Who in the entire world would believe that I shared a pond with three gorillas?

Finally, it was my turn. I wasn't sure why, but I had a premonition I would be gone longer this time. I packed enough food to last what I figured was twenty days' worth. That was about all I could carry. I set my compass for a south-by-south westerly course. Sadie was born in the jungle so she should have no problem. After about the third day out it was obvious she was right at home getting through the jungle. I had to machete my way through it. She went through it like it was wide open ground. The fourth day we came upon a neat little fresh water stream. I tested it and it tasted cold and clean. It was only about three feet wide at the widest. I checked up and down about a hundred feet upstream and downstream. My memory still had vivid pictures of the huge alligators I saw on the north end.

There were fish in it that looked like trout. I found a branch that I trimmed and cut a little branch off on the end that made like a one-inch hook. A very patient half hour later and I would be enjoying fish for dinner. I cracked up as Sadie barked herself silly as the fish flopped on the bank. I had no idea what kind of fish it was. I cleared an area by the stream and made a little fire. I ran a sick through the fish and Sadie and I had fish for dinner. By the end of the sixth day I was getting kind of tired of cutting my way through the jungle and all it seemed that I had to look forward to, was cutting my way through more jungle the next day. Once I had explored the entire island, what was there left for me to do? I began to get some off the wall ideas. One that may not be so crazy is; There was everything on the island to build a boat; A big boat. I knew I could put together enough food and water to last me for months. But then, what about Buddy and family? I had better be careful and not allow myself to be lonesome.

I had come this far and had to quit thinking about turning back and heading for home. There was no sense heading west as that was a very rocky part of the coastline. OK; I'll keep going until I arrive at the coast line. I'll enjoy some seafood and head home. Those made me laugh! I would have chopped my way through the jungle for over a week to have a seafood dinner. I had better look out; the mind can do strange things if we let it. I had been cutting my way through the jungle when Sadie began barking without let up. I had the AK ready when there it was; I wasn't sure if it was a boa constrictor or a python, but it evidently was thinking of having Sadie for dinner. It was almost like it was trying to trick us as it was changing direction and like feinting with its head. I had my AK in my left hand and my machete in my right hand. It made a lunge and my machete separated its head from its body. It was huge; I estimated it to be twelve feet long. I had heard or been told that snake meat was good to eat. No thank you.

Chapter Eight

I was getting close to calling it a day when I came upon what were four graves. They were each covered with rocks and wooden crosses that had fallen and mostly rotted. I found a spot about a hundred yards away and made my camp for the night. I had a hard time falling asleep thinking about the four graves. I finally fell asleep thinking about the possibility of a lost civilization. It was a windy misty morning that woke me up. I thought this could lead to a major tropical storm and I had better prepare for. I wanted to find an area that was clearer than where I had camped for the night. The mist was actually refreshing. I thought it could stay like this all day. As I cut my way through the jungle just west of where I saw the graves I saw old dead stumps that had been cut. There weren't any beavers on this island. Those had to be cut by humans a long time ago as the stumps were rotten. I came to an area that was evident it had been cleared a long time ago. It had begun to thunder and lightning. I knew it was but a matter of a short time that it was going to rain like only a tropical storm can rain. I had been caught in a storm here where it rained so hard it was difficult to breath.

    I had no choice; I was going to have to camp here soon as I could feel the heavy rain coming; and down it came. It was getting difficult to see; I thought I saw a rock pile on the side of a hill and headed for it. As I got close it looked like a cave. All kinds of varmints like caves and I got my flashlight out. The wind was so strong I could barely stand up. I shined my light inside and almost fell over backwards. There was a table and chairs and a human skeleton scattered around it. What was I getting myself into? I didn't want to use my batteries up so I took a candle out and lit it. It was like a man made cave out of rocks. It was very organized. Bingo; along one wall was an area where five people had slept. There were backpacks and four rifles leaning against the wall. The table and chairs were well made out of bamboo.

There was what looked like an oil lamp on the table and actually had oil in it. I took my fire making things out of my pack and got a small fire going. The makers of this rock dwelling knew what they were doing as there was a perfect draft that pulled the smoke to the opening in the front. I put my precious candle out and put a little more oil in the bowl from the can beside the table that smelled like diesel oil. It gave enough light that it lit the entire, I guess it could be called, a stone cave or structure. The thunder and lightning were so strong I could feel the vibration in the cave. I'll call it a cave as that is what it looks and feels like. There was a pistol lying on the floor beside the chair; the skeleton was mostly held together with what appeared to be a uniform. The Japanese flag leaning against the wall solved part of the mystery. There had been Japanese on the island probably since the Second World War.

It began to rain so loud it actually sounded like thunder as it pounded through the jungle. It was a pleasant surprise the cave didn't leak. Whoever the skeleton had belonged to no doubt committed suicide. There was a hole through the skull and an empty cartridge lying on the table. I thought, "What do I do"? There was no doubt that I could use this cave, especially now as the rain pounded down. Sadie knew how to handle things as she was sound asleep on one of the beds on the floor. I had a jillion questions going through my head. How did these five get here? Were there more? Why were they here? What I finally decided was I would bury the skeleton with the other four when the weather cleared up. In the meantime, I emptied what looked like a duffle bag. It had miscellaneous uniform parts and two thick blank tablets. There was a tablet lying on the table with a quill pen and what looked like ink. Evidently the suicide man had written a suicide letter as there was a lot more than a note.

I emptied what looked like a large shave kit and found the biggest treasure of all, a pair of scissors, a straight razor, a comb and a mirror. I had kept my knife sharp enough all of these years to not give myself a haircut or shave; just keep it cut back. I had my hair tied in a ponytail. I looked in the mirror and shook my head. I looked like a wild man. I decided I would do some major house cleaning and stay here long enough to get this place ready as I was coming back. The last entry in the paper on the table was 2005.

It had been a long day; I fed Sadie and my growling stomach and laid down on one of the beds on the floor and that's all I remember. I awoke to utter silence and Sadie licking my face. That was either true love or hunger. I took a look outside; Not a cloud in the sky. It must have been hunger and not true love, the reason Sadie was licking my face. She ate her breakfast and barked for more. I took the homemade shovel leaning against the wall and headed out to dig the four graves. The dirt was wet but perfect for digging. I had gotten down about three feet and hit what seemed to be solid rock.

I went back to the cave and put Charlie, which is what I named the skeleton, in the duffle bag I had emptied. I laid Charlie to rest and said some words to God for him. I made a bamboo cross and carved Charlie's name on it and what I thought was the date. I spent the rest of the day rearranging the cave. There was no doubt I was coming back here, and soon. The five past residents of the cave were well equipped. I stacked all of the personal things in the back of the cave. I stacked three of the thin homemade mattresses on top of each other and had a comfortable bed. I had weapons, writing paper and things to set up a barbershop. I kind of hated to head back but I didn't want to overstay my welcome. Ha! Sadie had a bed right next to mine. She had quickly become a very good companion and pal. I wondered if I could ever get Buddy and family to move up here. I was going to have to share a piece of my ham with Sadie and ration myself on food going back.

I awoke to a perfect day; there was a perfect breeze and it had cooled off. I remembered that after a bad storm like the one here was how it always brought the cooler temperature with it. No, there was no chance of a snowfall. For whatever reason, I felt energized even though as cool as it was I still had to wear a sweatband to keep the sweat out of my eyes. Swinging a machete all day will put muscles on top of muscles. I learned a long time ago to cut with either hand. Otherwise, there is no way I could go all day cutting with one hand. We even stopped at the little stream and had fish for dinner. Sadie let me know there was something not too far from us. We sat quietly for several minutes and sure enough, I caught a glimpse of the same kind of cat we had seen once before. I let out a holler and it went crashing through the jungle until we couldn't hear it anymore. By the time we got home to our clearing, I was hungry. I had rationed the food coming home and that was leaving me hungry. I made sure Sadie was well fed.

Everything was over grown and the entire perimeter needed pruning. Unreal; I just got home and I was ready to go back. There was something about the whole deal down there; it was south! Five dead Japanese from the Second World War! Everything was neat and well organized. But how did they get on the island. There was really only two ways to get on this island, by air or sea. There was no doubt they were not sailors. It had to be they were there by plane as they had aviator style hats and goggles. There either have had to be a landing field or they crash-landed. If there was a landing field they probably wouldn't have died on this island. About the third day home Buddy and family showed up. Skipper was becoming one big boy. He didn't even act like a little boy any more. He wasn't even interested in Sadie. But he was interested with the pond and was the first one in it. Here I was a seventeen-year-old boy with three gorillas visiting me and it felt like old home week. The little boy was still in Skipper as his mom gave him a swat to get out of the pond. As always, Buddy stopped and grunted goodbye before he disappeared into the jungle.

    I had a blast the first time I cut my hair and shaved. Thank goodness I found the razor strap and figured how to use it. I remembered my dad shaving. He said hot water was important to soften his whiskers up and the shave cream was so the razor slid across his face and cut the whiskers and didn't pull them out. The hot water was no problem. The shave cream? I thought, "OK, I'll experiment on my arm first". I got the water hot and rubbed a wild banana that I had smashed into a creamy substance on my arm. It worked perfect and I didn't cut myself once. OK, here goes; I did the hot water and my "shave cream" on my face. None of this would be possible except for the mirror I found. I couldn't believe the difference! I went from a hairy scary looking jungle man to I guess a good-looking teenager. I wished I had a camera so I could get a before and after picture.

    I found myself hurrying to get my place in top shape before I left again, left again? Finding the five dead Japanese airmen had my curiosity at its peak. It was almost a sure thing that they must have crashed; maybe not on this island, but if not on this island, how did they get here? It is unreal how the jungle can take over so quickly. As I trimmed the perimeter of my place I had to laugh; it was as if the jungle was chasing me. I had cleared a large area, which I called my yard. As I was pruning and trimming I thought by the time I get all of the way around, where I first started it would already begin to grow back. There is absolutely no comparison living in the jungle and living in the city. There is not a day in the jungle where I could say I had everything done and could take a day completely off. It is a matter of every day survival. If I want to eat, I have to hunt, forage or grow any food I am to put on my table.

I figured I would be gone about three weeks my next time out. I shot another pig and four of the birds I am going to call pheasants. They were more than twice the size of a pheasant but colored just like a pheasant. I smoked most of the pig and birds. I wanted to have enough food to last at least three weeks away from home. I have the entire southwest section of the island to explore. I was fairly certain it would take at least two trips to explore the whole area. I even thought of staying in the habitat the Japanese had built. But that would be about the same distance from my place and I had been lucky so far to find fresh water. As much as it rained here it was understandable how there could be fresh water. Sadie had me worried; she would disappear for a day or two and then show up. I had to realize she was a wild animal. Buddy and family were frequent visitors. Skipper was for sure not a "Little boy" any more. He was one husky gorilla. But Becky let him know she was his mama and the boss

I finally had my place as ready as it was going to be before I headed out. It was really neat that if I wanted, I could get three crops a year from my garden. By being able to dry most of my crops, I was assured vegetables until my next crop. Not only that, but the dried vegetables were very light and it was no problem carrying a three week supply of vegetables along with the pork and bird jerky. The night before I was to head out exploring saw me get very little sleep. I had so many things going through my mind. My dad would have loved this island. I am sure he would know every square inch of the island. My sister Stacey would be twenty-one years old now. I fell asleep wondering if I would be spending my entire life alone on this island.

I went to sleep late and woke up early; an early bird gets the worms; I wasn't a bird and worms sounded yucky, but I was raring to go. The first couple of days were true to form; I was one sore guy swinging the machete all day even though I was in very good shape. I rarely saw any wildlife but often heard them as they made their way through the jungle. I did see species I had never seen before. It was a dark grey cat that would probably go a hundred and twenty pounds. It was lying on a branch of a tree about thirty feet off of the ground. I did get a good look at it before it quickly disappeared when Sadie began to bark. I thought, "Now that was not the kind of "Puddy Cat" I wouldn't want to wake up and find sleeping at the foot of my bed. But I was going to be more careful watching over hanging trees. Danger surrounds anyone living in the jungle; In order to survive you develop like a sixth sense; you don't realize it, but your eyes are always searching.

The route I had laid out would be like an M; this would allow me to search the lower half of what I had to explore. The ground began to get more damp and spongy of which I did not like; my ninth day it had gotten so bad I had to do some evaluating. I had to use a tree to pull myself loose from a sandy mud that wouldn't let me go. There was no way I could continue in the direction I wanted to try. I would back out until I got to firmer ground and try going southwest. It seemed like all of the insects on the island called this area home. Thankfully my "home brew repellent" kept the insects at bay. I made it back to drier ground but the under growth seemed to be twice as thick. It was evident the area I had to back out of was like a swampy area. I kept to the edge of it and I couldn't help but think and wonder about the alligators I saw on the north end of the island. It took me three days to get around the swamp area. It was not a large area but I had no desire to go wading through it. The westerly area of the island was higher and quite rocky. The swampy area was round shaped of which I would have seen a plane if it had crashed in that area.

By the time I had searched the area I had mapped out I was

ready to head home. I decided to head for the Japanese encampment and rest up for a day or two. The swamp area was not to my liking. The vegetation around it was very thick and not only my arms, but my mind and body needed a rest. I kind of felt defeated, the only thing I accomplished this time was that the only thing I found which I could do without was the swamp area. By the time I made it to the Japanese encampment I had all of the exploring I wanted for a while. My homemade pigskin moccasins had seen better days. Needless to say, I didn't have a spare pair. They were actually beyond repair. Right at the present, I needed sleep more than I needed footwear. Thunder and lightning woke me up during the night and I could hear and smell the heavy rainfall. It continued throughout the next day. It was a good thing I planned on resting up for a couple of days. The quill pen, ink and paper saved me from getting cabin fever. I woke up during the night and had to chuckle; Even silence can wake me up; It had quit raining and the storm had gone to visit someplace else.

My footwear needed a major overhaul. There was a leather pair of boots but the leather would break instead of being pliable. I was about to give up when I found the bottom of a duffle bag had a rubber bottom and the rubber was still very pliable. I used the rubber, the shoelaces from the boots and I fabricated very useable footwear. No, they wouldn't take a prize at a shoe contest but they would get me back to my home. I would have to ration my food, but I wouldn't starve going home and had plenty for Sadie. This was my first outing that I just wanted to get back to my place. I think the idea that this was my toughest outing and I accomplished nothing other than there was nothing to take me back to that section of the island. Just the smell of the swamp was enough to keep me away from that area. I guess when I look at the overall picture I did find something; I found the second area on the island I had no desire to ever go back to.

Chapter Nine

Going back was a cakewalk after what I went through this trip; especially when my machete work was easier having cut my way through here once before. I hadn't been home two hours when Buddy and family showed up; here we go; it was like old home week again. Skipper made it look like the pond was his sole possession. When he was little it was fun to watch him splash water on himself; Now that he was older and much bigger, by the time he would get out of the pond he would have splashed half the water out. I didn't think there was any hope of teaching a young gorilla, which probably weighed close to four hundred pounds, not to splash the water out of the pond. The little creek and my bamboo pipe would fill it up overnight. If we didn't get rain for a few days I used the overflow to water my garden. I was always sad when Buddy would turn around and grunt goodbye when he and his family disappeared in to the jungle. If only they could talk. Even Sadie had high tailed it for the night.

    I put the map I had laid out of the island on the table and marked where I had been this time ; I only had one section of the island to explore; Then what? More than once I had thought about building a boat. I had the basic tools I would need. I had a compass, but what good would a compass be? I would have no idea which way to go. Plus I couldn't build a boat big enough to take Buddy and family and Sadie. Not only that but the island had always been their home and I don't think they would want to go sailing across the ocean in a homemade boat and I didn't know which way to go. I had to quit thinking about what I would or could do after exploring the entire island. Dad had taught me survival; but he never mentioned loneliness. I had maybe two weeks maintenance work to do here. Then I would head out again.

The cleared area around my place of which I called my yard was beginning to be more work than what it was worth. I built a sickle out of the remaining metal I had salvaged from the Gigo-Gigo rudder. I preferred swinging the machete through the jungle rather than swinging the sickle through the grass. I also built a lawn rake and would rake the lawn cuttings up into a pile that made great mulch. Every time I got ready to do some sickle work, I thought of the gas-powered lawn mower my dad used. First things first; I trimmed the perimeter which if I allowed it, it would have totally covered my home in a couple of months. It took all of two weeks to get my place ready to head out. I didn't want to attempt the swamp area or climbing over the rocky west shore line. The only way, to the best of my knowledge, as a safe route would be head for the easterly coast once I reached the ruins. If the beach jungle were "traveler friendly," I was probably looking at fifteen days to reach an area to where I could head inland on a northerly course.

That means I would need a minimum of three weeks supplies. I would hopefully be able to recover clams and crabs once I reached the shoreline. I had my share of surprises in my years on the island. This time I found myself getting very excited. It was almost a sure thing the Japanese airmen didn't arrive on the island in a boat. Unless the last area I was going to search showed signs of a place where a plane could land, the island survivors must have crashed landed someplace. If they had crashed in the swampy area, the plane could have sunk in the blackness of the muddy quicksand. That would mean the five survivors would have been swallowed up in the swamp. All of my thinking and figuring were getting me nowhere. I shot a larger pig this time. It was a hot sweaty chore to get it back to the smoker that, once again, I had built larger. By the time the last of the pig was smoked, the dried vegetables were ready to be packed. I wasn't too concerned about fresh water; So far I was lucky and found areas where fresh water springs would be running out of lava beds.

    I had my backpack on and was just ready to head for the jungle when Sadie showed up. I tried calling her but she stood her ground barking. When I went to pet her she ran about ten feet and turned and barked. After she had done this several times I followed her to an area where I had piled what was left of unused material when I built my home. It had a thorny bushy covering that had grown thick through the years. Sadie disappeared in a little opening. As I stood watching in disbelief, she brought five little pups out for me to see. She let me hold them and took them back into their safe thorny home; she then came out and sat down as if to tell me she was staying home and taking care of her kids. I went back to my place and got two large hands full of jerky; I went back to Sadie's den and shoved the jerky as far back in her den as I could. That should make her life a little easier. Looks like I was heading out by myself this time

    It was too late to head into the jungle today; I used the rest of the day to work on my ledger. If I were to spend the rest of my life on the island, at least my ledger would tell of my experiences if anyone ever discovered my ledger. Jungle noise woke me up early the next morning. A quick light breakfast and I headed for the jungle. The route I was taking to the old ruins was totally over grown from the last time I went this way. My third day out I heard the familiar sounds of a big cat; this really slowed my progress down as I was continuously checking the trees overhead. There was no way I had survived this long in the jungle to become a gourmet meal for a big cat. I slept with my AK at the ready the next couple of nights. I reached the ruins in the nick of time; Thunder and lightning were getting closer. I finished making my camp secure when a wind driven rain came crashing down.

I was always able to sleep soundly when it rained and tonight sleep came quickly as the rain sounded like a loud constant drum roll on my tent. Thankfully jungle noises woke me up. The sun was just coming up and the sky was as clear as a bell. I reached the easterly beach just as the sun was saying good night after tough day with the machete. I had less than hour to set up my hammock and get ready for nightfall. There was a full moon tonight and it was so bright it was almost like a silver daylight. Jungle sounds and the surf woke me up the next morning. I hadn't had a chance to check this area out before the sun set. There was a spectacular beach as far as I could see in both directions. The ocean looked like a dangerous place as there were various sized rock formations in the ocean as far as I could see. There was no doubt it would be suicide to land any size boat as far as I could see. I decided to walk the beach as far as I could or until it was time to head inland. The beach wasn't littered with debris; but every so often I would find wood that evidently was all that was left of what had been a boat. I continued walking the beach until I reached what I called the point of the island. Clams and crabs were in abundance and I did have a seafood dinner.

I had been cutting my way through the jungle over half of the day when I came upon a crystal clear pond in a lava bed. I thought "Wow", my own swimming pool; too bad it didn't have a Jacuzzi. The water was very cool but what a pleasure. I had been taking sponge baths since arriving on the island. I had to laugh when I found myself wishing I had this pond next to the place I had built and called home. This seemed like a great place to camp for the night. If a person weren't used to it the jungle night sounds could drive you bananas. I pretended it was rain on my tent and fell quickly asleep. Needless to say, it was the sounds of the jungle that woke me up. I was going to use a zigzag route to explore this area. It was about twice the size of the last area. By the time I had cut my way through the jungle for the next two days my arms needed a break. I went back to the pond, which was easy going as the trail I cut had no chance to grow back yet. A couple of hours in the pond and I felt like I was raring to go again but decided to spend the night here. I slept solid through the night and a quick dip in the pond the next morning and I was ready to hit it again. I hacked my way back and forth for the next five days and found nothing but more jungle facing me. It was a matter of survival and I had to head back home.

I was very glad to get back to my home but not very happy. I went over my map carefully and realized I had only covered about a third of the last unexplored area. The zig zagging back and forth was not only time consuming but was wearing me down. I had a feeling of almost desperation to search the entire last area. I could only carry so many supplies. I wouldn't be close enough to the beach to be running back and forth for seafood. My second day home Sadie showed up with one of her pups that had about doubled inside since I first saw it. It was a female. It didn't take long for it to follow me around after I gave it some pork jerky. It was very independent and wandered off by itself. Buddy and family showed up my third day home. Skipper was a big boy now. I figured it wouldn't be long and he would be out checking the island out for himself. My family consisted of three gorillas and two foxes. Polly and Molly had added I am not sure how many more parrots or whatever they were. My family was growing. The best part was, Sadie and her pup were all that I had to feed thankfully. Sadie's pup came back and I decided to call her Suzy. She was a playful little rascal but still kind of puppy awkward. She would begin running and get tangled up with her own legs and go rolling.

I checked my map out several times and decided I wasn't coming home until I had explored what was left unexplored. I knew it would take at least a month. It took three weeks to build my food supply up. I figured Suzy would have to keep up or I would spell her off and carry her in my pack. Buddy and family showed up one more time before I left. I always put a bowl of grapes on the table for them. It was neat to see how they would pick one grape up at a time and eat it until they were all gone. I always got a lump in my throat when Buddy would turn around and grunt something to me before he disappeared in to the jungle. There is no doubt he was probably saying, "See you later". I could save a lot a lot of time if only the trails I cut through the jungle wouldn't grow back as fast as they do. This trip I was going to take a new route, if it were possible, I would take the beach up to where I could cut straight across to where I left off. I could camp out at the ruins and at the last home of the five deceased World War Two airmen. Not only that, Suzy could probably make it on her own walking on the beach.

I always liked camping on or near the beach. There is no music such as that of the surf. Plus clams and crabs were readily available for seafood dinners, which would stretch the supplies in my backpack longer. I figured I saved at least three days walking on the beach. Plus it wasn't the steamy hot jungle that drained ones strength. I woke up each morning refreshed and ready to tackle a new day. I reached the old ruins late on the fifth day. Nothing had changed except all of the clearing I had done had become over grown again. No problem; I didn't come here to further explore the ruins. I had just finished hanging my hammock when it began to rain. It was too late and wet to pitch my tent, and there was no way I was going to machete my way back in the ruins. I had an extra canvas just for a situation such as this; I covered myself and hammock with the canvas and woke up dry in the morning; plus it had quit raining. The humidity was so bad it was difficult to breath. It took two very difficult days to make it to the Jap's encampment.

The heat and humidity had drained my strength. I spent two days recovering before tackling the jungle again. I am not sure if it was the heat or what. I kept thinking if I didn't find any plane wreckage this time maybe I would begin building a boat; a boat like Noah's ark so I could take my family with me. After what I had been through these past years and what I had learned on my own I felt like there wasn't much I couldn't do. Well, look out jungle here I come. Late the third day of chopping my way through the jungle I arrived at the clear pond. I was too tired to swim but took a cool refreshing bath. Sadie went in the water on her own; I had to catch Suzy and put her in the water. At first she tried to get out; when I was ready to go I had to take her out of the water. The cool water perked me up enough to enjoy dinner. I got my map and compass out; it looked like I had maybe four more days of searching. If I didn't find any airplane wreckage I may as well quit looking. The problem was; the jungle was so thick there was a good chance I was within ten feet of any wreckage and may not have seen it.

Chapter Ten

I had trouble sleeping and woke up early. I was trying to stay calm and not let the search get to me. As I ate breakfast I thought of all of the miles of jungle I had cut my way through looking for a downed plane that I wasn't even sure even existed. It was just another long hot day and nothing but more jungle waiting for me. I figured at the most three more days of searching; if I found nothing, it was time I resolved myself that there was no airplane. It was just about quitting time the next day when my machete hit metal. I frantically cleared and found what looked like a wheel and part of a landing gear.

I'm not sure but I either cried, or almost cried. Now I had a difficult time sleeping because I was so excited. I did get some sleep, but woke up just as excited as when I tried to sleep last night. I savored my breakfast and couldn't wait to begin my search. It was about mid noon when I uncovered part of the right wing and an engine. It must have been adrenalin kicking in as I had to calm myself down when I found myself swinging my machete like a madman. I was hungry and it would be getting dark soon when I uncovered the tail of the plane. I must have said "Thank you Lord" a hundred times. It would probably take at least two days to clear enough jungle to find a way to get into the wreckage. My supplies were getting very low. If I skimped, I had maybe five days left. My dad's words began ringing in my ears; "Survival first"!

I had enough food to make it back to the beach. I found the

plane; that was my main objective. I had enough pork to feed Sadie and Suzy until we got back. OK! It would be a lot easier getting back to the beach than it was getting here as I had a well-cleared path to follow. I could live on seafood until I made it back to my place. I would check things out and take care of whatever needed tending to at my home sweet home. I would pack as much food as I could carry. This trip all together had taken me almost twenty days. The worst was over and I should be able to make it back to the plane in maybe six days. That would give me maybe ten days to explore the wreckage and see what I could salvage that I may need.

I shot two pigs and kept the smoker busy for the next couple of weeks. I had made about ten pounds of raisins from the abundance of grapes. I saved a lot of my garden that had started to go bad. Buddy and family visited me twice and I had to hide my raisins as Buddy and family would have wiped my supply out in no time. I found myself constantly smiling. Not that I would? But I found myself smiling every time I thought of that plane; there was enough salvageable material in that plane to build a big boat. I had no idea what to expect if or when I made it inside the plane. I could only carry so much and food was the most important item. I would take the hacksaw and extra blades and a hammer and chisel. My backpack was a lot heavier this time. I was going back soon enough that the jungle would not have had time to overgrow what I cut away this last time.

For a change, I had something to be very excited about. Then I thought, "What if the plane was carting a load of unexploded bombs"? One thing for sure; If it did contain bombs I wouldn't be doing any salvaging. I think if I didn't have the pack, AK and machete I probably would have tried to run all of the way back to the wreckage. Just as I was approaching the ruins it began to thunder and lightning. It seemed like every time I got close to the ruins bad weather hit. Was it trying to tell me something? I had time to pitch my tent before the cloud opened up. Sadie, Suzy and I had a cold dinner in the tent. By the time I woke up in the morning it had cleared up. Sadie and Suzy were behind the tent and began barking like in a panic; I got my AK and as I walked around the tent, I would have been barking too. There was a huge boa or python thirty feet from the tent. I put five rounds in it and it was one dead snake. It took about a half hour to round the foxes up. There was no doubt they did not like the sound of gunfire. They were even a little leery of me until we were back in the jungle. A couple of days later we had made it to the Jap's camp. We should be at the wreckage in two more days.

    Living in the jungle had kept me in very good shape. But this past few months of cutting my way back and forth through the jungle was beginning to take a toll on me. It was becoming obvious that I needed a long break to recharge my physical batteries. I should be at the wreck in two days. Once I made it inside the plane to satisfy my curiosity I would head back home, spend some time working on my ledger, and take a break. I woke up excited and to a beautiful morning; I thought if I quit being in such a hurry I would be doing myself a favor. It was a lot easier getting to the wreckage. I had to fight the urge to begin clearing jungle away from the plane as by the time we had dinner it would be getting dark. I woke up early and excited. After breakfast I cleared enough to see it was a big three-engine plane. I figured I would clear to the middle of the plane and get lucky and be able to get inside. No such luck. That was OK though. Once I made it to the plane clearing the jungle away would be a little easier.

    I finally made it to the front of the plane late the second day. The front end was badly torn up but I would be able to get inside the plane tomorrow. I took the foxes to the pond for a quick swim before it got dark. By the time we finished dinner it was dark. Suzy reminded me of Skipper and the pond; Nether of them wanted to get out of the water. I awoke to thunder and lightning, but no rain. By the time I had finished breakfast the sky had cleared and it was just a hot humid morning. I had to be careful climbing through the wreckage as there were a lot of very sharp jagged places. It took all day to work my way through the wrecked front end. I was fairly certain I could get to the inside of the plane tomorrow. One thing for sure; I saw all kinds of things I could salvage and use. I had lucked out; I had a couple of bruises and scratches, but no cuts.

After breakfast the next morning I thought, "Here I go, the moment of truth today". If I had a wish come true, the plane would have a lot of tools that I could use. Thankfully I had brought the hacksaw and spare blades along; I had a lot of cutting to do to get mangled aluminum out of the way. I could have really used a crow bar. I was able to finally cut a pipe loose that I could use to pry metal out of the way. I had no choice but had to get out and replenish my drinking water. It was extremely hot inside the plane. I was finally able to bend the last piece of aluminum out of the way and made it through the wreckage. It was pitch black as there were no windows. I turned my flashlight on and wasn't sure if my eyes were deceiving me. It looked like there were wooden crates stacked on both sides of the plane. Inside of each crate were four gold bars strapped down. I cut the bands on one crate and picked one of the bars up; it felt like it weighed maybe eighty pounds. I counted a hundred and twenty five bars. That meant there was about ten ton of gold in the wreckage.

The bars were stamped with what looked like the rising sun. This was an unimaginable treasure; but other than that I could maybe use the metal, it was no good to me on this island. Now the wood the crates were made of was a different story. I could find a lot of uses out of the milled lumber. As I stood looking at the gold, I began thinking of what if I had to spend the rest of my life on this island? I have had many wonderful experiences; my animal friends and family were something totally unbelievably special. I decided I would like to leave the island for short times, never over two weeks. This had been my home since I was a very young boy. I barely remembered the outside world. I remembered it was noisy and smelly. Not only that, and I had to laugh, I was the wealthiest person on this island. I claimed this island to be my very own. I had written enough in whatever it could be called. It wasn't a diary; more like an ongoing story that should be published someday.

I had better quit admiring my treasure and find what must be a door. There was a door but on the side of the plane I hadn't cleaned. I was able to unlatch it and get it open maybe two inches. That was my tomorrow project. The gold was the only cargo. I figured it was a maximum load. There was a tool chest and a set of acetylene torches. I couldn't tell if the plane was strictly a cargo plane or a converted bomber. I had to be just as careful getting out of the plane as I did getting in. Once I had the jungle cleared away from the door it would make everything a lot easier. The foxes were glad to see me. Time had slipped away and my stomach was growling loud enough to scare anything away. I had to make a serious decision. Whether I would spend my life on this island alone or not, I wanted that gold.

I was sure there was close to ten ton in what seemed to be eighty-pound bars. My supplies were running low. I had better get back home and do some serious thinking, and make some plans. I wanted to take a bar of gold with me, but what would I accomplish except wear myself out more. I must have gone to sleep a happy camper as I slept in for the first time in a long time. I had enough food to get back to the ocean and get the foxes back to home base. It was easier going getting back to the ocean as the jungle had not grown over the path I had opened up. The foxes surprised me and they liked fried clam. Well one thing for sure, we weren't going to run out of clams and crab.

There is no place like home and it felt great to open my front door. I cleaned up my garden area and was planting for my next crop when Buddy and family showed up. I figured they would be wandering in and had a big bowl of raisins waiting for them. As I sat and watched them enjoy the raisins, I knew I could never leave them for good. Two weeks? OK! But if I had to make a decision, I already made it. I was spending the rest of my life on this island.

Chapter Eleven

I couldn't get my mind off of the gold. If I were to ever try and get it off of the island I would have to rework it to get rid of the rising sun. I imagined if those with authority knew about that gold they would reclaim it for Japan. I figured they probably stole it in the first place. That meant I would have to get rid of the plane and anything the Jap's had written before they died. There was no doubt the pilot and copilot died in the crash because the cockpit was totally disintegrated. The plane was made mostly of canvas and wood. I would have to bury the three engines but could take most of the plane apart and burn small amounts at a time. There was enough salvageable metal to make a smelt and molds. That means I would have to live on this end of the island until the plane was gone and the gold reprocessed. It was a streak of luck the plane must have been built near the end of the war when any metal in Japan was very scarce.

If I ever had the opportunity to leave my island, I decided I would spend three weeks here and one week at home. I had no idea how long it would take to erase any signs of the plane and reprocess the gold, but what else did I have to do? Actually other than my garden, I would be fine here. Buddy and family were jungle animals, they would find me. That was it, my mind was made up; I would burn what I could of the plane and bury the rest. That meant clearing and keeping a large area free from anything that could burn. I spent three weeks at home prepping for my first month away from home. I shot seven of the pheasant like birds and smoked them along with two of what the dictionary described as wart hogs. Food would be all that I was taking back, along with some seeds for another garden. I made a shrill loud whistle out of bamboo and had Buddy and family follow me to the beach and up the beach for a way. I did this twice and it was evident they got the idea I wanted them to follow me. It was too bad I hadn't trained them to carry a backpack.

    I packed as much food as I could carry with a few pounds of raisins for the gorillas. We must have made quite the scene; three gorillas, two foxes and me with a backpack hiking up the beach. Twice when I woke up I thought the gorillas had returned to wherever they stayed but they would show up that day. Once we got to the plane I put my backpack inside the plane and headed for the pond. Skipper didn't hesitate or slow down and was the first one in the pond. It was more than big enough for the three gorillas and me. Once again, skipper did not want to get out. I am not sure what Becky was saying when she grunted angrily and took about two steps into the pond. Skipper couldn't get out fast enough and disappeared into the jungle. Once back at the plane I began preparing a decent camp area. Buddy and family disappeared the third day I was there. I had a cleared area big enough for a comfortable campsite. I would hold off planting a garden until later. It took two weeks to cut up and burn one wing.

    It took almost a week to dig a hole big enough for the first engine. I dug the hole right next to the engine that I shimmed. When I was sure the hole was deep enough I pulled the shims and the engine rolled into the hole. Another long day and one engine was covered and gone forever. It was break time and I headed home. It was easier every time I made this trip now as I had a trail that was easy to maintain. Once I got home I blew my whistle for a couple of minutes, it worked, about an hour later Buddy and family showed up. Being home now had become a routine. Weed the garden and gather what vegetables I could and replant. Go bird hunting and shoot at least one hog for smoking. My being at home cycle was about two weeks each time. It was mostly pruning my area and keeping up on the garden. Through all of that, I was getting my food supply to take back.

I was up early on the morning I would head back to the plane. I used the whistle as soon as I was up and outside. About an hour later, here came Buddy and family. Sure enough, we all headed up the beach together. Getting back to the plane amounted to no more than a long walk and camping out a few nights, which is basically how I lived anyway. It had become standard procedure to head for the pond as soon as it was feasible. Skipper should have been a fish. He was a show to watch at his various antics in the water. I am not sure if he was trying to dunk his mom, but she gave him a good swat and he let out a yelp. He stayed on the far side of the pond by himself and it looked like he was pouting. The third morning Buddy herded his family into the jungle; He turned and grunted at me and I grunted back. Oh boy; now I was beginning to talk like a gorilla.

The second wing section was larger; I still had about a fourth of it to cut up and burn when I knew it was time to head back home. I was losing ten or more days every time I headed home. Not counting the time at home I was losing about a month of which I could be disposing of the plane. I also had one hundred twenty five bars of gold to contend with. There was an area just south of where the Jap's had built their camp that was about thirty feet higher than then the rest of the mostly flat terrain. I checked it out and decided when it was time to begin disposing of the fuselage I would dig a cave and shore it up to hide the gold while I worked on it. In fact, I would build a structure and process the gold there. There was no sense in putting more to contend with until it was time to move the gold. But on a trial run, I made two trips to the high ground with a bar of gold each time. Two bars a day would be my limit, which meant

I was looking at two months or more just to move the gold. It was time to head home. There were always things to do when I got home. But once home I realized how hard I was working at the plane site.

I had a brainstorm while home this time; I began thinking of the deer north of here. The gators were far enough west and would be no problem. Those T Rexes, or whatever they were, could be a problem. I took the projectile out of five of the AK rounds and plugged the shells with enough candle wax that I could shoot a T Rex and scare it and maybe sting it a bit, but not severely hurt it. If that didn't work I wouldn't be smoking deer venison. Going on memory, it looked like a medium sized deer would dress out at less than a hundred pounds. I should be able to get one back to my place no problem if I could walk the beach until it was time to head inland. I would give it a trial run and see how it went. I packed enough supplies for six days. I didn't think it would take over four days round trip but it was better to be safe than sorry. In two days later, I was on high ground looking at a herd of deer grazing. No T Rex in sight so I put a good round in the chamber. I picked out a medium sized male and dropped it and the herd immediately scattered. I was just about finished dressing the deer out when I heard a screech; Two T Rexes were running toward me. I popped the first one and it let out a shriek, turned around, and beat feet. It took two rounds to change the second one's mind and he retreated to the jungle.

I tied the deer's four legs together and put my arms through the legs I tied which had the body resting on the top of my pack. This freed my arms up in case I had to use the AK. It took two hot sweaty days to get back home. By the time I got there my butt was dragging. I did butcher the deer and get it in, the once again enlarged, smoker before it got dark. I didn't remember going to bed. I woke up to a brainstorm; Why not build a smoker at my southern campsite. There were wart hogs north by the swamp area. The only reason I was going home now was to stock up on food. By the time eighty pounds of deer was smoked, it only weighed maybe sixty pounds. I had a total of ten or twelve pounds of raisins and another fifteen pounds of dried vegetables. Buddy and family stopped by once to see me. They polished off a bowl of raisins I had for them and Skipper got to play in the pond. The morning I was ready to leave I didn't whistle for them to follow me.

The hike to the downed plane area never got easier. The longer I planned on staying, the heavier my backpack got as I carried more food to stay longer. Building a smoker there should make my life easier. The front of the plane was aluminum of which I would build a smoker out of. I had enough vegetable seeds to start another garden and there was a variety of plants that were edible. I would upgrade from living in my tent. I knew I had a huge project on my hands. I had been on my island for many years now; it didn't look like I would be leaving anytime soon. Staying busy was very important; I had come close to depression several times and fought it off with a new project. I had to laugh; between getting rid of any signs of an airplane and reprocessing the gold, I was going to be kept busy for a long time.

First things first; I would use the big metal tool box to keep my food in; The small spring about two hundred feet from the plane was cold water; A little work and I would sink the tool box about half way to where the spring water would run around it; A perfect place to store my food. It would be safe from animals and cold enough to preserve my food. I had so much to do it could be mind-boggling. I arrived back at the plane about mid noon. I hung my hammock and emptied the toolbox. It was too big and heavy to carry so I dragged it to the area I would sink it in the ground. The ground was soft and I soon had the box where I wanted it. It was plenty big enough to hold the food that I brought. I was a muddy mess but now I didn't have to worry about my food supply going bad or animals enjoying it.

Sadie and Suzy liked the smoked deer a lot more than the pork and hung around while I got the box ready for the food. I gave them both a generous piece for their patience. I didn't need to be rocked to sleep. Putting in a hard day's work in the hot steamy jungle would help anyone go quickly to sleep. Sunup and jungle noises woke me up. Today I was cutting bamboo to make my shelter. Three days of hard work and I had a one-room "bungalow" built. It wasn't fancy, but would protect me from the elements. Once again, I could hear my dad's advice, "preparedness was essential for survival". Another week and I had a garden planted and a security fence out of bamboo and a thorny bush I spread around the base of it. There was an empty metal locker in the plane that with a lot of hacksaw work made a perfect smoker. The food supply I had brought was going down. Tomorrow I was going pig hunting and hopefully get a few of the pheasant birds.

The next day I had to circle half of the swampy area before I saw any hogs. The good thing about this swamp area was, there was very little water; it was just a muddy dangerous area. It was more like quick sand than mud; I found that out the hard way when it tried to suck me in. The good thing about it was, there were no alligators. This was a much larger herd of hogs than the one closest to my home north of here. I picked out one that I thought I would be able to get back to my new camp and fired. It ran about ten feet and dropped. I circled around to it and dressed it out. I would skin it back at camp because I thought I would cure the skin and make a bellows out of it. There were some trees that looked like crab apple trees close to the downed plane. I had cut a big pile of saplings to use in the smoker. By the time I got back to camp it took the rest of the day to get the hog cut up and in the smoker. Thankfully, everything grows so fast in the jungle. My garden was showing green sprouts. With any luck I wouldn't have to go back to my northern home for a couple of months.

Tomorrow I would start on the second wing and motor. I had

a better plan; I would carry a gold brick to the spot I was going to stash it; then I would spend half the day working on the cave where I would stash the gold. I would spend the rest of the day working on the second wing. I would rotate like this every day. I would use wood I salvaged from the plane to shore up the little cave I was digging. By the end of the fifth day, I was ready for a well-deserved break. I was going to go bird hunting tomorrow and pay the pond a visit. I had made good progress on the cave and the wing. Rather than work myself into the ground I would work five days and scrounge for food, and make good use of the pond. I woke up the next morning feeling good about not working for a couple of days. I had to laugh; I only had one hundred twenty gold bars to move. I finished breakfast, fed the foxes and headed in the direction I felt the birds might be. About the time it was time to head back I saw a flock of birds. It was too late and I didn't want to be cutting my way through the jungle after dark. Not only that, but my backpack was heavy with the grapes I had found.

It was getting dark when I got back to camp. I would build a screen to dry the grapes on for a raisin supply tomorrow. I was up early the next morning and I had just finished spreading the grapes out on the screen when Buddy and family surprised me; they acted about as excited to see me as I was to see them. I had kept a bowl of grapes for myself of which I shared with them. We still had time for a dip in the pond. Skipper was a water bug and was quite the show. When we got out of the pond they headed for the jungle; Buddy turned and grunted to me and yes, I grunted back.

Chapter Twelve

Five more days of hard work and I had the hole dug for the second motor and over half of the wing cut up and five more gold bars stacked up. I went bird hunting the next day; an all-day effort, and I had four and a half birds in the smoker. The foxes and I had the other half of one for dinner. It would be quite a while before I began reworking the gold. Just for the heck of it I brought a bar to my camp and made a handle for one of the wood rasps; about an hour of scraping and I had about a fourth of the bar scraped off. There was a half dozen one-gallon oilcans in the plane. I would make a tumbler out of one to put the gold scrapings and a couple hands full of small gravel in it. The little spring had enough water to turn the tumbler. A couple of days in the tumbler and the gold scrapings would look like recovered gold from a stream. I woke up to the welcome sound of my family. I had three gorillas and two foxes waiting for me to get up.

As I ate breakfast, who would believe that I was having breakfast with three gorillas and two foxes. After breakfast I went to the plane to get an oilcan to clean out. The screw on cap was big enough to easily get the gold and gravel in. I didn't want to waste the oil; it may be of use down the line. I used sand and water to get the can squeaky clean. A little hacksaw work and the tumbler had a three-foot axel through it. The gorillas had been very patient, and all I said was "pond" and Skipper was on the way. He was splashing in the pond when we got there. The gorillas were a welcome relief whenever they showed up. Kind of like some company is better than no company. By the end of the next week I had the wing cut up and the motor rolled in the hole and covered up. I made the cave just big enough that it could easily be big enough to hold all of the gold bars; I didn't attempt to make it a live in cave. I had worked on the gold bar every night and had it ready for the tumbler. I figured I could do five pounds of gold at a time. Leave it tumble for two days and do another batch.

Buddy seemed to have my work schedule figured out; He and family always showed up on my second day off. I called the pond Skippers pond even though it was obvious Buddy and Becky enjoyed it too. And me too! By the end of the week, the wing was burned and the tumbler, after a couple of adjustments, worked perfect. I had what I figured to be ten pounds of gold that looked like it came from a riverbed. I had four different sixed rasps. By using all four of them I had basically four sizes of gold and mixed together looked like natural gold from a stream. Buddy and family didn't show up this time and I missed them. On one of my explorations up north, I thought I had seen four or five gorillas but the distance and jungle made it almost possible to be sure. There had to be more or how did Buddy's mom get pregnant?

I had plenty of work to do and could take a pass on socializing on my days off. I harvested a decent crop from my garden and replanted. The gold tumbling was going well. I took pleasure in looking the outside of the plane over and not working on it. I decided to begin taking the fuselage apart starting with the tail section. I made an axe of sorts out of one of the propellers, which worked great when there was wood chopping to be done. I did go to the pond and enjoyed myself but missed the gorillas. I enjoyed my two days off; my food supply was holding up but I would need meat within the next two weeks. I thought I could save time and head for the beach, and load up on seafood. I knew that I could smoke clams, but wasn't sure about smoking crab? My final decision was work two more weeks and head north. I could spend a couple of days at home and bring a deer back with me; Maybe get a few birds on the way back. I was ready to go to work on the fuselage.

It rained hard during the night. There was something about rain and sleep. I seemed to sleep totally sound through a rainstorm. I actually liked a storm, especially if there was a lot of thunder and lightning. It had stopped raining by the time I woke up; the fresh smell after a rain made me want to take deep breaths. I checked the spring to make sure the tumbler was OK. It was turning a little faster but was doing fine. My goal for the day was to get the entire tail section cut loose. I had to be careful as it was about five feet off of the ground. I cut around the bottom first and had both sides cut by quitting time. It was hanging from the top, which needed cutting about four feet and it should hit the ground. I would be able to drop it tomorrow and begin cutting it up. There looked to be three days of burning to get rid of it.

I was up bright and early the next morning to the barking of the foxes. I got my AK and opened the door; I didn't see anything at first and then I saw a tiger looking our way. I hit it in the rear end with a wax bullet. It leaped in the air and let out a howl, and was gone. I doubt if it would ever be back. The shot scared the foxes who calmed down when I walked towards the smoker. They got a special treat this morning for waking me up. I was anxious to get to work and get the tail section on the ground. About an hour of sawing and the tail fell, but didn't hit the ground. It was hanging by the cables that controlled it. I had to get inside the plane as the cables were hanging from the bottom of the plane. I looked through the tools but there were no bolt cutters. I rolled the cutting torches up and made short work of the cables and the tail crashed to the ground. It took three days but I finally had the tail in three separate piles to burn.

I decided to work on the front of the plane next. It was mostly aluminum and presented a real challenge, as I wanted to save as much as I could. The motor was shoved back into the cockpit area and made it even more dangerous to work in that area. I would do some cutting tomorrow and get a better idea how to dismantle the front. I was working on the third gold bar and that would be the last one I made into "Gold Dust". I had emptied some aviator gear out of a neat wooden box that could easily hold two hundred and forty pounds of gold. I would put about eighty pounds of gold in the box and take it up to the cave. It would take two more trips to take the remaining one hundred sixty pounds up to the box. I woke up early anxious to get started on the front end. Today would be mostly exploring, the rest was to take the front end apart. It turned out to be a good day; I wound up with three large panels of aluminum.

Buddy and Becky showed up and spent my two days off with me. I wondered and worried about Skipper. He had proven to be a young active rascal. I thought of Buddy's mom and how she had died. Buddy and Becky had just got to the edge of the jungle to leave when Skipper showed up, with another gorilla. Well how about that, Skipper had a girlfriend! I put a bowl of raisins on the table; Buddy and Becky came back. Skipper came to the table and began grunting to the female. She slowly made her way to the table and cautiously began to eat the raisins. I decided to call the female Katy. I thought "Skipper you sly rascal, you have been holding out on us". As per usual, Buddy stopped at the edge of the forest and grunted his goodbye. I waited a minute to see what he would do. He grunted a couple more times and I grunted back, and he disappeared into the jungle. I guess I was talking a gorilla goodbye. I had to laugh as I thought "One of these days Skipper and Katy would be bringing a little skipper along with them".

I woke refreshed and ready to get to work. I kept thinking of Skipper and his girlfriend. I was actually laughing when I thought one of these days they would come wandering in with a little Skipper. That reminded me that Suzy had been wandering off for a couple of days at a time. I hoped if she had a litter of pups she didn't bring them here. Feeding two foxes was OK but I didn't feel like feeding a pack of foxes. Taking the front end apart was a real challenge; there seemed to be a maze of wires. I saved the longer lengths of wire as I found many uses for the salvaged wire. I saved one of the seats, which would make a comfortable seat in my one room. I saved seven big panels of aluminum, which should be more than enough for me to make what would be needed when I began smelting the gold. The biggest and best find were two small stainless steel hydraulic cylinders and two large ones. I could make molds out of the two smaller ones and melting pots out of the two big ones. The two pigskins I had been working on were very pliable now. I would for sure need a bellows when I began smelting.

Another week and I should be ready to bury the front engine and anything I couldn't use from the wrecked nose. Between working on the plane and hauling gold bars, by the time I could take a break on my two days off I was ready to do anything that didn't require physical labor. Sure enough, Buddy and family showed up. Skipper no longer acted like a playful young gorilla; He was very attentive to Katy. This would be their last visit before I had to take a break and replenish the grape and raisin inventory. I too ate a handful with my breakfast every morning. It was one of my few sugar sources. I discovered a way to make pancakes out of the fruit I dried and pounded into flower and I made decent syrup by boiling a bunch of raisins. There was one thing for sure about this island; there was more than enough food here if you knew how to get it. As I waved and grunted goodbye to Buddy and family I wondered what life would be like without them. Very lonesome no doubt! I laughed and thought maybe I could catch a baby T Rex and train it, if I survived trying to catch it. A bad idea!

I decided to gather grapes and do a little hunting the next day. I woke feeling good knowing this was a work day and I wasn't going to work. Grapes were in abundance and I soon had my backpack full. Hogs were nowhere to be seen but I did shoot four birds. The foxes and I were going to enjoy a good dinner tonight. Both foxes began barking and it was evident why there were no hogs today, on the far side of the mud bog were two tigers. I changed the ammo to wax heads just in case. As I headed south so did they. No sense in taking a chance and I cranked a round their way. I doubt if the wax traveled to them but the guns noise did the trick as they both jumped and disappeared to the northwest. By the time we got back to camp I was one pooped guy. I dressed the birds and got them in the smoker, and spread about eighty pounds of grapes on the drying screen. I had found a spot for the screen where it got direct sunlight. The two scarecrows I made and hung over the screen kept the birds and everything else away. The foxes and I enjoyed fried bird for dinner. I felt much rested up and looked forward to tomorrow.

I woke up to a windy tropical rain. No problem. I had wanted to take the crates apart that held the gold. It was inside the plane out of the rain. I could be stacking the gold bars by the door and save myself dragging it out one bar at a time when I hauled it to the cave. What I thought would be a piece of cake turned out to be one sore back, and I had only moved about half of it. I was sure there would be another rainy day and this project would be there waiting for me to finish. It was a bright sunny morning the next day. I was determined to finish the front end in the next three days.

That didn't happen. The motor was in the way but I had to get everything clear before I could begin digging a hole big enough for the engine and scrap what was left. The middle motor was much larger than the wing motors. I dug in front of the motor to about a third of the way back on the motor. I had to be careful as the front of the motor was much heavier than the back. I used some of the lumber from the gold crates to safely hold the motor while I dug a little further under it. When it was evident the wood frame I made was holding the motor up I quit digging when I could see a slight movement in the motor. I tied two of the longest cables together that I had salvaged and tied it to one corner of the frame I built. I pulled the frame and it fell in the hole; the motor tilted forward but didn't fall. I cut a thick bamboo and made a pole about eight feet long; I got behind the motor and put the pole under it. It wiggled twice and the third time fell into the hole. I dropped the pole and called it a day. I was dirty, tired and hungry.

Buddy and family didn't show up on my two days off. It was just as well as I just needed to take it easy and rest. I spent a couple of restful days working on my ledger and doing minimal clean up around my place. Sadie and Suzy showed up and were full of burrs. I spent a couple of hours "de-burring" them. It was the two most rest full days I had in a long time. I was getting antsy and ready to get back to work. Cutting up what was left of the front end was more of a chore than I had planned on. I was close to putting the rest of the junk in the hole. I figured when I got up tomorrow, if I was lucky, I could have all of the junk in the hole and the hole covered in two days. That wasn't going to happen yet because thunder and lightning woke me up. Next, it began to rain as only it can rain in the tropics. It was like Heaven was pouring every last drop of rain on me. I brought the foxes inside and we had breakfast together.

I was going to work inside the plane today. I opened the door for the foxes to go out and they both lay down as if to say "No thank you". I propped the door open so they could get out if they wanted to. I ran for the plane and was completely soaked when I got inside. It was OK though as it was hot and humid in the plane. I finished moving the gold and taking the crates apart. I had a nice pile of wood and a big pile of nails that I salvaged and straightened. My stomach told me it must be getting late as it was doing a lot of growling. I never did get dry while working in the plane. It was hot enough to dry me except the humidity kept me soaked. I decided to make a run for my place. The foxes had decided to spend the day in my dry place. Good idea; I got out of my wet clothes as soon as I could. I had vegetables and fried venison which is why I think the foxes stayed inside all day. I had smoked certain parts of the deer for my foxes and they wasted no time in putting it away.

It quit raining while we ate and as soon as Sadie and Suzy had cleaned their dishes, they were out the door. I am not sure how much it rained in inches, but the hole for the motor and parts was almost half-full. It was a cool day so I hauled gold bars over to the tunnel. I thought about taking two at a time until I picked two bars up of which I quickly set down. Two bars of gold weighed more than I did. I had seen something of interest as I cleaned junk out of the cockpit. I knew it was my two days off but curiosity got the best of me; the water in the hole had begun going down already. I threw junk in the hole as I dug back behind where the cockpit had been. Jackpot! I found what looked to be an oblong stainless steel pan about a foot deep. It was about a foot wide and a foot and a half long. The main component of stainless steel was chromium, which had a very high melting point. This would be the charcoal burner.

Chapter Thirteen

It had been a couple of weeks since I saw the gorillas; I am sure they could take care of themselves. I did a thorough cleaning job around the plane and threw anything that was junk in the hole with the motor and covered it up. One way or another I had been going nonstop and even lost track of time. I decided to head out for my northern home as I am sure it needed tending to. I wasn't wrong. A few more weeks and my home would belong to the jungle again. I put two hard weeks of pruning and trimming in. I hadn't replanted the garden which was now totally over grown with weeds and junk vegetation. I wasn't replanting so I let it go. I decided to take a deer back; I made eight wax bullets but made the wax projectile twice as big as last time. I didn't want to kill a T REX, but I didn't feel like being a gourmet meal for them either. My second day put me at the base of the big hill where the deer grazed below it. I got up at the break of dawn and in position to get a shot as several deer cautiously came in to view. It was like they were scouts and then quite a few more appeared. I picked out a medium sized buck and dropped him where he stood. The herd disappeared in the blink of an eye.

    I didn't have to be in a hurry and waited a while but no T Rexes. I gutted and beheaded the deer and had just loaded it on my back when three T Rexes came screaming out of the jungle. It took seven rounds of wax to get them running back to the jungle. I only had one wax round left and I would have had to hit them with real rounds.

They were about as scary as the alligators. I was glad to get the heck out of there. Those big wax rounds must have hurt but they just kept coming. I lucked out this time. No more deer hunting there unless I figured out how to scare them mean rascals away. By the time the deer was cured in the smoker I was ready to go back and get to work on the plane. Buddy and family still did not show up. Maybe they found something better than my raisins. I am sure the foxes were happy that I had bagged a deer. I saved the heart and tongue for them for their special treat.

We made it back to our southern camp just as a tropical storm came crashing in. This was a lot worse than the usual tropical storm; it was a worrisome fierce storm. There were a couple of times when I thought my hotel Ritz was going to blow away. If I thought we could make it, I would have got the Foxes under my arms and ran for the plane; I am sure it was probably safe. The third morning the wind had stopped as well as the rain. The foxes made it evident they were glad to get outside and so was I. There were a lot of branches and palm fronds to clean up. Luckily, there was little or no damage in my area. Two days of clean up, and it was time to get to work on the plane. I needed a ladder tall enough to get to the top of the plane. The horizontal bracings on the plane were perfect for the ladder's verticals and pieces cut from the ribs were just right for the horizontal steps. The nails I salvaged put the finishing touches on my ladder. It took the remaining three work days to cut a four foot section off of the body. I decided to haul gold my first day off. I had the pile down to seventy-three bars. I was definitely gaining.

It took a week to cut the four-foot section up and burn it. The planes diameter grew larger as it progressed to the front of the plane. The next section took almost two weeks to cut a three-foot section loose and burn it. No matter how tired I was I always took a gold bar up to the smelting area. I had no idea how long it would take to dispose of the plane and redo the gold; Just the plane would take at least a hundred days. I still had to bury the landing gear I almost tripped over. I was going to work from the back to the front until I got close to the gold; then I would work from the front to the back. It didn't make any difference if the weather got to the gold. The worst the weather would do is wash the dust off. The day before my day off I stood back and looked at what was left of the plane. What plane?

I wasn't in a hurry to get up; I decided to work straight through for the next seven days and then head for the old homestead. The traveling back and forth between my places was taking too much time when I could be getting rid of the plane. I decided to make one more trip to my northern home and not return until there was no trace of the plane. After six long hard days I had eliminated and burned another four foot section and had another four foot section on the ground ready to be cut up and burned. I figured if nothing went wrong I could finish up the plane project in just over a month and a half. I decided to put two days in hauling gold from the plane. There were fifty-eight bars still in the plane when I ran out of steam. I sat looking at what was left of the plane. There was about thirty-two feet left. It would take about ten more days to get the last of the gold out of the plane. That meant I had less than two months and I could begin working on the smelting equipment. I had to chuckle when I thought "Or I could burn what was left where it sat". That could turn into disaster. Plus I was saving the cable and a lot of screws.

It was good to be heading north. There was no doubt the foxes knew we were heading home; they would run ahead and wait for me. I had a real good feeling as I entered my cleared area that needed a lot of pruning and clearing. There was no sense in putting the cart before the horse; I went hunting the next day and by that evening had a hog and five birds in the smoker, which filled it to the max. For the next few days I kept the fire in the smoker on slow smoke and had to turn the hog and birds more often which worked out fine. Every time I took a break I would tend to the smoker. I had about fifty pounds of raisins about ready to take off of the screens when Buddy and Becky came hurrying out of the jungle. Two big gorillas hugging on little old me could have been disaster if I wasn't careful. They had no idea of their strength but I did. The three of us sat on the ground enjoying a bowl of raisins when Skipper and Katy came out of the jungle.

I should have known; but I still couldn't believe my eyes. They were coaxing a beautiful baby gorilla in front of them. He was determined to go his own way but his parents kept him heading towards us. I wanted to pick him up and hold him but he wasn't quite ready for that. He saw the bowl of raisins and knocked the bowl over getting to them. I quickly got the raisins back in the bowl and on the table. He was bound and determined to get up on the table. He was a little guy and I was sure he shouldn't be eating too many raisins so I put a few in my hand and held them out to him. He tried to get them all, knocked a couple on the table, and scrambled to get them. I picked them up and gave them to him. His parents and grandparents were just finishing up the remainder in the bowl. I got two and gave them to him. I picked him up and put him on the ground. He climbed up my leg into my lap looking for more raisins on the table. His mother picked him up and grunted something, and gave him a swat. He lay down in her lap and was sound asleep.

There was some grunting and Buddy headed towards the jungle, and his family followed. Buddy grunted and waved and then disappeared. I decided to call the baby Little Guy. As he grew and got bigger, I would just call him Guy. This whole thing was unreal; it all started with my rescuing Buddy when he was a baby like Guy. My family was growing. I left the gate to my garden open. There was little or nothing worth harvesting. I hoped Buddy and family would visit me at the southern location. It didn't bother me to head south this time as it always had before. I think the worst part was the time it took traveling back and forth. Unless there was a good reason, I wouldn't be back until the plane was totally gone.

I did feel sadness as I turned to look at my old homestead before heading into the jungle. I almost felt like I was making a fool out of myself; I felt sadness when I left my southern place also. I believe I heard my dad say once "Danged if I do and danged if I don't". That's how I felt about my two homes, but then a thought made me laugh; I could build another home half way between my two homes and really complicate things. By staying in my southern home it would make it too far to get a deer and bring it back. I had thought about going deer hunting before I headed south again. The plane project was wearing me down. I don't know why I was pushing as hard as I was. I had nothing to prove and I wasn't going anywhere. What was not so funny was; I had millions of dollars in gold and couldn't spend a penny of it.

As I entered my clearing I thought, here we go again; I was glad to be home again. I actually had it better at my southern home. I had everything here including the pond, which was a great swimming hole. The only thing I didn't have here were the deer. I stood looking at what was left of the plane; I could salvage seven horizontal two by fours thirty-four feet long. I had been saving a lot of the screws that held the frame together. That meant I could build a boat thirty-four feet long. But I would need a Noah's Ark to take my family. I had better be careful and not go getting wild ideas that weren't going to happen. I would bet if they had the chance the gorillas would not want to leave this island. Plus I would have no idea which way to go. If I were all alone I would build a boat. I had enough sail material left for one set of sails. I thought 'Let it go, neither I nor the gorillas are going anyplace".

The foxes had become somewhat domesticated as they liked sleeping inside with me. I slept in as I had carried a large load of food back this time. I was in great shape but the load had worn me down. I took care of putting the food where it belonged and even transferred four bars of gold. I decided to save the horizontal frame. I would stash it in the jungle but not with a boat in mind. Not only that, If I did build a boat for me and my family it would have to be big enough to carry twenty ton of bananas just in case for the gorillas. The whole boat thing was bizarre and I decided to not think about it again. I got a brainstorm and decided to take all of the screws out of the frame before I began cutting it apart. I used a small pipe wrench to hold and turn the screwdriver. I could remove the screws twenty times faster this way. The canvas still would not come loose from the frame as it was also glued to the frame. Actually, the glue held the plane together better than the screws.

I put two hard weeks in. I burned three panels, hauled ten more gold bars, and was beginning to see light at the end of the tunnel. I lost a day of work when Buddy and family showed up. It was evident Skipper wanted to head for the pool. Why not? It seemed like a good day for a family swim. Katy was hesitant about going in at first; when she finally came in Little Guy was clinging to her back. I could tell he has afraid as his eyes were wide open. After getting wet a few times he wanted to go in by himself. His mom sat him in the shallow water and he was a little Skipper all over. He put up a regular little kid fuss when he was taken out of the pond. It took swats from his mom before he gave up and snuggled his mom on the way back to the camp. A couple hand full of grapes calmed him down and they headed back into the jungle. I woke up early the next morning; I felt like I was on a roll and wanted to get to work. I heard the foxes barking like crazy and picked my AK up. Sure enough, there was a tiger by the smoker. I put a wax round in and hit him in the rear end. He was gone in the blink of the eye. I gave Sadie and Suzy venison treat; I was reserving the venison for them. I had like a double whammy going;

I was close to disposing of the plane, but I was beginning to feel drained at the end of each day.

As I began sawing on the next panel I knew it was good I was nearing the end of disposing of the plane; I knew I should be excited that the day wasn't too far off when I was no longer sawing or struggling with each panel. That didn't get me through the day any easier. I continued to fight the urge to burn what was left without working on it anymore. I had been on my island a long time and this was the first time I had to push myself to go to work each day. I thought "Here we go", I had a brainstorm. A couple of years ago, I wondered what a cup of coffee would taste like: I experimented with various plants, berries and roots. I even boiled a root that tasted like sassafras. The last berry I boiled and tried made me very dizzy. So dizzy I didn't do one productive thing the rest of the day. I would treat myself to a cup of whatever it was at the end of each fifth day; maybe I had better wait until just before I went to bed. I felt I deserved something for the way I had worked all of these years; especially after disposing of the plane.

After work on the fifth day A went to get a cup full of the berries I named, "The merry berry". I remembered the last time I boiled a handful. This time I boiled a half of a handful. I worked on my ledger while I sipped on a cup full of my merry berry tea. I began having a problem focusing my eyes. I raised the wick on my lamp but even the lamp flame was blurry. I had only drank a half of the cup, plus I only boiled eight beans. I thought," I'll just lay down for a bit and rest my eyes". The sun woke me up shining through the door opening. I was fully clothed and hadn't even closed my door. One thing for sure; If I ever had trouble going to sleep I would do an eight beaner. For experiment sake only, tonight I would add a half cup of water to the left over tea. If that put me out, I would cut back to two beans. This was supposed to be a treat and not knock me on my butt.

I decided to begin working on a smelt today; or at least begin laying things out to get an idea where I would start. Better yet, I would haul four bars before I began, and I had to laugh, before I began smelting. My mom's dictionary was probably the greatest treasure I had. It was almost like an encyclopedia; I learned so much from that big thick book. Mom had started me reading and arithmetic when I was four; otherwise, the book would have been useless to me. Mom would be proud of me as I was continuously learning something from that dictionary. I had no idea of the melting temperatures of gold and stainless steel until I researched it in "The book". Gold was almost two thousand and stainless steel twenty six hundred. I salvaged a large stainless steel cup off of the planes brake assembly. It had one hole in the bottom of it of which I closed with the acetylene torch. I then welded a long handle on it and formed a pour spout. I made thick mittens out of pigskin. I had the cylinders for molds. I realized I had gotten carried away from excitement at the smelting equipment I was making. I would put extra hours in for the next four days.

I got up early in a hurry to see what I could accomplish in four days in ridding the plane of another section. I did torch a four-foot section in four days; but I wouldn't try that again. I could barely crawl in bed on the fourth night. I woke up according to my outdated calendar Saturday morning sore from top to bottom. One sure way to work the soreness out was to see how many bars of gold I could get moved. The best I could do was six bars, which earned me a long relaxing dip in the pond. I took Sunday off and did some cleaning around my place. I had fried bird for dinner of which the foxes waited patiently for their dinner. I did weed the garden, which was a week away from harvest. I looked at what was left of the plane and wondered if I did the right thing eliminating any trace of it

Chapter Fourteen

I had been on my island fourteen years and never saw another human being. But then I could hear my dad say; "Always be prepared". Between eliminating the wrecked plane and hauling the bars of gold every night, I did not have to be rocked to sleep. I was prepared to sleep in on my two days off. I would haul gold both days. The pile in the plane was down to thirty-four bars. I wasn't sure if it was Saturday and Sunday or not. It didn't make any difference; the island was my world; not only that but those that have the gold make the rules. Sunday a commotion woke me up; Well how about that? Buddy and family were waiting impatiently for me to get up. As soon as I joined them, Little Guy began acting up. I knew what he wanted and headed for the pond. Guy splashed his mother and she gave him a good swat; He retreated to the end of the pond and sat for a few minutes and there was no doubt; he was pouting. The foxes and I hadn't had breakfast yet and I headed home.

I finished breakfast with my foxes and got a bowl of raisins ready, and headed back for the pond. I was just in time to see Guy trying to evade his mom as she tried to catch him and get him out of the pond. All of a sudden Skipper jumped in the pond and dragged a very noisy Guy out of the pond. In the human world I believe he would be considered a problem child. Guy was unruly all the way back to camp until he saw the bowl of grapes. He was going for two hands full when his mother sat him on the ground and yup; she whopped him a couple of times. By the time he finished the raisins he was ready for a nap. His mom picked him up by an arm and put him on her back. Guy was a hand full. Buddy went to the edge of the jungle and called his family. Guy had made sure it was a busy day. I hated to see them go but I still had time to haul some gold. I was down to thirty-four bars.

I put in a hard week and had the plane down to three sections and twenty-four bars of gold to haul. I spent the weekend harvesting my garden and filling the drying rack to the brim. I didn't have any choice, I was low on meat and had a taste for seafood. I decided to head for my old homestead next weekend. I needed a break from the everyday routine of eliminating the plane and hauling gold. I decided to go for a deer and maybe some birds when I got home. I would be on the beach four days coming and going; I was going to enjoy seafood for four days. The foxes weren't into seafood other than fried clams so I saved the last of the venison for them. My place had survived the weather but the jungle was closing in. Four days of swinging the machete to clear my place had me thinking that eliminating the plane wasn't so bad after all. The garden fence needed repairing but I wasn't going to be planting. It was evident Buddy and family were using the pond here. It needed minor repairs.

The deer had moved further north to more rugged high country; after two day's I shot a medium sized male. I didn't see any T Rex but heard them just west of where I was. I stayed on top of the high country and headed west. It took me in the direction of the large alligators. I was being very careful as I heard what had to be the T Rexes. Below was the swampy area and then I saw them; four T Rexes were tearing a very large alligator apart. A fifth T Rex came screaming out of the jungle and joined the four having dinner at the alligators expense. The biggest T was about seven feet tall; I was thankful they stayed on this end of the island. If they ever began showing up anywhere close to my homes I would not hesitate to shoot them. It would not do well for a person with a weak stomach to watch them tear that alligator to shreds.

I had my deer and that is what I came for, I was careful heading back for the beach; I could scare the tigers off with a wax bullet or two but I wasn't sure if my AK would even stop one of those carnivorous creatures. About halfway to the beach, I made an amazing discovery; I found a dead T Rex and a dead big buck deer. I hadn't given it much thought; but these deer did not have antlers, they had like two slim horns up to a foot long. The deer had impaled the T Rex, which killed the T Rex, but the deer, evidently because of the T Rex position, couldn't get its horn out. This may be the reason the T Rexes were leaving the deer alone. But then I came upon a second herd of deer. It was a big island and hopefully room for me and all of the wildlife.

The deer I shot was a big one; it still weighed over a hundred pounds dressed out. My camp never looked as good as I entered the clearing. Fortunately I had time to get the deer cut up and in the smoker. Of course, the foxes had a great dinner as well as me. I stayed another week at the old homestead. I shot five birds that went in the smoker with the deer. It was a good thing I enlarged the smoker when I did. The deer had shrunk down to about seventy-five pounds and the birds about three pounds each; that meant I had about ninety pounds to pack back. I was beginning to feel guilty. I needed a break from my daily routine at my south camp, but I had no intention of taking a two-week vacation. The clam and crab dinners on my way back eliminated some of the guilt. I wished my camp were closer to the beach; I could live on seafood.

I was glad to get back to my south camp or home. I think the foxes were just as happy. If it weren't for the deer on the north end of the island I would probably give up on the north camp. I knew once I had gotten rid of the last of the plane I had one big project facing me. I had no idea how long it would take me to rework the gold. But, it wouldn't be the brutal hard work of taking the plane apart and disposing of it. I had salvaged various metal parts from the plane that I thought could become very useful as time went by. I had saved a few pieces of stainless steel pipe of various diameters and thought they could be used in making my own gold coins. In the meantime- get myself mentally ready and finish the plane and hauling ingots. I got up early and found renewed energy as I began cutting another section loose. I paced myself and hopefully the renewed energy would last. I almost wished I had planned on working with the gold on the area where the plane had been. It would have saved a lot of back breaking carrying it to where I would work it. I think that is called hindsight. By the time I had finished burning the last section I had cut loose and hauled gold, I had two sections to go and ten bars of gold to transfer.

I was really tired of eliminating the plane. It was hard work and if I had it to do over I'm not sure if I would have tackled that project. I planned on taking a break Sunday and Buddy and family made sure that I did. They showed up just after I had breakfast. I let them empty a bowl of raisins and devour the six banana type fruit I had picked. Then we wasted no time heading for the pond. Guy should have been a fish; he rolled, jumped and splashed us all; I had to laugh. His mother instead of whopping him began to splash him. He did not like that and once again went to the end of the pond and looked like he was pouting. He was not a baby anymore. He had become, what in human terms, I would consider a twelve year old. He was a rascal and full of the devil. If he was human he would have been the clown in any neighborhood. But a well-loved clown I am sure. Here I was spending a Sunday afternoon in a pond with five gorillas; I thought, "Maybe I wasn't a human anymore"?

When they were ready to go Guy came over and gave me a hug. It always bothered me when Buddy would grunt goodbye and wave as he followed his family back into the jungle. The foxes and I enjoyed a venison dinner. I was anxious for tomorrow and primed to get back to work. I did a two-bean drink that evening; I didn't feel silly but felt totally relaxed. For no better name, I renamed the drink or tea "Goodnight". I slept like a baby and woke up raring to go. I had lost track of how long I had been taking the plane apart. As I stood watching the next to last section burn I laughed and thought I ought to leave the last section alone, it could be a memorial. But that would defeat my purpose of no trace. By Sunday afternoon I had transferred the last gold bar. I had one section to go and the landing gear I had stumbled on. I spent the weekend planting in my garden. I was kind of glad I had no" company". I was always glad to see Buddy and family, but it cost me a day of productivity.

I finished up at the garden and went over to the pond to rinse off; it always seemed strange whenever I went in the pond by myself. By the time the foxes and I had a late dinner I was ready for some "Goodnight". It did the trick and Mr. Sandman was quick to visit me. As I took the last section of the plane apart I was kind of sad to see the last of the plane go. The pounding rainstorms we had had basically eliminated a big ash pile. I burned each section away from where I burned the last section. There must be something in the ash that plant life liked; Areas that were three or four weeks since I burned there had various plants rapidly sprouting up. I should have been very happy but I was really sad to look where the plane was and saw nothing. The jungle was already beginning to take the area over where the plane had laid.

I found the landing gear I had stumbled on; it had at least two days of clearing that would enable me to dig a hole big enough to bury the wheel and assembly. I was so thankful that the soil stayed moist and soft. One more week and I believe I'll celebrate. Saturday I went over to where I would be working with the gold. I had a lot of work to do before I even touched the gold. One thing for sure; I didn't have to look far for building material to build a structure out of. I would build it big and tall enough as I would be working with fire and I for sure did not want to burn the structure down. Sunday I worked on the garden and finished the day with a dip in the pool. I was having difficulty going to sleep; I got up and made a two beaner of Goodnight, which did the trick. I had been excited last night knowing this was the last week of disposing of the plane. Goodnight allowed me to get a good night's sleep and I was raring to go.

Just like I figured; it took two days to clear the area to dig the hole for the wheel. Another three days to dig a hole big enough. The only easy part was I was able to roll the wheel and assembly into the hole. I did not want to come back Monday to finish filling the hole so I worked Saturday and thankfully finished early Sunday afternoon. As I walked across the area where the plane had been it sank into me what a major project I had undertaken. It wouldn't take long and the jungle would take over the entire area. By the time I got back to my place a major storm was brewing. This was going to be a major storm as the thunder shook the ground and the lightning was actually frightening. The foxes were more than glad to be inside with me. It rained so hard I became concerned; this was more rain than I could remember. I was glad I didn't have the tumbler working. I'll bet the pond was going to look like a lake. I worked on my ledger for a while and decided to call it a night. Working straight through the weekend had me ready for a much needed good night's sleep. I didn't need Goodnight tonight, the pounding of the rain on my roof lulled me to sleep. I woke up and had to smile, the storm was gone and the air smelled so fresh. It had cooled off but once it warmed up the humidity was going to be something to contend with.

After I ate breakfast it felt strange not to be heading for the plane. I laughed as I could now say "What plane"? I packed a lunch for the foxes and I and took enough drinking water for the three of us. The area in front of the cave was overgrown but flat. Something seemed to get my curiosity and I went scouting around the cave area, and I lucked out. About a hundred and fifty feet from the cave was a small spring. I took a couple of small sips and it tasted like an artesian water flow. First things first and I spent the next two days clearing the area for the work structure. Then I used bamboo for a pipeline, or water line, it was a chore cutting and fitting the pipe together. It was a small spring; three days of tedious work and I had a water flow next to where I would be building. I decided to save a lot of time and stay in the Jap's place they had built. I would go to my place on weekends if I wanted to.

I spent Saturday hauling what I would need to be staying in what I decided to call "Habitat three"; or just call it "Three" for short. I stayed at my southern place Saturday night as I had one more load to take back to three. As luck would have it I was just ready to head back to three when Buddy and family showed up. They were as glad to see me as I was of them. We did the pond, which was still much larger from the huge rain we had. It kind of tricked Guy as it was over his head and his mom pulled him out. He stayed on the shallow end; it was obvious he wanted no part of the deeper water. While the family enjoyed the pond, I picked a half dozen banana fruit. I waited and sure enough, here they came for raisins and fruit. I walked about ten feet towards three and waved them to follow; it took a while but I finally got them to follow. It helped to hold a banana up for them to see. When we got back to Three, I sat the raisins and fruit down and enjoyed watching as they cleaned the treats up. They walked around checking everything out and headed for the jungle. Buddy grunted more than usual and waved as he disappeared into the jungle.

Chapter Fifteen

The ladder I had built was sixteen feet. I would build the workshop fourteen feet tall. That would keep it high enough to be away from the heat from the smelter. I thought, "Here I go again". I am building a work area to smelt the gold of which was going to be guess and by golly. Needless to say, I had never smelted gold or anything else. I would enclose the back and two sides and leave the front open. It took a week but I had four vertical bamboo planted firmly in the ground. It would be fourteen feet deep and twenty feet wide. It seemed to take forever to put the roof on it. I double layered the roof with about two-inch diameter bamboo; it had to be strong as I would be working on top of it as I installed the palm fronds. Putting the back and sides up went easily. Getting the right materials to trim and install took a lot of time. My family showed up the fourth Sunday I had been working there. I had the back wall up and had just started working on a side wall. I thought "why not?" and we headed for the pond.

The water had gone down and guy had grown; but he went in the pond very cautiously. He splashed his mom and she reached over to whop him, he got away and I swear he was laughing. I fooled them and while they were enjoying the pond, I went to my south home and got a bowl of raisins. On the way back I picked six bananas. We picnicked beside the pond. It was still early but I didn't want to go to three in the dark. The bowl was almost empty and Guy started to pick it up. His mother whopped him and he quickly sat it down. He was a rascal but the day was not too far away when I don't think his mom would be correcting him the way she did. He seemed to double in size each time they visited. He was going to be one big boy. Buddy and I waved goodbye and I put it in overdrive and headed for three. It was almost dark when I got back. The gorillas once again made it a great Sunday.

I laughed and thought, "If or when I don't have a major project to keep me from going bonkers, maybe I could go live with the gorillas". For whatever reason, my mind seemed to be racing. I did not like that and drank a Goodnight. That did the trick. I woke up and almost jumped out of bed; I wanted to finish the walls and begin building the smelt. I had just finished the last wall when a tropical storm seemed to come out of nowhere. I headed for three just as a seemingly solid wall of water hit. There wasn't much thunder but the lightning kept the sky lit up. I would find out tomorrow if the roof leaked on the shop. I lay thinking about the smelt and finally got up and made a cup of Goodnight. The last thing I remembered was making a charcoal pit. Smelting called for using charcoal. I slept until the foxes barked and woke me up. I did it again. I slept in. The sun was up and shining bright. I was hungry and no doubt the foxes were. As soon as they had food in their bowls, they were too busy eating to bark. After breakfast I checked the work shop and it was dry.

I dug a pit and filled it with the wood I figured would make the best charcoal, it was a hard wood that would burn slowly. I would keep it stirred up and when I thought it was ready, I would cover it to smother it. I would let it cool for three days and recover it, and start a new batch. Next I made a bellow out of pigskin. I would eventually mount it on a frame and make it foot operated. There was so much to build and put together; I knew better than to rush building a smelt area; haste makes waste. Next I built a frame to hold the box

I salvaged from the plane that would hold the charcoal. Trial and error coast me a lot of time. The hardest thing to build was a frame to hold the bellow, which had to be foot operated. I remembered an antique sewing machine my mom had; she called it a treadle machine. I had to build something along the same principle. Five days of putting something together and taking it apart when I finally had it working to my satisfaction, I was one happy camper.

I wasn't overworking myself physically, but everything I built was something new to me. I called it the pan that would hold the charcoal; it fit nicely on the frame I built for it. I built a small workbench on each side of the pan. The next and final challenge was to rework one of the large stainless steel cylinders that were more than big enough to hold a bar of gold. I built a frame to hold the cylinder as to where I could lift it, swing it, and pour the gold into the two smaller cylinders that would be my bars. I had engraved an S on the inside bottom of each of the molds. It was time for a trial run. I fired the charcoal in the pan; I needed to make a narrower, wider, opening on the bellow, which was the beginning of my trial and error. I used rocks for weight instead of gold and it was a good thing. I had to totally rebuild the swinging frame for the big ladle. The frame had to be at least twice as strong as the one I built. The second test run went much better; I decided to do one more test run just to get me familiar with everything and get the feel for it.

I put one of my bar molds on a table on either side of the smelt; Trial day was tomorrow. I probably went over the whole procedure a hundred times before I went to sleep. I woke up early very excited even though I didn't get a good night's sleep. I slammed a quick breakfast and went to the cave, and got a bar of gold. It took about an hour and the charcoal, with the help of the bellow, was ready. I put the bar in the big ladle, swung, and lowered it into the charcoal. I was about ready to lift the ladle, as it didn't look like the gold was going to melt when all of a sudden it just in the blink of the eye melted. I carefully but quickly filled both molds and swung the big ladle away from the pan to cool down. The molds were burning the wooden tables; I slid them across the tables or they would have burned through the tables.

That shut production down for the day. I figured out how to solve that problem; I would make two pans out of hard wood and put an inch of water in them; the molds would set in the middle and the water may boil but the gold would cool fast enough not to do any damage, or so my planning said. First things first, I needed to go hunting for a pig and do some harvesting in the garden. I picked the molds up with two branches I squeezed together and set them in a pan of water I had ready. I was starving and realized I hadn't eaten since breakfast. I had a decent quick dinner and went back to the smelt. The molds were cool enough to pick up. I turned them over on the table and got a smile that felt like it was going to break my face. There were two beautiful bars with my initial S on them. Now I wished I had more molds. If everything went right I should be able to get two batches a day. That meant if nothing went wrong I could finish this project in about three months.

I took the bars to my home away from home and sat them on the table. They were beautiful and I was very proud of myself. Even more so, I was thankful that the smelt had worked out. I went to sleep with a smile on my face, it was a great day. I was awakened by the sounds of company; the gorillas were all waiting outside for me grunting and the foxes were barking. OK! I'll go hunting tomorrow. I realized I hadn't taken a day off in quite a while. I went over to the cold storage box and got a bowl of raisins and some jerky. We all headed for the pond. Wouldn't you know it? Guy was in the pond when we got there. I had a great day sharing time and the pond with my friends. As usual, Buddy was the first one out of the pond and called his family. They finished up the last of the raisins and headed home. I told Buddy to hurry back as he grunted and waved goodbye.

There was still plenty of light and I went back to the smelt building. I was having another one of my brain bombs; I had thought of it earlier but had too much going on to give it a try. I had three sizes of stainless steel pipe. I would saw them an eighth of an inch thick. I had the sheet of stainless to braze to the bottoms and make coin molds. I had plenty of time and the tools to do it; I would engrave "Scott's Island "and the date on the bottom flat plate. But first things first, the foxes and I had to eat; the foxes weren't into vegetables and that is about what we had left! I decided I would go after a hog and birds. I may be out for three or four days. I hadn't slept in my hammock for quite a while but I was ready. A day and a half of swinging my machete and I reached the mud bog. The hogs were normally there in early morning. I hadn't cut my way through the jungle in a while and my whole body could tell it. By the time I had my hammock hung and had something to eat I was ready for a good night's sleep.

Chapter Sixteen

I woke up early as my hammock was kind of moving and there not a breeze or wind. I heard a scratching noise just above my head; God was watching out for me; I looked up and a boa constrictor was about six feet from my head. I always slept with my AK on one side of me and machete on the other side. We both made a quick movement about the same time; I was able to roll on my side and grab my machete and get a good swing. He was a big one but no match for my machete. I hit it about a foot behind its head and it dropped out of the tree and fell to the ground. It was about twelve feet long. There is no way he could have swallowed me but he could have caused major damage or crushed me. The foxes were barking and making a lot of noise as the boa kept thrashing around. I had to shut the foxes up or there wouldn't be any hogs today. I got up and rolled my hammock up, and departed the area.

    About two hours later I was dressing a medium sized hog. I would have liked to have shot a bigger one but I still wanted to go bird hunting and the one I dressed out was about a hundred pounds on my back. We took a different route home, which meant cutting my way through the jungle. I did get five birds and picked some fruit. I slept in my hammock that night but think I slept with one eye open. I woke up just as the sun was coming up. The foxes had barked a couple of times during the night and sure enough, there were tiger tracks about thirty feet from where I slept. I was going to be glad to get back to my camp. I was very anxious to get back to work smelting the gold. Actually, for the first time ever I wanted to be out of the jungle for a while. The boa pretty well unnerved me; and a tiger that close to me while I slept was not a good thing. It was good to get back to camp. Between getting the hog cut up and in the smoker and cleaning the birds and getting them in the smoker there was a good day's work awaiting me in the garden.

I spent five tedious days making twelve coin molds. I had to guess the weights; so I had six, inch and a quarter, four one-inch and two three-quarter inch. Making the molds went quickly and smoothly, engraving them tried my patience several times. I put in some long late hours but was proud of the twelve molds. I didn't need any Goodnight as I worked late every night to finish the molds. I found a large flat slab of stone from which I chiseled a piece about a foot long and six inches wide. I put it on the table with the brick mold. I laid the coin molds on it and tomorrow I was back in the smelting business. This gold smelting thing was keeping me excited; I did make a cup of tea before going to bed. I believe if I were to ever leave my island, I would patent my tea.

I put fresh charcoal in the tub and waited anxiously while the gold melted. I poured the bricks first, then I melted enough of the fine gold dust I had tumbled for the coins; I misjudged, but got eleven coins poured. By the time I cleaned the work area up I removed the bricks from the molds. The coins turned out great and I decided to celebrate tonight. I took the bricks and coins home and put them on the table. The coins were shiny beautiful and made me smile so hard that once again my face hurt. I had fun making the coins. I was going to bring a couple of the eighty-pound bricks home so that I could file them and that is what I would use for smelting. I could use the eleven coins I poured and make a balance scale and perfect just how much gold it took to pour twelve coins. I found that the entire gold thing was a lot of fun. Sure it was hard hot work;

and then I laughed out loud when I thought what a hundred sixty some pounds of gold coin would look like stacked up on the table.

I got another brain buzz; I could make a stamp out of the sheet metal. Now that was going to test my artistic skills. I would engrave an eagle and write "In God We Trust" and USA on the stamp. I would have to be quick and stamp as I poured. This was getting very interesting. Maybe the day would come when I could weigh the coins and put a monetary value on them; or the amount of gold in them. I wouldn't pour any more coin until I had made the stamp. Once again, I had to laugh, here I am alone on my island and busy enough that it seemed I was always behind trying to get caught up. I was always planting, weeding or harvesting my garden, or gathering grapes for the raisins or pig, deer and bird hunting. Tomorrow I had to haul wood to make more charcoal. It was also about time to go deer hunting. I think once I have the wood hauled I'll harvest and clean the garden area up and then go deer hunting. I would enjoy seafood on my hunting and coming back I would pick a backpack of grapes. So much for smelting gold! The foxes and I did have to eat though. A cup of Goodnight and it was goodnight.

I dragged and carried a large pile of wood; I thought of my dad and his chain saw, getting wood for the charcoal would have been so much easier if I had a chain saw! I got a good harvest out of the garden and took a couple arms full of weeds out. Curiosity got the best of me; I went over to where I had dismantled the plane. It was totally over grown and not a trace of the plane could I find. The foxes and I were both hungry and I treated us to generous portions. It was, as always, going to be jerky for them on our hunting trip. I had left the gold coins on the table, as I did every night, and enjoyed stacking them and restacking them. I had put in a couple of fast paced days and didn't need to be rocked to sleep. I slept a little later than I intended; it was a breezy cool morning, a great day for hiking. It was good to get to the beach. The smell of the ocean was almost hypnotic, invigorating or something. It was just a special smell.

    I fried a few clams for the foxes who decided that they did like fried clams, I had my specialty, crab! We made good time but weren't in a hurry. I had made a few extra wax rounds just in case. I was up early the next morning and as I got closer to the area where the deer sometimes grazed I cautiously climbed to the top of the hill as it was evident the T Rexes were on to something. I looked down at what was a spectacular sight; there were seven T Rexes circling what looked to be five adult water buffalo that formed a ring and a young one inside the ring. Every time a T Rex got a little closer the closest buffalo would let out a warning sound and shake its head and the T Rex would quickly back off. It seemed evident the T Rexes wanted the young one but they weren't going to give the adult buffalo a try. The buffalo had wicked looking horns. I was about ready to head for the beach and head south to where I shot the last deer when the T Rexes gave up.

    I wished there were deer on the north end of the island. I had only gone inland about a quarter mile when I saw three deer eating grass by a little stream. I took the biggest one out. I quickly dressed him and tied the four legs and put him on my back. I had laid everything I trimmed on a couple of palm fronds; It was a lot more work but I dragged the guts and whatever to the beach, It was low tide with high tide just coming in. I would rather the fish eat the remains than have the T Rexes get a smell of them. I still had a few hours and headed up the beach. It was getting dark when I built a fire and the foxes had fresh deer for dinner, I stuck with crab boiled in sea water. I was up at the crack of dawn; I wanted to try and make it back to camp by nightfall. That would be pushing it but I just wanted to get back home.

    There was just a trace of pink in the sky when I woke up. I had cold crab for breakfast and the foxes made out and had venison again. I usually walked the beach in a casual pace, today I turned it up a couple of notches. I wanted to sleep in my bed tonight if I could. I never stopped for lunch but it became evident I may as well hook my hammock up; It was about ready to get dark and I still had a least three hours to go. I was asleep as soon as I crawled into my hammock. I slept in and I didn't care. Carrying eighty five pounds of deer on my back and walking as fast as I did had plain wore me out. The walk to camp was a piece of cake, I made it back in what I thought to be about three hours. By the time I had the deer in the smoker I was ready for dinner and bed. The foxes and I shared a fried deer or venison steak. Just sitting at the table moving the gold coins around had me looking forward to morning.

    I slept in again but it was OK; I deserved it. I fired up the wood in the charcoal pit and spent most of the day hauling ten bricks to the smelt area. After dinner I went back to the smelt and worked on the stamp. I had to continuously sharpen and temper my homemade engraving tools. There was a perfect size and picture of an eagle in my mom's dictionary. I traced it and that is what I used to engrave the eagle

    It took me three nights to engrave the stamp. I melted just enough gold to cast twelve perfect coins. The stamp worked perfect; in fact so good I remolded the eleven coins and redid them with the stamp. Casting the coins was time consuming and I had to push it to cast two ingots and twelve coin in one day. I decided to try something different; I was going to see how many coins I could get out of one eighty pound brick. That worked out good as it took me a week to file one brick for smelting. I cast ten ingots that week. I figured the three coin sizes combined would weigh close to two and a half ounces. That meant I could get three hundred and eighty four coins out of an eighty pound brick. If I made eight more coin molds and did two pours a day it would take forty eight working days to pour an eighty pound brick. If I did four coin pours a day I could finish eighty pounds of coins in twenty four days. Between the weather, garden, hunting and my gorilla family, and the gold, I had my work cut out for me. In two weeks I had cast thirty ingots and eighty coins. I was building boxes to store the coins in.

    I was just cleaning up the work area and was going to take the day off when my family showed up. Good timing! My entire body needed a rest. The pond never felt so good. Oh no; I just had another brain storm. I should build a steam room. That would be a piece of cake. I would have rather had a Jacuzzi, but with no electricity a steam room would do just fine. I could heat the stone in the charcoal pit. I could add some more bamboo pipe to my existing irrigation system for the water. About then Guy woke me up when he splashed me right in the face; I splashed him back and he wanted to rough house, He was too big to be rough housing with. His mom growled a menacing growl at him and he actually fell backwards. It looks like mom still rules but it was evident Buddy was still the boss. When he got out of the pond his family got out, when it was time for them to head home Buddy led them to the jungle. Guy was definitely growing up; his manners had become more mature. As always it always bothered me to wave goodbye.

    That evening I put a couple of steam room ideas on a drawing. I was young; but I had pushed my body to the limit many times; my lifestyle required a lot of physical stress. Just to swing a machete all day long was a total physical drain. Working the gold project the way I was required a lot of physical requirements. I was up early and excited about building a steam room. I began framing it right next to the habitat I had taken over. I wanted it to be oval; bending and tying bamboo for a frame worked out well. In three days I was ready to seal the igloo looking frame. I made a plaster out of mud and grass. It is a good thing I had the pond to rinse off in I am sure I looked like a mud pie when I finished each day. I worked ten straight days and was happy with my finished project. I used the lid off of the chest the Jap's had used for storage for the water. I used the remaining metal from one of the planes propellers to fashion a scoop to get the rocks out of the charcoal pit.

It is a good thing I built my mud igloo next to my living quarter; I spent about an hour in it the first evening and I was ready for bed when I exited but I felt like I was physically rejuvenated. I was anxious to get back to work with the gold. About another week and I would need to go hog hunting. The garden needed harvesting and weeded. The "igloo steamer" was turning out to be a great help to keep me physically fit; it took care of most of the aches and pains. I went in it almost every night. Because of it, I kept the charcoal pit going every day which meant my charcoal stockpile grew instead of shrank. Hopefully the hunting went well as I was anxious to get back to work with the gold. Depending if I was successful hunting I would come back with a pig, birds and grapes.

One thing for sure, I had learned a lesson on where to hang my hammock with the boa scare. I picked two smaller trees with no surrounding "hiding place" for a boa to come sneaking up on me. I shot a good sized pig the second day; I filled my backpack with grapes and got four birds on the way back home. I had about a hundred pounds of pig, birds and grapes on my back. All of the way home I was thinking of the igloo. By the time I had the pig and birds in the smoker I laughed and thought "if I didn't get to the igloo now I might have to get to it on my hands and knees". One of the trees on my island looked like eucalyptus but it had sort of a sweet smell to it. I put a couple of hands full of leaves in the water and when I put the hot stones in the water it gave off a very pleasant smell. It had sort of a reverse effect on me; I would feel drained when I exited; I had no problem going to sleep and always woke up feeling refreshed and ready for whatever awaited me that day.

It felt good to get back working with the gold. I had refined the entire process after trials and errors; the entire smelting and casting was hard work but I enjoyed it and actually had fun trying different methods. It took me almost two weeks after work but I made a mold the shape of the island and engraved "Scott's Island" on it; I wasn't happy with the first casting. A little more work on the mold and the second casting turned out perfect. A nice thing working with gold; if you are unhappy with whatever it is your doing, just re melt the gold. I cut a cord out of the pigskin and tried it on. It looked great but would be dangerous to wear when I was working with the gold or cutting my way through the jungle. It could get caught on something and cause a serious injury.

Chapter Seventeen

The same old thing day after day was finally beginning to get to me. I enjoyed what I was doing but needed something else to break what was on the verge of being repetitious or boring. I needed to do something just for the fun of it. I decided to build a sailboat. Not an ocean going vessel, just something to sail around my island and fish from. I would allow myself two days a week to work on the boat. It would take weeks just to accumulate the materials to build it out of. Plus I would have to build it close to the water. It would not sit well to build the boat but couldn't get it into the water. On the southwest end of the island was kind of a natural bay; I would build a slide ramp that extended out into the ocean about six feet at high tide; I would grease the slide up with lard from the pigs I had shot. When the boat was finished I would launch at high tide. I had no idea if there was a strong current or rip tide; so just in case I would build it with a set of oar locks and a pair of ocean going oars with a spare. I would build the boat for strictly pleasure with no thought of leaving the island for good.

Building the boat was a good idea; I would work the gold project five days a week and the boat project two days a week. I went to the scrap metal I had salvaged from the plane; none of the metal was recognizable from airplane parts. I made a draw plane I would use for making the boards that I would need. There was a particular tree that the wood was soft enough. I could plane it but would make great planks or boards. The launching ramp was a piece of cake; I built it out of bamboo and wired it together with the salvaged copper wire. Between working the gold project, keeping food on the table and working on the boat with an occasional visit from my family I didn't need to get any wild ideas about any more projects. It was too bad the five Jap's died on the island but very lucky for me that my island is where they crashed the plane. It was a huge undertaking to dispose of the plane but I was thankful every day as the material I salvaged made processing the gold and making the boat project possible.

 Something else had me thinking. I wasn't low on ammunition for the AK yet; I had used about a third of the ammo I had salvaged. The only alternative weapon I could think of that I could use to conserve ammo was a bow and arrows. I thought of the ruins and the weapons that were there. There were a couple of different style bows and different kinds of arrow heads. It all had to be made from material on my island. When I needed a break from work I would do some exploring back at the ruins. The bows and arrows may be useable; they were in an area that had never been wet. If not useable I could use them for patterns on how to make new weapons. In the meantime I was ready to try the stand I made to hold the wood as I used the draw plane on it. Trial and error before I had the stand as to where I could work from either side of it as I planed to the dimension I would need. It took two days to plane one board;

 I cut one edge at a forty five degree angle; put together it would have a quarter of an inch gap on the outside and an eighth of an inch gap on the inside. This way water pressure couldn't push a quarter inch of caulk through an eighth of an inch opening. Whether it is good or bad I figured it would take a good two months to plane the forty five boards I would need just for the hull. With all things considered, I was probably looking at a year to build the boat. I decided to work on the boat three days and the gold two days. Whenever needed, I would include my two days off when I went hunting or worked on the garden?

I remembered my dad telling me a busy mind is a happy mind. Just trying to survive on my island could keep me busy enough; With the various projects and things I had to take care of, I couldn't be much busier; then how come I wasn't happy? Maybe I was and didn't understand what happiness was all about. My parents both worked to pay the bills. I had no bills; I worked to eat and keep myself busy. If I didn't have the various things I have to work on I could never have survived on my island alone. The gorillas were an interesting family and I loved them but they weren't humans who I could share conversations with. I kind of chuckled; I was building a thirty one foot sailing boat for pleasure. Maybe I should use it for a pattern to build a boat big enough to be ocean going. I am not even sure if I ever want to leave my island; this was basically the only life I had ever known. If I ever needed money I figured I had around twenty five million dollars depending on what gold was worth now. Twenty five million dollars that had no monetary value on my island! I was lucky as I enjoyed everything I was doing.

I wouldn't even begin laying out the boats hull until I had the forty five boards I thought it would take. I found the caulk I would need to seal the hull up by accident. I had leaned on a tree without looking and got a sticky resin, or gummy material, that I had to use diesel fuel to get off. I collected about a pint of it and found by heating it, it was very strong and pliable. I made a blunt faced wooden chisel and caulked a couple of short boards with it. I took it up to the pond and put it in the water and weighted it down with a couple of rocks. I really didn't want to stop working but I would need to go deer hunting soon. I would check the weapons out at the ruins and maybe bring a bow and arrows home with me; I wouldn't use them even if they were useable; this way I could figure out what they were made of and use them for a pattern. It was time for a break on the beach anyway; I hadn't had seafood for quite a while.

The first night on the beach I stuffed myself on crab. Sadie and Suzy wasted no time in cleaning up the clams I cooked for them. It was too bad I couldn't smoke the crab meat. I tried a couple different ways and it didn't work. It was like the crab shrunk down to little or nothing and was hard as rocks. I would just consider it a special treat whenever I came to the beach. I didn't see any T Rex or water buffalo this time but got what I came after. I tried sneaking up on the deer just to see how close I could get; I was within seventy five yards when the wind shifted and the deer shifted. I dropped a nice size male.

Sadie and Suzy always got excited whenever I was cleaning the deer; they knew they were going to have venison all of the way home. I decided to take a pass on getting grapes or bird hunting; I would save that for another day. We made it back to the ruins in the nick of time as the wind had turned from a gentle breeze to a wind that made it difficult to walk. I gathered just enough dry wood before it all hit at once; the wind, lightning, thunder and a wind driven downpour. I hoped the skulls wouldn't mind company tonight. I would have pitched my little tent, but the weather caught me first. Whoever built these structures knew what they were doing; there were no leaks and there was a perfect draft for a fire. The foxes and I enjoyed a fresh venison fried dinner. Lucky for me the weather had cleared up; I stepped outside to a blue sky. I laughed and thought I sure slept the night away. I checked both of the bows; the owners knew what they were doing as the strings were unattached at one end. I restrung the one I liked the most and it was like it was brand new. I tried drawing the string back as hard as I could. Whoever owned this weapon must have been a powerful guy.

I gathered about a dozen arrows out of two quivers; I didn't take the ones that looked like they had been dipped in something dark; no doubt a poison. It was an uneventful walk home the rest of the way. I was always glad to reach my clearing even though this habitat had been made by someone else. It was heading towards dinner time by the time I had the deer in the smoker. The foxes and I enjoyed a venison dinner except I had vegetables with mine. I put about an hour in the igloo and I didn't need to be rocked to sleep. The foxes woke me up early; it was just getting light; there was a tiger walking slowly around the smoker; it was too hot for it to get anything out of the smoker but I hit him on his flank anyway; he was gone in the blink of an eye. I doubt if he would venture back this way again.

As long as I was up I had breakfast and headed for the smelt. I couldn't have worked the gold if it weren't for the bellow I made. The brick pile in the cave was not nearly as big as it was when I stacked it all in there. I worked on the gold for two days and then went bird hunting and to gather grapes. It was a good couple of days; I had five birds and a backpack of grapes when I headed home. I would take a day and get the birds in the smoker with porky; spread the grapes and check the garden. Dropping the trees for the planks was no problem; clearing the jungle to get to a tree and dragging it back to the work area took the time. Three days of back breaking work and I had five trees to work on. I spent the next day with my family; Guy was bigger than his mother now; He had a ways to go to catch up with his father; but he was acting more like an adult now. He was such a cute "Little Guy". We were lucky the pond was as big as it was; five adult gorillas take up a lot of room. If I had to guess, I would guess the pond and raisins were a highlight in their lives. They were a highlight in my life.

I put two days in casting the gold and then went to work on the five trees. Smelting the gold was like taking a break when it came to milling the trees. It took four days to get five boards added to the stack which now numbered twenty boards. As I put the last board on the stack I had to laugh; there was the beginning of Gigo-Gigo two. It had been a long time now, but I always got a lump in my throat when I thought of my family I had lost. If I were to ever become a part of the human world, whatever I did I would do in the hopes they would be proud of me. I decided to just take one day off from now on; I would do two days smelting and four days getting more planks. I got kind of excited when I thought of actually putting the Gigo-Gigo two in the water.

 I decided to work on the gold two days and the boat four days. The igloo had turned out to be a great salvation. I would be almost woozy when I got out and was asleep as I lay down. The best part was I always felt refreshed when I got up. It made me wonder about the leaves I put in the water. It made the steam feel great but I wondered if was the reason I was so woozy when I got out. Well I liked the smell and being a little woozy was OK. My dad would have called me an air head. I put two hard weeks in; my lumber pile was growing. I wanted it to grow faster but was happy to be progressing. I had backed off eating the venison; it was too time consuming and a rough haul to get one deer back to camp. I would save the venison for the foxes; I preferred pork anyway, although the porkies here had a strong taste. My family showed up which meant I would need to replenish the grapes and raisins soon. While we were at the pond I recovered the boards I had sunk there. The caulk worked perfect. That was a big plus.

 I only took two days off the next month. I stood looking at the forty five boards in the lumber pile and was one thankful guy that part of the boat would be curing and waiting to be installed on the hull frame I would be building next. I decided to take a break and go hunting for the wood that the bow I brought back was made from. It seemed to be of the ironwood family as it was almost as strong as metal. I found a small stand of the right trees and cut a young tree; it took a while to cut that tough little guy. I gathered a backpack of grapes and shot two bird's on the way back to camp. Working on the bow would be an evening thing when everything else was done for the day. The next day I began cutting the bamboo I would need for the hull. I would cut and drag them to the ramp I had built. It took a lot of bamboo to build a thirty-one foot boat. This is where the boards I had salvaged from the plane were going to save me a lot of extra work. I soon found out building a thirty one foot sailboat was a lot more difficult than I had figured on.

There was no sense in trying to hurry as every step seemed to be very tedious. The screws I salvaged from the plane were a great help. I was going to be glad when the last of the gold was processed. I didn't realize how much of a project I got myself into when I decided to build a boat. Working alone was going to take extra time; I had to frame, brace and crib much of what needed to be done to build a boat frame. I was tempted to quit working on the gold and dedicate all of my time to the Gigo-Gigo. I had to keep convincing myself that building the boat was supposed to be a fun project. All work was beginning to get to me; maybe I should quit working on the boat and finish the gold project. Working on the boat was almost becoming an obsession with me. It seemed to be taking forever to finish the hull frame. It was actually at the end of the tenth week when I finally stood back and looked at the finished frame. My food supply as well as my patience was getting very thin. I hated to stop to go hunting but I had no choice. It was going to be a hog hunt in order to save time.

Chapter Eighteen

I shot a good size hog the second day the first thing in the morning. I got a backpack full of grapes but never got a good shot at a bird; no fried "chicken" till the next time. I saved the venison for the foxes; I think the pork didn't agree with them. Once back home I spent a day getting the hog cut up and in the smoker and pulled a lot of weeds in the garden. I checked the cave to see what I still had to smelt. There were twenty eight bricks left. That meant seven more working days and all of the gold was smelted, worked and done. A few extra leaves in the steamer and I was falling asleep before I made it to my bed. I woke up anxious to get to work on the boat. I put two of the boards on my shoulder and headed for the hull frame. It took all day to get the two boards fastened exactly where I wanted them.

The first two boards would determine how the rest of the boards would go on. I took four boards the next day but only got three on. I cut a dozen three eighths of an inch spacers. I never built a boat before. The boards I was covering the hull with were bound to swell once in the water. The caulk I was using was flexible. Even if the wood swelled leaving a quarter of an inch between boards the caulk would insure the hull did not leak. I decided to bevel the sides of the boards to insure the caulk couldn't be forced out. About the best I could do was get two boards on a day. At the end of two weeks Gigo-Gigo was beginning to look like it might be a boat. The gold was down to twenty bars or bricks and the garden needed some serious tending to. I had been working on the wood that would be my bow every night after work and it was ready for stringing; I had unwound about seven feet of the nylon rope I was conserving. I used the wax from the last candle to wax the string before I strung it on the bow. My mulch pile was about twenty five yards away. I used one of the arrows from the ruins and let it fly; not bad! It fell about five feet short and about a foot to the right.

I retrieved the arrow and tried again; it had the distance but off to the right again. I basically bulls eyed on my seventh try. I decided to go cut a bunch of arrow material tomorrow. I unstrung the bow as the nylon had stretched a bit. I tied a rock on the string and hung it from a branch; that should take the stretch out of it. There was like a grove of tiny trees on the east side of the mud bog. That was my project for tomorrow. I reworked the mulch pile to where it was about four feet wide and five feet tall. That would be my practice target. I was up bright and early the next morning; I was hoping to get at least three saplings to take home and remove the bark. Things never go quite as planned; the saplings or whatever they were, grew out of the mud. I took my shoes off and took two steps and had to lie down to get out of the mud. That was a scary close call. Snow shoes were the answer; I would probably have to travel several thousand miles for a pair of snow shoes. Better yet I would build three mesh like screens out of bamboo; the saplings were close enough together I would use the screens like a sidewalk. First of all get to the pond and take a bath and rinse my clothes out. One day shot!

I was up early and it took all day to build the screens, but I was ready. The screens sunk in the mud; but I was able to stand on them long enough to gather forty saplings. There was no way to save the screens; but I got what I came after. I still had time when I got back to camp to take the bark off. I bundled them together and wrapped nylon string tightly around them. I would let them slow dry for about a week and hopefully they would be straight. I put in two days smelting and my family showed up the third day. I needed a break and the pond was enjoyed by all. We had our usual raisin picnic before they headed for the jungle and Buddy grunted goodbye and waved. I put five hard days in putting the boards on the hull. It was beginning to take shape; the Gigo-Gigo was beginning to look like a boat. Oh boy, here I go! I just got an idea for putting a seal coat on the hull. I would collect a few gallons of the resin and cut it with the diesel oil. I would get a little resin tomorrow and cut it and put it on a couple pieces of the cut off lumber and let it set for a few days. It was time I got lucky.

The area I picked to build and launch the boat was on an old river bed; the boat would need at least a ton and a half of ballast. It took me two weeks to build thick screens to line the bottom and lower sides of the boat; this was needed to protect the boat from the ballast bouncing around in bad weather which could severely damage the hull. The sap cut with diesel oil worked perfect on the sample boards. It cured in less than two weeks. My family showed up and I needed a break.

I had to laugh as they played in the pond; if the family got any bigger the pond would have to be enlarged. When they began frolicking I got out as they would not mean to; but as big and as strong as they were, I could have accidently gotten hurt. They cleaned up the last of the raisins; I had been rationing the pork and venison; I wanted to get the ballast in the boat before I went hunting. I removed three feet of boards on one side and began the back breaking job of loading river rock ballast in. I shied away from round stone as they could easily roll and cause damage. The steam igloo was a Godsend. I would load rock into the boat until about an hour before sunset; then I would get in and spread the rock evenly. I surprised myself and had what I considered two ton in the boat and spread in seven days. I needed a break and I needed food.

The garden needed harvesting of which I took care of; there was enough venison to feed Sadie and Suzy for a couple more weeks. I checked my bundled arrows and they were ready to be worked on when I found the time. I shot a large hog my second day out; by the time I filled my backpack with grapes I felt like I was overloaded. I wanted to see about getting a couple of birds and some bananas but I had all I could carry with the hog and grapes. I made it back to camp a couple of hours before sundown. There was just enough light left after loading the hog in the smoker to spread the grapes out so they wouldn't spoil. I was too tired to eat or use the steamer. I needed to lie down before I fell down. The sun was up and shining bright when I woke up. I had almost slept the morning away and I didn't care. I decided to do light duty today.

I spent the entire day working on arrows; of the forty shafts I had bundled, thirty seven were good ones. I made heads out of sheet metal from the plane and feathers I had saved for the shafts. Not a bad day; I finished fifteen arrows before darkness set in. I almost fell asleep in the igloo; I laughed as I got out thinking I had better cut back on the leaves. It was almost with pleasure when I worked with the gold for the next two days. It wouldn't be long and the gold project would be history. I was pretty danged proud of the smelting system I had set up. Crude but very efficient! My family woke me the next morning; I figured they were about due. I had fun with Guy; I would pitch one raisin where Guy was sitting; he would grunt as if to say thanks. He would pick the one raisin up and eat it and look at me and grunt. There was the big bowl of raisins on the table but he was content to pick up the one raisin I tossed his way until he threw a raisin back at me and reached over and took a handful out of the bowl. I was always sad when they left; but I couldn't spend my life feeding gorilla's raisins.

I woke up anxious to get back to work on my boat. Most of all, my body was thankful to have the ballast in the boat. I reinstalled the boards I had removed to load the ballast; everything went without a hitch and in eight days all of the planks were installed and ready for caulking. Caulking was one messy job. No matter how careful I was I still managed to get caulk on me someplace. Beveling the boards had been very time consuming but it was insurance the caulk would stay where it was supposed to.

It took ten days to caulk the hull; the reason it took so long, I had to climb in and out of the hull to scrape the caulk flat with the hull. I would fill about eight feet inside and get outside to scrape it before it set up. I was so thankful I salvaged about thirty gallons of Diesel from the plane. I had collected about five gallons of the resin I used for the caulk to make the hull sealer out of. The one and a half diesel to one resin worked great on the boards I used for a sample. I made paint brushes out of a heavy vine that grew everywhere. It was time consuming to fray the end of a branch; but it made a workable paint brush. I had the first coat on the hull in two days; The Gigo-Gigo was beginning to look like a boat. I needed a break and was just about out of venison. Seafood sounded just like what I needed. I would take the arrows I borrowed back to the ruins before heading for the beach. It was like Sadie and Suzy knew we were going hunting as they woke me just as the sun was coming up. The weather was good and the two day hike on the beach did me good; or maybe it was the crab I had for dinner each night.

I bypassed the area where the T Rexes abounded. I didn't need any drama, I was after food. It was late afternoon when I reached the area where the deer hung out. There wasn't a deer in sight! Not good! I went back and camped on the edge of the beach. There had been about thirty deer in that area the last time I was here. If they weren't there in the morning I would go back to the other area. I had ten bullets loaded with heavy loads of wax I brought along just in case. The smell and sound of the surf lulled me to sleep. Loud surf woke me up in the morning; the tide had come in and the sea was kind of wild this morning. The sky had a strange color to it. I hoped there wasn't a major storm coming in. I fed the foxes and settled for a piece of pork jerky. I headed for the deer's feeding ground and hoped that I was rewarded.

There were about twenty deer grazing. I shot a medium sized buck and of course the herd quickly disappeared. I made short work of dressing it as I didn't like the looks of the weather. By the time I camped that night the wind had picked up but no storm yet. It was coming because I could smell it. I thought about staying at the ruins the next day as the wind was getting very wild and a wind-blown mist stung as it hit the bare skin. The dense jungle was some protection and I headed for home. I was just entering my clearing when it hit. I prayed the boat was safe. I had secured it when I first began building it knowing that a big tropical storm was possible. It also had two drain plugs of which I had left open. I wasn't sure what I would do if the storm took the Gigo-Gigo. I couldn't stand the suspense and had to go check on my boat. I was just barely able to make forward progress as the wind was trying to push me back. I finally made it to the boat; it was rocking slightly from the wind and the water was still about three feet from it. It had survived what I figured was the worst of the storm. I think I said "Thank you Lord" all the way back to my place.

The wind died that afternoon and the rain tapered off to a sprinkle. I hurriedly got the deer in the smoker and went over to check on the smelting area. It had survived. I was wet and hungry and a venison steak for me and the foxes sounded like a good idea; As Sadie and Suzy tore into their dinner it was evident they thought steak for dinner was a good idea too. I had a two beaner tea and headed for the igloo; I fell asleep and almost fell off of the bench I was sitting on. I don't remember going to bed. The sun woke me up and I think I yawned and stretched a few minutes before I got up. I decided to ease into the day and spent a pleasant day working on one of the last bars of gold. Four more days of smelting and the last of the gold bars will have been reworked.

I was tempted to work on the gold until the remaining bars had been reworked; but Gigo-Gigo was calling. I had made a couple of sketches how to make the rudder; it seemed like it was all coming at me at once. I would need about forty planks for the deck and cabin. I had making the planks down to a science. I had picked out a tree for the mast. I would use the lumber I had stashed from the plane for the base framing for the mast; its main function was to keep the mast from kicking out at the base. It took four days to build and secure; I was sure there was no way the mast could get loose. The planks were my next project; it took two weeks to cut and haul the trees I would get the planks out of. I was finishing breakfast when my family showed up. I had to laugh as Guy still got excited and showed it when he saw me. Guy and I had a water fight in the pond until he got too carried away and I got out of the pond just in case. It seemed like they knew when I needed a break; there I was sitting on the ground with five gorillas eating raisins.

I put long days in trimming the planks; it was the hardest work I did since I washed up on my island. I started early and worked late and the best I could do was four planks a day. The fifth day I had twenty planks cut and curing; my arms and back needed a break. I worked in the smelter for two days. Two more days and the smelting would be done, although there were a few things I wanted to try casting for fun. My next project with the boat was going to be kind of tricky to build. It was the top frame for the mast. It had to be the strongest thing on the entire boat. I didn't have a lot of canvas left for a sail and a spare. I did not want a tall mast. Once again I made some sketches; a picture of a Chinese boat gave me the idea. I believe they called the boat in the picture a "Junk". It had a short mast and an almost square sail. The top mast frame took a week to build and install. I would install the mast before I began planking.

I cut the tree I would use for the mast; I skinned the bark and laid the mast in five stands I had built. I would rotate the mast every day while it cured. I spent the next long hard days finishing the planks so they could be curing. I needed a break and worked the remaining gold for the next couple of days. I was kind of sad when the last bar was recast. But, if time permitted, I was going to do some serious experimenting casting various items. I had plenty to do before I could make that happen. I decided to make the rudder assembly next. That was going to be a trick project. First the garden needed tending to; I harvested the last of the vegetables and put them on the rack; next I weeded the entire area and when it was clear I reseeded. There was still some day light left so I got my bow and arrows. One arrow of the twelve I made curled; it was a reject. I shot the eleven arrows three times; I got five bull's eye and seven close enough to be a kill. I had better stick with the AK if I was going to eat.

Chapter Nineteen

The next five days were productive get food days; I shot a medium sized hog; got four birds, filled the backpack with grapes and picked a dozen not quite ripe bananas. It seemed strange not to be working with the gold anymore. But then it seemed strange when I wasn't working on the plane anymore. Making and installing the rudder was quite the challenge. While I worked on it I figured out how I would go about installing the mast when it came time. There were trees all around where I was building the boat; of course there were a lot of trees; the jungle was covered with them. There was a tall one that had a thick branch that was almost directly overhead of the boat. I would have to climb up to where I could put the nylon rope over the branch. I would hoist the mast high enough and physically put it in the sockets I made for it. I would tie the rope off and lock the mast into place with the boards I had ready. Before I did this I would have to put the rigging on for the sail.

This was definitely not going to be a walk in the park. Once I had the mast securely locked into place I would install the horizontal pole complete with rigging, which would be the next project. I was happy with the rudder and glad it was done; I was anxious to install the mast; that was going to be a challenge. My family showed up and that cost me a day to relax. They made short work of the bananas and raisins and to my surprise, Guy and Buddy both waved good-bye. Guy was becoming a well-mannered gorilla. I woke up excited;

today was the day I thought about installing the mast. I ate a good breakfast and put some deer jerky in my pocket. I knew I was in for a hard day's work. Carrying the rope and climbing the tree was not my most favorite thing. But I was very nervous when I had to crawl out on the big limb about four feet to drop the rope over. If the limb broke that would probably be the end of me and the boat. The rope kept trying to tangle and I had to jiggle it to get it to drop down. I was very glad to get my feet back on the ground.

This was going to be tricky. I tied the top of the mast with the rope; I had to hoist the mast in the air high enough to clear the boat, hold the rope and guide the mast into the sockets I had prepared for it. As I lifted the mast it began to drag on the side of the boat which was good; I can reach it and still hold the rope. I lifted the mast some more until it cleared the boat and swung my way; now I was able to move the bottom of the mast to and through the top brace. This is where it became tricky; I lifted the mast slightly and put my left shoulder on it; when I thought it was straight enough I let the mast down slightly; it wasn't straight enough and I had to lift it again. I was running out of strength after the third try and miss. I changed my position slightly and thought; if I don't get it this time I'm going to have to put the mast back on the ground. I lifted it again; as I began to lower it, success! I could see it was in the base in the hull but before I locked it in place on the top brace I went down in the hull to make sure it was in the socket. It was; the easiest thing I did all day was install the boards that locked it in place.

It had been a stressful physical day; I wanted and needed food and sleep. I woke up the next morning not in a hurry to do anything. Climbing the tree and wrestling with the mast had drained me physically. I had a very specific bracket to make for the horizontal part of the mast; It would have to be stationary on the main mast but hold another bracket that could rotate on the solid bracket; then it would have like a cup that the horizontal bracket slipped in to and was secured and attached to the swivel collar on the vertical mast. I had installed a pulley and ran the rope through it before I set the big mast. I had given up on the idea of a Chinese type sail. I was building the Gigo-Gigo for pleasure, not for oceanic travel. It took ten days to make all of the metal fittings needed to put the sail on. I needed a break; I also needed a place to lay the canvas out to make a sail. The only large covered place was the ruins.

I packed up ten days' worth of dried vegetables and jerky. Between the grommet equipment, the sewing supplies and the roll of canvas I was packing a load. It was almost dark when I reached the ruins. I put everything in the big room I would be working in; by the time I hung my hammock I had one eye open. I ate a piece of cold jerky and never woke up once until the sun coming up woke me. I spent two days sewing two major seams up and almost another day installing the grommets. I treated myself to a day on the beach the next day. Having crab twice in one day seemed to energize me a bit. The way I cut the sail out of the canvas actually left another sail ready to be sewn and grommets installed. That wasn't needed yet. Before I went sailing I would finish the other sail. I left all of the sail making items in the safety of the ruins.

I was anxious to get back to the camp and made it just as the sun was going down. Hopefully I could hook the sail up tomorrow and pray it didn't need any modification. I woke up to sounds that let me know I wouldn't be checking the sail out today; I had five gorillas outside looking for me. All five got excited when I stepped outside. They were all grunting something so I grunted back at them. I had lucked out and picked some bananas on the way back from the ruins. Just like old home week; we sat around until the bananas were gone. Guy jumped up and took off at a fast pace for the pond. There was still a little bit of child left in him. Buddy was the first one out of the pond and with a couple of grunts the family got out including me. We had been in the pond quite a while. Soon after the raisins were gone Buddy headed for the jungle with his family following; He and Guy both waved goodbye.

By the time the foxes and I finished dinner the sun was saying good night as it disappeared behind the ocean. For whatever reason I was feeling strange tonight; I didn't like the way I was feeling. I looked at the picture of my family; my sister would have been twenty five; I tried to imagine what she looked like now. I was just a little boy when I washed up on my island; I was a twenty one year old young man now. I drank a two bean tea and headed for the igloo. A few extra leaves in the water and I was soon feeling better. In fact I felt so good I was going to have another tea. I dozed off a couple of times and thought I had better get out of here while I still could. I carefully made it to and put the beans away. I had thought of having a second beaner and thought better of it. I almost fell on the floor as I sat down for the edge of my bed and almost missed it.

I woke up hungry and anxious to get to the boat. If hanging the sail went smoothly I would begin putting the deck on today. The sail went on without a glitch; it was a little long which was OK; once it caught the wind it would be perfect. I took it down and folded it and set it aside. By the end of the day I had five planks installed on the foredeck. I had to smile; Gigo-Gigo was beginning to look like an ocean going sailing ship. I decided I wouldn't take any kind of a break until the entire deck was on. Putting the deck on was the easiest thing I had done with the boat so far. I was going to need about thirty more planks to finish the cabin and cabin floor. I must have found renewed energy as milling the rest of the planks went easier than all of the rest. I wanted them to cure for at least two weeks. I made up another couple of gallons of sealer and sealed the entire deck. I was going to give the hull and deck one more coat before launching.

If only I didn't have to eat; the garden needed tending to and the pork supply was running low. I was out of grapes and it really irritated me that I had to take time off from the Gigo-Gigo project. It irritated me more that I had to use the machete as much as I did; I didn't get into the jungle as much as I used to and it could over grow in two weeks. The hogs showed up early the next morning; one looked like it was hurt and had a broken front leg; I put it out of its misery with one shot. I figured as long as I was taking time off I might as well stock up; I filled the backpack with grapes and headed home. I still had a couple hours of sunlight left; by the time the hog was in the smoker and the grapes spread out I was ready for dinner and bed because I wanted an early start tomorrow. I was up and it was still dark. I ate a piece of jerky and headed out. By the time I was headed home I had four birds, bananas and six coconuts. I almost stayed in the jungle that night. It was dark by the time I got home. I would clean and smoke the birds tomorrow. I was beat and needed sleep right now. The sun had been up for a while when I woke up.

I had to boil water to pluck the birds, once they were cold there was no way to get their feathers off. I put the bananas and coconuts in the cooler. I saved a lot of the bird feathers; the day may come when there was no more ammo for the AK and I would be hunting with the bow and arrows. I put the birds in the smoker except what I was going to fry for dinner. I wasn't a sailor and didn't know the sailors language; I had built the rudder assembly to be manually steered or steered from a wheel. I had just enough pulleys' left to set the steering gear up. I decided not to go to the boat until I had the wheel built. It took three days but I was proud of it; it looked like it came off of an old time sailboat.

It took three days and I finished the cabin floor. I gave it a coat of sealer. I had buried several small round windows from the plane; I could use four of them when I built the cabin, which was the next project. I actually had fun building the cabin. I missed working one day to spend the day with my family. They got here just in time or I would have lost the bananas. They didn't stop until every banana was gone. There was no getting around it; I was going to have to enlarge the pond someday. Once again as we waved goodbye I was hit with a wave of emotions. I'm not sure what was going on but I didn't like it. I went home and made a two beaner; I finished up the cold fried bird and headed for the igloo. I had put the stones in the charcoal pit before heading into my place. I thought why not and put a handful of leaves in the water. As I was waking up I thought "Oh the sweet smell of the steam"; except there was no steam; I must have slept for a couple of hours. I barely remember going to bed and once again I slept in.

It was kind of a cool morning; I thought a good morning for digging. I had buried the windows between three tall coconut trees which made it easy to locate. I only buried them about two feet deep and covered them with a piece of unrecognizable canvas. I set four of them aside and reburied the other two. It took two trips to get them to the boat; they made me more anxious to get the cabin done. Four more days and the cabin was done, now I could install the windows. As I stood admiring my work I thought wait a minute; the cabin needs a door. I had just enough planes left to make a door. Another glitch; it needed hinges and a latch. That irritated me as it seems there was always "One more thing". I actually liked black smith type work; the metal scrap yard once again had decent metal to work with. Having the bellows saved the day. Well actually, it took two days to make a pair of hinges and a latch. I hung the door and after a little trimming it worked perfectly; except what is a door without a window?

I woke up the next morning and headed straight for the window stash. There was two left; I was tempted to take both of them but reburied the one. I had to use hacksaw blades to cut the holes. I made a handle for the blades but still got major blisters. The best I could do was two holes a day. That gave me two front windows, a window on each side and the door window. I decided to recoat the hull and cabin floor and deck with another coat of sealer. I was struggling to hold back my excitement. The only thing left to caulk was the windows when I installed them. I was getting low on diesel fuel; It took three days to collect enough sap or resin or whatever it was. I could only mix five gallons at a time as I only had one can. Five gallons just finished the hull the second coat. The first coat on the inside and outside of the cabin took just under three gallons. I used the last pulley I had on the bow for hoisting the anchor. Anchor? I still had to build an anchor; I pulled enough scrap metal out of my junk pile that was almost gone. Two days of cutting and brazing and I had an anchor fit for an admiral's ship. I put a day in on the garden and spent a day with my family. Someday I was going to follow them to see where they lived.

    I stayed up later than I should have. I caught up writing in my ledger; I did sleep in and didn't care. I could finish coating the cabin today and take the anchor to the boat. For a change luck was on my side; I did have a little coating left; but my last brush was trash. Instead of cutting a hole in the fore deck for the anchor and rope I had built a low box for them. I used all of the rope from the last spool which gave me one hundred fifty feet of anchor rope. The only thing questionable now was the fin I had installed on the bottom of the boat. I had seen what looked like a big fin on the bottom of dry docked sailing ships. I didn't see one hanging that far down so I installed one about sixteen inches deep and one a foot away on either side, a foot deep. I had yet to explore what looked like the perfect bay to anchor Gigo-Gigo on the southeast side of the island. I had installed the oar locks I had built; but still had the oars and hardware for them to build. I decided to install the windows and take a break.

Chapter Twenty

I wanted to let the second coat of sealer dry really well. It was time to go exploring; I packed up a week's worth of supplies and headed south. There were some more totally over grown ruins of which I would come back and explore someday. The south end had a couple of very tall hills. I climbed the tallest one and got a good look at a small but beautiful bay. It had an opening about seventy five yards wide. Perfect! It was a beautiful blue which meant it was probably more than deep enough. The beach was narrow but also inviting. I was going to take a different route going back; there was a clearing between the two hills and I froze. There was about a dozen what looked like deer but had strange, like twisted, horns. I was tempted to shoot one but had a little more exploring to do. They heard me and it spooked them; as they ran for the jungle, about fifteen more came out of the jungle and ran after them.

This meant another food source; things were looking up. The jungle was very thick here and I came upon some more ancient heavily over grown stone structures. One was about three stories tall but as were the others, totally encased with jungle. I thought it was another hill until I got closer. I would be back to do a lot of exploring. I headed home; I found what I hoped I would find. It was the perfect place to anchor Gigo-Gigo. I had another one of my brainstorms on the way home. I would build a little dinghy to tow behind the Gigo-Gigo. It would be perfect to get back and forth in the bay. I was glad to step out into my clearing; my arms needed a rest. I am sure Sadie and Suzy were glad to get home. It was rough going for them and twice I put them in my backpack and carried them. They didn't complain. I would have to go hunting in about two weeks; I thought about going back and get one of those twisted horned whatever they were.

I cut five trees and had it down pat; I had them milled and drying in five days. I cut two trees for the oars and spent two days making the hardware for them. It was time to go hunting; my pantry was bare. There was a little deer jerky left which I would share with the foxes; it was nice to get back into the jungle I knew. I laughed as I hung my hammock on the two trees I hung it on the last time. I was up early and had been watching the far side of the mud bog when a couple of big hogs showed up; They must have been scouts as they grunted and snorted and about a dozen and a half more of various sizes came out followed by nine little ones. I just watched them for a while. I picked out a medium sized male and dropped him; in the blink of an eye the rest disappeared. The one I dropped was heavier than he looked. I carried him over to where I always butchered. He dressed out heavy. More meat for the table! I got the usual backpack of grapes and headed home.

This was the heaviest porker I had ever brought home. I was glad to be walking across my clearing. I just finished getting porky in the smoker as the sun was going down. The igloo was very welcome tonight; the porker on my back and swinging the machete had me ready for some smelly steam and my bed. It was strange how the steam would seemingly drain my strength at night; but I would wake ready to make it a productive day. I spent the day building the oars and installing the hardware on them. I had enough coating for the first coat. After building the Gigo-Gigo, building the little boat seemed like I was playing with a toy. I built it right next to the sailboat. It was a little boat but why carry it? It would be part of the launching. I lost a day gathering the resin to make the coating. I gave it and the oars a coat and had enough for a second coat. I hadn't been to my old homestead in quite a while; I could only imagine how overgrown it was. In fact, as I looked around, this place needed a couple days of pruning and trimming; and the garden needed harvesting and replanted.

I gave everything that needed a second coat of finish the final touch. I was going to leave for the old homestead early tomorrow but was awakened by my family. They were worth every minute I spent with them. I tried to tell them I was leaving for the old homestead tomorrow; there was a whole lot of grunting back and forth; I would point north when grunting. They would look north when I pointed and I do think they understood me. As I waved goodbye I wondered if I would see them up north. I hadn't had seafood for a while and just the thought of it got my mouth watering. My usual route to the beach was totally overgrown; by the time I reached the beach I had time to get a few clams and a couple of crab. I hung my hammock first; the sound of the surf and smell of the sea had me ready to call it a night, but dinner first. The foxes got their usual two fried clams cut up. I am sure this was a treat for them like the steamed crab was for me.

I was going to chance the T Rexes this trip; I would save two days not going farther north. I was up at the break of dawn and was soon on the hill above the deer's feeding ground. I hadn't been there long when the first deer appeared very cautiously; they munched their way further into the field and then about a dozen and a half came out of the forest; it was evident,as it was with the hogs, the first ones out were scouts. One of the young doe was limping; I had a feeling if I was going home with a deer I had better shoot now; I dropped a younger buck where he stood; the herd quickly disappeared into the forest. The crippled doe tried to run and fell. As I approached the fallen buck it was evident the doe had a badly broken front leg and the other front leg was skinned up badly. She wasn't going to make it so I shot her to put her out of her suffering. Once again, timing is everything; after I shot the doe I reloaded with the wax bullets.

I had just started to gut the buck when here they came; five screaming T Rexes, I hit the fourth one before they stopped. They just stood there making that ugly screaming noise. They must have remembered the last time I hit them with the wax bullets. They were getting braver and moving slowly closer; I had the buck ready to be loaded on my shoulders. The T Rexes could cover a lot of ground quickly; Rather than take a chance I hit two of them in the flank and that sent them running for the jungle. As I headed for the beach I kept looking back until I was well into the jungle. Once I started walking up the beach I thought about them, I guess they were some kind of a deer I saw on the southern end. They were closer than these on the northern end; but it was thick jungle all of the way. I would go for it one of these days. It was getting dark when I thankfully entered my clearing.

I had no choice and finally with the moon shining bright, put the last of the deer in the smoker' I did the igloo less the leaves before basically sleep walking to my bed. The sun was high in the sky when I woke up. I had decided to take a pass going to the old homestead; there was no doubt it was overgrown. I had too much going on to spend a week or two clearing it; if I would be living there soon, I would have cleared it. There was a good chance I wouldn't be using that homestead again. It seemed there was a lot to explore on the southern end. There was no doubt I would keep Gigo-Gigo in the bay. I slammed my breakfast down as I wanted to get over and check the boats over. The second coat of sealer had set up; I sat down and smiled as I looked at Gigo-Gigo; she was a beauty; it was too bad I couldn't paint her. My parents would be so proud of me. I climbed aboard and checked everything over; the Gigo-Gigo was ready, complete with a sea anchor.

If the sky was clear and the water calm I would launch tomorrow; I would launch at the break of dawn as I had no idea how long it would take to reach the bay. My dad had let me take the helm on our sailboat, but he was there to coach me. I was on my own now. I had worked just as hard, maybe harder, building this boat as I did getting rid of the plane. When I launched I would use the oars to get me away from land and then raise the sail. One thing about it; I had a big ocean to practice in. I spent the day re-greasing the launching ramp and getting supplies aboard. I had even made a little hibachi and had a box of charcoal. I had built a special life jacket that I hoped I never had to use. I even made a harness to wear if I was ever caught in a storm and a chance that I could be washed over board; It had a rope on each side of it that I could hook on each side of the helm; because I was alone I made sure I would be as safe as possible. I would have to take the foxes with me and hope they didn't or wouldn't jump overboard.

Chapter Twenty-One

There was no doubt I was nervous; after dinner I made an entry in my log and drank a two beaner before I headed for the igloo. I went easy on the leaves and was totally relaxed as I went to bed; but I woke up early, nervous and excited. This was it! All of my weeks of hard work was about to be tested. I put the foxes in with a couple bowls of feed; food always seemed to be the most important thing to them. I removed the two chocks in front I had put there for safety's sake. I untied the two ropes I had wrapped around the tree directly behind the boat; I was able to let the boat slide slowly to the water. I kept the dinghy on shore with me just in case. When Gigo-Gigo was finally in the water I sat looking at her and almost cried. I put the dinghy in the water and rowed over to the boats side; Preparation is everything. I climbed up the rope ladder and tied "Me-Too" on the back of the boat. I tried the oars, it was tough rowing, but did move the boat.

    I slowly raised the sail about half way; I was so nervous I knew I had to get control of myself if I was going to control the boat. There was a gentle breeze and I was soon smiling; I was soon able to go in the direction I chose. After about an hour of practicing tacking I headed a little farther out to sea. Oh my God; I was so thrilled I felt like jumping up and down and screaming with joy. I was actually sailing on the ocean on the boat I built! The wind picked up a little and I was ready for it. I had my island on the port side as I sailed merrily along with a smile that hurt my face. The Gigo-Gigo was made for the ocean and handled great. It took about four hours and I saw the opening to the bay. It looked a lot narrower than it did when I saw it from the hill top. I brought the boat around in a big circle which lined me up where I wanted to be. I thought, here goes, and began to tacking towards the opening; something was going wrong as I seemed to be pulling southward. I headed back to sea.

I realized there must be riptide; OK, I had a different plan and tacked northward; there was no way there was a riptide in the bay. This time I used a full sail and the rudder. This had to work as I was cutting through the water very fast; I was actually a lot closer to shore this time. I gave the sail and rudder a full starboard and practically shot into the bay with room to spare. There was just enough breeze to carry me as close as I wanted to get to the sandy north beach when I was ready. I decided to sail around the bay and check it out. This was the prettiest area I had seen on the entire area so far. I smiled and thought I had discovered a tropical paradise. I anchored about seventy five yards from the beach. Just for the heck of it I had put knots in a string every five feet with a weight on the end to check depths; cool! It was right at forty five feet at seventy five yards from shore.

I loaded the supplies and foxes in the dinghy and headed for shore. I had never felt this good since washing ashore on my island. Finding all of the gold was a thrill; but nothing compared as the dinghy reached the beach. One thing for sure, the foxes were glad to be on land. It was evident I came in at high tide. When I was ready to leave I would leave at high tide. I had locked the highest hill on my compass. It was late afternoon so I figured it would be best to camp on the beach tonight and begin exploring tomorrow. I pulled the dinghy well up onto the beach and hung my hammock from a couple of coconut trees. I couldn't help myself and kept looking at Gigo-Gigo anchored in the bay. There was a little waterfall coming off of the lower of the two hills. That must mean there was fresh water close by. I could get spoiled over here as I sat feasting on fresh boiled crab. My wheels were spinning; the perfect place to keep Gigo-Gigo, deer, seafood and what looked to be a lifetime of ruins to explore. I was moving up in the world.

I wondered if I could get Buddy and family to follow me here. I had to laugh, I had been sitting here patting myself on my back admiring what I was thinking might be my new homestead and it had gotten dark. The sound and the smell of the sea and with a gentle breeze rocking my hammock, I thought "Who needs a two bean tea and steam igloo to fall asleep" The pink sky of morning was turning to gold when I woke up. I lay in my hammock for a while just enjoying the smell and sound of the ocean. The foxes must have known I was awake as they sat under the hammock barking at me. They were probably hungry because I was. As I sat eating breakfast I had to laugh, here I was sitting eating breakfast admiring the Gigo-Gigo as she rocked gently in a soft breeze. That was it; I found myself happier than I had been in a long time; I liked where I was.

Like I had discovered when I was here the first time; the jungle was thicker here; I knew I had to follow the route I laid out with the compass. It took a lot longer but I cleared the path wider, as I knew if this would be the route I would be using, it would need cleaning every couple of weeks. It was the shortest route to the highest hill. It may have been the shortest route but it took me all day to make it half way up the hill. It took about nine hours to make it this far and about an hour and a half to make it back to the beach on an open path. I carried the foxes most of the way up; they ran back and stopped every so often and barked at me like" hurry up". Aha! They were hungry. I had given them a little jerky for lunch. I think the whole deal was, they had accumulated a taste for seafood. My butt was dragging; I don't care how good a shape a person is, swinging a machete all day through a heavy jungle would wear anyone out. I decided to make it to the top of the hill that I named "High Hat" and head over to see if I could make it to where the fresh water was coming from.

I rose early to get a good start. It was a good thing as the terrain was bad. I gave it my best shot but would need another day as the going was treacherous; it was not only very rocky, but covered with very thick jungle. On the way back to the beach it began to thunder and lightning and a light rain began to fall. The rain actually felt good as I was wringing wet with sweat. The weather got worse the closer I got to the beach. Not good! I was going to have a wet hammock. The sea was looking a might ferocious but the bay had gentle rolling waves. I wasn't prepared to ride out the storm on the beach. The wind wasn't bad so I decided to load up in the dinghy and head for the boat. It was kind of a rolling ride and the wind kept trying to push me, but I finally made it to the boat and up the ladder. I had built the boat so any water hitting the deck would flow out a two by four opening just above the deck in the aft.

I'm sure the foxes were glad to get out of the backpack to the dry warmth of the cabin. It was going to be a cold dinner tonight. I thought why not! I had a two beaner after dinner and the rocking of the boat and I was sound asleep. Lightning flashes and thunder with a pounding rain woke me up once. When I woke up again the storm was gone; it was a lot cooler which was OK; I would spend two more days looking around. If I found an area I would like to make habitable I would sail back and load up everything to get me started here. I had only been using the machete about an hour when I came to a very rocky area that had a bunch of little trickles and streams of water that formed the little stream and created the little waterfall I had seen. I carefully tasted the water, it was cold and tasted great. It looked like it had a rock dam around it at one time. There was a large plateau on the east side of this hill. This was it! It was the perfect place to set up housekeeping and have a large garden. I could cut a path from here and be much closer to the beach.

I decided to spend the night here; it would be getting dark soon. I cut a bunch of the tall grass and made a mattress and unrolled the canvas I used if or when it rained. The foxes I am sure thought heck yes and snuggled under the canvas with me. Noises woke me up; it was just as well as it was getting light out. I sat up and looked around; off to the southeast at a lower level there were about twenty of the twisted horned deer or whatever. They were grazing. Evidently the wind was right and they hadn't picked up my scent. No, I didn't stink as I bathed almost every day! I rolled over to where they couldn't see me and got up. I headed back for about an hour and stopped so the foxes and I could have our cold breakfast. It was an easy hike not having to cut my way through the jungle. I loaded up the dinghy and headed for Gigo-Gigo.

Chapter Twenty-Two

There was a gentle breeze so I went for full sail. We weren't flying through the water; but moving towards the opening at a safe controllable speed. As I reached the ocean the water became a little rougher and the wind picked up. I only messed up once and got the boat sideways in the swells and took a heavy spray; a lesson learned. The rougher water and a stronger wind kept me busy getting back to my camp. I dropped anchor about twenty five yards from shore and stayed aboard for about an hour to make sure the anchor would hold. When I hauled the anchor to the boat I thought I might have made it too heavy. My thought was it was better to have a heavy anchor and be safe. I had to laugh; it was a piece of cake dropping anchor but it was a bear bringing it back in. The deeper it was the more difficult it was to raise it. I had cleats to where I could lift and cinch. This way I didn't have the constant weight of the anchor testing my strength. The dinghy was perfect; it wasn't too big and hard to handle; but big enough for what I would use it for.

It was good to get back. I decided to erase anything that resembled a smelt; I would keep the area looking like a black smith shop, which it was that also. I harvested the last of the garden. When I headed back south I wanted to take everything I could to set up living there. I had pretty well given up on my northern home. It had served me well and I would always have pleasant memories of it. There seemed to be endless ruins on the southern end. Plus everything I needed was closer. Thinking of needing; I wasn't out of anything but wanted to take plenty of food back as I was going to be busy setting up house down south. I checked on Gigo-Gigo and she hadn't dragged the anchor at all. I had to do a lot of machete work to get back to the mud bog. An early bird gets the worm or a hog; I didn't have to wait long and I had my choice. As per usual I picked a medium sized male and dropped him. I quickly dressed him out and headed for the grapes.

I had just about finished filling my backpack when a thought came to me. I remembered when I use to play my flute Buddy would show up. If they showed up this time I was going to try something. I would play the flute and go south a hundred yards or so; I would do this several times and see if he knew what I was doing. I figured if I was on Top Hat and the wind was blowing north he may be able to hear the flute and know I was calling him, or them. I lucked out and got three birds on the way back to camp. I saved myself some work and plucked the birds as soon as I got back to camp. I built a fire big enough to see what I was doing and put the hog and birds in the smoker and spread the grapes before I had a snack and went to bed. I was up early as I had a lot to do before heading south. I retrieved ten of each of my coins to take with me. Of course I couldn't spend them; but my dad's words rang in my ears, "be prepared". I resealed what I called my vault to where you couldn't tell where it was.

And then, there was my beautiful family coming out of the jungle as happy to see me as I was them. It was really neat; I hugged them each very carefully and they were all grunting (talking) at once. We had a great time in the pond; I decided to try something and got out and went back to camp and got my flute and blew some high notes. A few minutes later here they all came. I did the hundred or so yards five times and they all came. We went back and I set the grapes out. While they snacked I took five of the little bread cakes I made and put a generous helping of my jelly on it and gave each one the treat. I had to laugh; they devoured them quickly and Guy went around looking on the ground for more. Buddy stood up and I held the flute up and pointed south; He grunted and hit his chest with his fists which meant he understood. Anyway I think that is what he meant. Well, I would find out. As Buddy and Guy waved I hoped they would come south and find me.

I had my home and grounds pretty well cleaned out; it took five trips back and forth in the dinghy to get everything on the boat I wanted to take south. I was going to miss the igloo but if things went well I would build another one. Actually I thought of so much I had learned as the years melted away. I couldn't allow myself to think or wonder about other people or humans in general; how much can a six year old know about people? The gorillas had been a salvation to me. I knew that humans got married and had babies and gorillas had babies; but it was evident I knew more about gorillas than I did about humans. I was excited and sad at the same time leaving this camp. I had accomplished so much while I lived here. But on the other hand; I was had mixed feelings when I left my northern home. I did smile as I thought "At least I am still on my island". And yes, I knew I had a job on my hands relocating.

The most important thing, Gigo-Gigo would be much safer in the bay. I was smiling again as I thought I would be sailing again tomorrow. Excitement woke me up early; the foxes and I had a hefty breakfast and headed for the boat. As I neared the edge of the jungle I turned and looked and got a big lump in my throat. This had been a great place and I had some great memories. The sea was calm with a slight breeze. By the time I rearranged everything I was taking back I thought "Wait a minute, I had to carry all of this stuff to the new location". I would only make a trip when it was necessary. When I had everything secure and made sure the dinghy would be there when we got there I pulled the anchor; it was a good thing I put the two cleats where I did, pulling the anchor required muscle.

I put Gigo-Gigo under full sail and it handled it perfect. I went farther out to sea this time; I wrote down various compass settings just in case. I figured I was about five miles from my island and headed back. Gigo-Gigo handled perfectly; I wasn't afraid of the opening this time and sailed right through it. I really liked sailing Gigo-Gigo; it was like a freedom that I had never known. I loved my island; but it was like I was not necessarily imprisoned, more like I was totally contained within a certain boundary. I often thought how lucky I was to be alive. I anchored farther east this time. I had taken a compass setting where the springs were; I knew I was going to have to cut a new trail but it would be much shorter than the one I cut when I was exploring. I stayed on the boat that night; I had my bedding and had a great gentle rocking sleep.

The foxes and I had a generous breakfast and I enjoyed rowing to shore. I took enough food and water for lunch as I planned on Sadie, Suzy and I having a seafood dinner. I took the first swing with my machete, I was going to make the path four feet wide and very clean; unless something unforeseen came up I would possibly make this area my permanent home. I was sure I hadn't scratched the surface of how many structures there were to explore. A lunch break was much welcomed. Because I was making the trail as wide and clean as I was, I figured two more days to make it to the springs. I had one of my ideas buzz through my head; I may as well haul or carry whatever I could handle when I came back tomorrow. I had a good looking trail started when my growling stomach told me to call it a day. I had hung my hammock before I started cutting the trail. I had to laugh when I thought I better build a steam igloo the first thing. My arms and back could use that igloo right now.

I made good headway the second day and figured I could be at the springs early tomorrow afternoon. I was glad I brought a load from the boat; it wasn't bad hiking up the new trail and I would bring another load tomorrow. There was some thunder and lightning but no rain that night. Something across the bay caught my eye; I would bet there were more structures over there. I would save that exploration for another day. I woke up sore but figured I would work it off. It was a hot muggy day; I reached the springs in early afternoon and enjoyed splashing the cold water on me. There would be no problem tomorrow making it to the plateau I remembered seeing. I would scout the area and from the way I remembered it, there were several places to set up housekeeping. I would continue hauling things from the boat according to their importance.

There was a lot of stone on this end of the island; that is probably why, whoever it was, settled on this end of the island. They must have been here a long time to build what seemed to be a lot of structures. My island seemed to be a lot bigger than what I once thought it was. As much as I thought of human beings, I was glad there were no other humans here. No wars or disease, just an overabundance of solitude.

I had been here a long time; in that time I had seen five high flying airplanes and one freighter off in the distance. My island must not be a very popular place. I found it strange with all of the ruins here why it had never been explored. I got off to a very early start the next morning; Depending on how it looked, I figured on spending the night on the plateau. I was anxious to be doing something besides swinging a machete. I made it to the plateau in the early afternoon. I liked what I saw; I was for sure going to spend the night here. I found a couple of trees in a fairly clear area to hang my hammock. Then I went looking; the spot I liked was the closest to the springs. As I looked the area over there was a short cliff that looked like an area where stone had been taken from; it was a strange type stone, almost like flagstone, the thickest pieces were three inches thick or less. After walking the entire perimeter of the plateau I found two more places where it was evident stone had been mined or taken from there.

I still liked the spot closest to the springs, plus the bay was mostly visible from there. There were plenty of trees if I wanted to build a log structure; I preferred a stone structure except I wanted my dwelling to be at least five feet off of the ground. Just a safety measure! I hadn't stopped for lunch and just realized why the foxes were following me around; they were probably as hungry as I was. They got venison and I got the last of the birds. The spot I picked to build on was about two feet lower than the springs; I could actually use bamboo and pipe water right to my place. I could even build a stone retainer and pipe water to it for a cold storage area. I changed my mind about spending the night here; I had a lot to haul up from the boat and I still had enough daylight to make it back to the boat. It was just getting dark when I climbed the ladder to get on the boat.

I was carrying as heavy of loads as I could carry walking up hill. I looked at what I had left to take up to the plateau. I laughed and thought maybe I should build a beach house. It was like a reward when I lay down on my bed. I thought it is a good thing I am young; the way I was going I would be an old man before my time. Two weeks of hard work and I had the eight vertical logs solidly in the ground and had begun milling the floor boards. I was in a hurry to get the floor in as I could store everything under it until I could build a storage area of which I had started building out of stone. I only had about three loads left on the boat, it was mostly things I did not want to get wet. I figured about another week and I would have to go hunting. Either that or live on crab and clam. I do like fried clams and boiled crab but too much of anything can tire one of it.

I was beginning to burn out working. I needed some kind of a break. I wondered how long it would take me to sail around the island. Why not? I only had myself to answer to. I would only sail in the daytime and anchor off shore at night. I would finish the floor first which was actually a piece of cake. I would have to go hunting. I had noticed a couple small patches of grapes as I cut the trail. Three more days and I should have the floor in. I had quit working on the storage structure and built a good sized smoker. There was kind of a bushy short tree that had something that looked crab apples; the fruit was bitter sour but the wood seemed to smell better than the fruit. I built a little fire out of a couple small branches and liked the smell. I cut a pile of branches to be drying. I was one happy camper when the last floor board was in. Early the next morning I circled the area where I had seen the deer, or whatever they were. There was a small herd about in the middle of the clearing. I had a choice between two bucks. I dropped the larger one. The others were gone in a few fast hops. Without dressed he probably weighed a hundred and forty pounds. I didn't want to cut up him there, so slung him over my shoulders.

I found a grungy rocky area and dressed him out there. I cut some tongue for the foxes which was one of their favorite delicacies. Luck was on my side and I found a large patch of grapes on the way in. I wouldn't have time to build a drying screen but the new floor would work fine for now. I still had plenty of light to dress out the days kill and get him in the smoker. I figured ten days on the grapes and smoker; so I spent ten days cutting logs with about a five inch diameter. I debarked them and covered them with palm fronds. I really needed a break now. Over half the grapes were ready and the deer was ready to come out of the smoker. I built a wooden box about two foot square and three inches deep. I had put a little pile of sand on the boat deck previously and the foxes did their duty there. I hoped they would use the box with sand in it as they were going to be spending a lot of time on the boat. I even made a little screened pooper scoop. I loaded enough food and water for two weeks as I had no idea how long it would take to sail around the island. I was smiling as this was a major adventure.

Chapter Twenty-Three

My mom's dictionary said May through October were the best weather months in the south pacific. According to my poor old calendar this was about the first of July. I woke up early to a blue sky and gentle wind. I had to smile; one of the foxes had pooped in the box, thankfully! I pulled the anchor and stowed it and raised a full sail. I had the tacking procedure down quite well and left the bay at a "full run". I would never have dared that the first time out. I took Gigo-Gigo out about two miles and loved Gigo-Gigo even more; the waves were kind of choppy and Gigo-Gigo went through them without a bounce. I laughed and thought maybe I had missed my calling; maybe I should be a ship builder. Uh-uh, I would be an engineer but not a laborer. I really busted my butt building Gigo-Gigo!

I had no idea how long it would take to sail all of the way around the island. I would sail from sun up and drop anchor and take the foxes with me when I rowed the dinghy to shore. I wasn't in a yacht race and had no reason to be in a hurry. I thought about doing some exploring but had a new homestead to put together. Not only that, there was so much to explore just around the perimeter of the bay. I practiced various maneuvers with Gigo-Gigo; I wanted to know just what she was capable of in case I ever ran in to severe weather. I knew that I built Gigo-Gigo as water proof as possible. It had stayed bone dry so far. I did have a close call when under full sail. A very strong blast of wind caught me; I quickly dropped the sail and minutes later went under full sail again. I spent the first night at sea on the Gigo-Gigo. Both foxes used the box I built for them. I call it the "Fox box".

    I remembered how monotonous it had been sailing for weeks on my parent's boat. My mom did her best to keep us entertained with her home schooling and various games she brought along and dad let Stacey and me take turns at the helm, but the days could still get very long. Sailing Gigo-Gigo kept my mind active as sailing a larger sailboat in open water ocean meant, whether you are aware of it or not, you are always doing something to keep your boat going where you want; otherwise you could quickly run into trouble. Most sailboats have an auxiliary motor; I had a sail, and oars if needed. I was ready to go ashore my second day at sea. I dropped the sail and tested for depth and it was thirty feet deep. I dropped the anchor and got things ready for a night on the beach. The foxes were excited as they could smell land. We were about seventy five yards from shore. It had been about an hour and the anchor was holding firm so we loaded up in the dinghy and headed for shore. It was a wide sandy beach about forty yards from the jungle. Crab and clam were in abundance and the foxes and I enjoyed a seafood dinner. The rising sun woke me up. I felt great and was ready for another day at sea.

    I about wore myself out rowing out to the boat; It was a windy morning and there was a moderate riptide. I pulled the anchor and hoisted the sail. It was a very gusty wind so I dropped the sail a bit and was more comfortable with about a three quarter sail. We were what I estimated to be half way around the island by late afternoon. It wasn't as windy as it had been but I decided to stay on board for the night. Gigo-Gigo rolling in the swells woke me up; it was just as well as the sky was just beginning to turn pink. There was a gusty wind, the reason for the rolling swells. The foxes and I had a hearty breakfast as it looked like I may be busy today. After pulling the anchor I found I had to sail with full sail if I were going to make any headway. I actually liked riding the swells; it was like slow going up and racing coming down. The wind eased up and the ocean calmed down; I had a busy day working the sail and helm; I was ready, as were the foxes, to head to shore.

For whatever reason crab and clams were scarce on this beach. It was getting dark when the foxes and I ate. I hadn't brought food ashore so I had to find us seafood for dinner. The foxes each got two clams and I had one small crab. Between the sun and a growling stomach I woke up and was ready to get back to Gigo-Gigo. Getting the dinghy through the surf proved to be a chore. By the time I was able to get in the dinghy and start rowing I was still breathing hard when I reached Gigo-Gigo. There was a moderate wind and I was under full sail all day. I took Gigo-Gigo out farther than I ever had before to get a better look at my island. It was much larger than I first thought it was. I thought maybe I might be losing it. I have been alone on my island for many years and here I was sailing the ocean blue and loving it. Staying busy had been my means of keeping my sanity. It was a great day for sailing; the sky was a deep blue; The Sea was a bit choppy but Gigo-Gigo didn't mind and the wind was perfect for full sail sailing. I decided to stay on the boat for the night; I laughed and thought "either stay on board or take food ashore as the foxes and I returned to the boat hungry this morning".

Gigo-Gigo rocking woke me up; it was just as well as there was early morning pink in the sky. It was a gusty wind and the water was very choppy. I would have to do a lot of tacking today. I had to go farther out to sea; there seemed to be a very strong riptide that extended to maybe two miles out to sea. I got my sailing skills tested today; I was edgy all day; Getting out of the riptide was very trying. I was too far out to sea to drop anchor; I began thinking "OK dad, what do I do"? I sailed at an angle to get as close to shore as I dared. There was very little riptide closer to shore; I tested and had about twenty five feet of water. I was beat and hungry and dropped the anchor. I had figured maybe five days to sail around my island. I had two great days of sailing and finally began to go south by southwest. The landscape had changed; the jungle had been mostly flat since I cleared the north end of the island and headed south. The terrain was much higher now.

The beach was narrow and I cautiously sailed towards it. There was no riptide pulling at me so I took Gigo-Gigo in as close as I dared. The wind had let up and there was a gentle breeze. I dropped the anchor in about thirty five feet of water. I wasn't taking any chances and put food and foxes in the dinghy. As I pulled the dinghy farther up on the shore the foxes jumped out and there was no doubt they were glad to be on land as they raced up and down the beach. This was one of the times I wished I could have found my dad's binoculars before our boat sank. There was an abundance of seafood; the weather was perfect and I needed no help falling asleep. The foxes barking woke me up; they were barking at something in the jungle of which I never saw.

I never turned my back on the area where the foxes were barking; I kept the AK handy and we still enjoyed a seafood breakfast. It was easy rowing back to Gigo-Gigo. About half way back two tigers appeared on the beach; now we know! Having lived in the jungle as long as I have, I found I am never intentionally looking but my eyes and ears rarely miss anything. They were not as big as the Bengal tiger but they weren't the kind of pussy cats I would care to bring home. It was a great day of full sail sailing. The south end of the island was much more interesting than the north end. I liked the higher landscape. It made me anxious to begin exploring; careful exploring as the two tiger were still clear in my mind. Tigers or no tigers we stayed on the beach. I kept two large wax bullets in the AKs. The only way I would kill any wildlife is in self-defense or food for the table. It was a quite good sleep night. Two hungry whining foxes woke me up; it was good timing as it was going to be a bright sunny day.

I took Gigo-Gigo out to sea about as far as I dared; My Island's high south country tapered off lower to the west; I now figured my island to be nine miles long and five miles wide. No wonder it took so long to machete from point A to point B. We spent a calm peaceful night on the beach. The wind rocking my hammock woke me up; the weather seemed to be slowly changing; the sound of a rougher sea got my attention in the morning. I took a pass on a beach breakfast and headed for Gigo-Gigo. It was a bouncy ride in the dinghy getting to Gigo-Gigo. The foxes and I were both glad to get aboard. I was hoping to make it back to the bay before nightfall. About midday I knew I was close to the bay entrance except it was difficult to see. A light rain had turned into a wind driven heavy rain. With great difficulty I tacked back and forth until I finally saw the bay entrance; I was down to half sail.

There was one thing about me and the storm; I would beach Gigo-Gigo before letting the sea take us. This was not good. It was getting dark very early. The thunder and lightning with the wind driven rain was very unnerving. I was absolutely thankful for the large lightning flashes; otherwise I would not be able to see the bay opening. There were no large lightning flashes for a couple of minutes and I had no idea where I was. All I could do was hold on and hope. A huge flash lit everything up; I was about a quarter of a mile from the bay opening. I pulled up full sail and figured I would either sail through the opening or run Gigo-Gigo up on the beach. There was another timely lightning flash and I was close to shore on the starboard side but was about to enter the opening. I cut it to the port as hard as I could and was inside the opening and in the bay. The storm was a wild one but the bay was much calmer than the ocean. I looked up at the stormy sky and said "Thank you Lord". I was able to get Gigo-Gigo over to my spot to drop anchor.

I was too tired to try to make it to land, plus I was soaking wet and it had turned very cool. Thankfully I kept extra clothes on board just in case. The bunks had very thin padding but I could have slept on an iceberg I was so physically and mentally worn out. If the foxes hadn't started barking I might have slept all day. There were clouds in the sky, but it was a warm sunny calm day. My two little alarm clocks were as hungry as I was. We didn't have to be in a hurry as after last night, I was very thankful to have Gigo-Gigo safely back in the bay. I hung my wet clothes out to dry and we headed for shore. What a pleasure it was to row the dinghy in the bay; no waves or riptide, just easy rowing. I was just as happy as the foxes to be on terra firma. I had to do a little machete work to get to the plateau. There were a lot of palm fronds and broken branches to clean up. Other than that, everything came through the storm OK. I totally enjoyed sailing around the island but was anxious to get to work and put my new homestead together.

Chapter Twenty-Four

The logs I peeled before my ocean adventure were ready to install. I decided to cut and peel or debark another load of logs before I begin using the ones already cured. Needless to say; using small diameter logs was going to take a lot more logs. At the end of two weeks I had a total of seventy six logs curing and I had laid the pole vertical frame out for a sixteen by twelve building. This would be the biggest I had built yet. I kept a generous amount of grapes curing along with a good inventory of raisins. I took a break before I began putting the logs up and spent a week stacking stones to build a pond. There was no shortage of stones and they were close by. I packed grass between the stones. I had to leave the end of the pond open as it was filling before I wanted it to. The pond leaked which was good as the water wouldn't mildew up and there was enough water from the springs to overcompensate for the pond leaking. In fact, when I closed the end up I made a spillway as there was a lot more water going in than what was being lost. I took my first dip in it and it was a good thing I was used to cold water as the pond got my immediate attention. I was in it about fifteen minutes and wasn't sure if I was used to it, or my body was numb.

It was time consuming but every third day I would climb to the top of the highest hill and blow the flute as loud as I could. I had reworked the flute to blow louder but it was useless for music now. I had just started to put a log on the structure when my family totally surprised me and came out of the jungle. It was funny as they were all grunting and hurrying to me and; I threw caution to the wind and we all hugged; it was possibly the happiest day I had ever had on my island. After things calmed down a bit I motioned for them to follow me to the pond; you bet Guy was the first one in. They didn't seem to notice how cold the water was, but I about froze my butt off. I got out and Buddy got out and we headed for the grapes and raisins I had set out. Soon the whole family was polishing off the grapes and raisins I had set out and grunting all at once; I had no idea what they were saying but there was no doubt they were happy as I was so I grunted back. Buddy finally stood up and looked at me and grunted and I grunted back and hugged him. He turned and headed for the jungle and Guy gave me a hug and they all headed for the jungle. Buddy and Guy grunted and waved and I grunted back and waved.

I am sure humans would think my association with the gorillas was stupid but if humans had survived alone and as long as I had on a deserted island they would welcome anything that seemed friendly. I spent the next week notching the logs. They would all need touching up, notching as I laid them which would be simple hammer and chisel work. I knew once I began laying the logs I wouldn't stop until my home was built. So I built a very nice steam room out of stone and plastered it with mud strengthened with grass. The roof was crisscrossed saplings with a couple layers of palm fronds. I built a charcoal pit in front of it and the water basin out of sap and sand. To celebrate the first night I used it I made a two bean tea. I dozed a couple of times and when I got out I think I could have slept standing on my head.

I laid logs for a week and liked the results so far. I had eight rows up, that meant if everything went right I had about three weeks to get the walls up. That was allowing me three days for hunting and gathering fruit of which I had better do first. There were more deer in the herd this time; I dropped a good sized buck and filled my backpack with grapes and a few bananas. Once I had the grapes drying and the deer in the smoker I went down and checked on Gigo-Gigo. There was not a drop of water in the hold. The foxes and I had a seafood dinner and I was soon lulled to sleep by the sound and smell of the surf. The sun woke me up; I just lay in the hammock for a while enjoying the sound and smell of the sea.

My family visited me two more times in the next few weeks. My cabin turned out just like I hoped. I was glad I brought the basic smelt along and the last of the scrap metal; I built a pair of hinges and latch to hang the cabin door. I thought the next time I go back to my "oriental" home I would bring back the last round window and install it in the door. I decided to call that home Oriental as calling it "Jap" sounded crude. I fenced the area where my garden would be and ran bamboo pipe for the over flow from the pond and plugged the end of the bamboo. I graded the ground so that if or when I pulled the plug on the bamboo it would irrigate the entire garden. As fate would have it, the day after the last of the seed were in it rained. Lucky for me it was a soft steady rain. I treated myself to a two beaner as I totally enjoyed the steamer. Every time I looked across the bay the adventure in me was aroused. I decided the next time my family stopped by for a visit I would take Gigo-Gigo across the bay the next day and begin exploring. I had saved all of the cut offs from the logs and had built a picnic table and benches when my family showed up.

It took a lot of raisins to feed five healthy gorillas; it was too bad I couldn't train them to do various things like take a basket and fill it with grapes and bring it to the drying rack and spread them. If they brought any more family with them I was going to have to do something as the five of them could polish off a lot of raisins. Good timing! We had the usual family reunion the next day. Guy was no longer a little gorilla; he had grown to be a big boy. I hoped there weren't any young female gorillas for him to hook up with; I was maxed out getting raisins ready for them. We had a great day as I laughed and grunted with them. I thought back when I had rescued the baby gorilla I named Buddy. Buddy was an exceptionally large gorilla now, and thanks to Buddy. I was curing a large amount of grapes to have raisins for five of them. That night as I slept I had a scary dream; I dreamed I saw about twenty gorillas exiting the jungle and headed for me; that woke me up. I wouldn't be able to feed raisins to more than one more.

I was up early and filled my backpack with food. I trimmed the trail down to the beach and hung my hammock on the usual trees. The foxes and I enjoyed the best of seafood dinner. I rowed out and put the backpack of food in Gigo-Gigo for safety sake. It was a beautiful night, an easy night to sleep. The sun woke me up and I was raring to go. I put Gigo-Gigo under full sail and the foxes and I had a cold breakfast as we sailed slowly across the bay. The beach was very narrow and the water deep close to the beach. I had been thinking about the two tigers I had seen; I put four large wax rounds in the AK; if I did encounter any tiger the large wax rounds should do the trick. If not I would use live rounds. As I had said before; I wasn't ready to be a Puddy cat's dinner.

As I neared shore there seemed to be a dock built out of stone; I dropped anchor far enough away from it to make sure Gigo-Gigo didn't get damaged. I tied "Me- Too" to what had to be a stone dock; it was totally over grown; I had to start using the machete and that was as good of a place as any. The stone dock was a surprise; the four foot wide steps going up the hill were a bigger surprise. One surprise led to another; at the top of the steps was what looked like a very large courtyard. I cleared a path straight ahead and there were four steps that led to a large doorway. I was able to step inside a huge room filled with all kinds of statues; this must be a temple or something like that. There was a large thick stone slab that was evidently used to secure the entrance door. The inside was over grown, but not near as dense as outside. There were stairs at the back of the room which were easily cleared of tangled vines. On top the roof must have once been made of wood, but was completely gone; and there was like a four foot wide walkway below a five foot wall.

There was no doubt this had been some kind of fortress. The entire complex was on different levels and extended as far as I could see through the jungle. There must have been a large population here at one time. It would probably take months or maybe years to explore this whole thing. I had brought about a ten day supply of food; I decided to stay on Gigo-Gigo at night but take a few days to explore what I could. I was hungry and I'm sure the foxes were too so we headed for" Me- Too". On my fifth day of exploring I hit the jackpot; near the center of the huge complex was a building about a hundred by fifty feet; it had walls like the entire perimeter of this complex. The thick wooden door was very rotted and easy to get through.

I was conserving the flashlight batteries as I had one unused set left. There seemed to be a front and a back room; there was no doubt the front room was an armory as it was filled with various kinds of weapons. There was a very thick door for the second room. I couldn't get it to open. I got a huge axe from the weapons room and was finally able to break the latch loose. I pried the door open and shook my head in surprise; I had figured this was a dungeon or something like that. There were all kinds of gold statues surrounding three walls. There were boxes of a variety of gold coins and small boxes of precious gems. Unreal! There were at least twenty different kinds of coins; I took one of each. I took a gold statue that looked like it was probably a king and queen that was about four inches tall. This must have been the treasury. I was getting hungry so it had to be getting late.

Just as I stepped out of the entrance the foxes came yipping back to me; two large tigers appeared and they were too close for comfort. I had to hit both of them twice on their rear ends before they high tailed it back into the jungle. I had done all of the exploring it took to satisfy my curiosity; It felt so good to be back on Gigo-Gigo that I sailed around the entire bay. I had a feeling the bay held some interesting secrets. I had seen sharks outside the bay but never in the bay. When I was totally caught up on everything I may do some exploratory swimming. It was so good to get back to my homestead. The ruins had a heavy musty smell that I was glad to leave there. I had plenty of gazelle jerky; yes the animal I shot was not a deer, but a gazelle. It tasted the same as deer venison. I was going to collect grapes and see if I could get lucky and get a couple of birds. The grapes were plentiful; the birds were scarce but I did get two.

I spent the night in my hammock; it would have been well into night if I tried to make it back to my place. I lucked out and got some bananas on the way back. I retrieved the raisins and filled the drying rack with new grapes. The foxes and I enjoyed a fried bird dinner. I made a two beaner and headed for the steamer. I put some leaves in the water and sipped my tea. Life was good; I fell asleep in the steamer. I lucked out and made it to my bed before the sun came up. Nothing like a wild night out!

I slept in as I had things well under control here. I spread the coins on my table and looked at the little statue. It was a nice piece of work, not crude at all. The coins were a mystery; they were very old; like the late seventeen hundred and early eighteen hundred. It looked like they were from four different countries. This was something for an archeologist of which I most certainly was not. I took a quick dip in the pond and thought about my family, the gorillas that is. I had time to climb High Hat and see if I couldn't call them in. The trail I had cut leading to the top needed very little trimming. I blew as hard as I could several times and was about to head back down when something at sea caught my eye. It must have been just beyond the horizon. It would appear, and then disappear. Each time it appeared it seemed a bit closer. There was no doubt; it had to be a ship.

Chapter Twenty-Five

I hurried back to camp and got my mirror. The sun was in the west which was in my favor. It was getting closer and I began to get very nervous. It wasn't a big ship and it wasn't moving fast. It seemed to be maybe five miles out and I began flashing with my mirror. I didn't know codes, so I would go one long flash, a short flash and a long flash. It had closed in to about three miles and there was less than an hour of sunlight. With a heavy heart I was about to give up when, oh my God; a light from the ship blinked long, short and long. We flashed that signal back and forth as the sun disappeared. I made it back to camp and my wheels were spinning.

I had to chance it; I had never tried to cut my way through the jungle at night, but I had to try it tonight. There was a bright moon which would help; I was on the last set of flashlight batteries. I set my compass as I would have to rely on it to get me to the beach. The poor foxes probably thought I was crazy. Maybe I was! I could have cried when I exited the jungle to a moonlit beach. Thankfully I had brought extra water. I figured I could still get maybe four hours of sleep and hung my hammock. It felt like I had just closed my eyes when a pink sky woke me up. I looked seaward and the ship was very close. It had National Geographic on the side of it. The sun was just coming up in the east which made my mirror useless. This was my first chance to connect with humanity in almost seventeen years.

I built a big fire on the beach and threw green grass on it and it did smoke. The foxes and I munched on jerky and I rationed the water. If there was no contact we would have no water to make it back to camp. Just as I put more green grass on the fire the light began blinking a long, short and a long. I was sure they were close enough to see me so I waved my arms. I saw a large rubber boat being lowered with three people in it. I think I had better keep my eyes dry as I wouldn't want the first people I would see in seventeen years to see me crying. My heart was pounding as I heard the sound of the motor and the raft was quickly approaching. I stood on the edge of the beach and pulled it up on the beach. All I could do was nod my head and hold my hand up; I was too choked up to say anything.

The man in the bow got out and introduced himself as first mate Hanson; He introduced the young lady as Charzad Carlton and the man in the aft as Larry Morris. I told them my name was Scott Christian. They told me they found this island by accident as it was not on any of their charts. I told them I was the only human on the island and had been here almost seventeen years. I asked if they had water on board and they did. I took a big drink and asked what the funny taste was. Charzad said there were chemicals in the water to keep it safe to drink. She offered me another drink and I thanked her and told her no thank you. I told them I had a comfortable camp if they would be able to stay awhile. The first mate said they would have to get back to their ship. I heard a familiar sound in the jungle behind me. The first mate had a weapon in a holster. I told him to keep his hand away from the weapon and I would treat them to something. Charzad asked what that might be. The first mate handed me his weapon.

I turned and grunted a few times and Buddy stepped of the jungle; I walked over to him and we bumped heads; He looked at the people a couple of times and I grunted to him. He went back to the edge of the jungle grunting and after a minute my family stepped out. I greeted each one of them and motioned them to follow me.

They followed slowly until they were about twenty feet from the astounded people

To the amazement of three human beings it seemed five gorillas were talking to them. I told them the gorillas accepted them because I told them it was OK. Charzad told me she was an archeology major at Arizona State University. I told them my dad was a survivor instructor for the Marine Corps. We were on a south pacific adventure in our boat and we were hit with a massive storm. I woke up on the beach. I found our wrecked boat washed up on the rocks. My parents and my sister were gone. Because of my dad teaching me survival I was able to live a hard but decent life alone for the past seventeen years. Buddy grunted something to me. I grunted and motioned like I was eating and pointed towards my camp. We bumped heads and he and the rest headed for the jungle. He and guy stopped and grunted and waved. The three arrivals were in total shock. I told Charzad there were ruins here that were an Archeologist dream.

She asked me to describe them; I told her there was a very large area with various types of structures in two different locations. The first mate told me they had anchored for a minor repair and were waiting for a helicopter to bring the necessary repair parts; if they hadn't anchored where they did and saw the flashing mirror signals and smoke coming from the beach, they would have weighed anchor when the repair was completed. They didn't even see the island until they saw the mirror and smoke signals. They were all three asking me questions; I finally told them I was hungry and thirsty; if they liked I would take them to my camp and show them around. Charzad had shorts and sneakers on; I told her that was not the way to dress in the jungle. She asked the first mate if he would take her back to the ship to get her gear and bring her back.

He told her no problem; the parts wouldn't get here until tomorrow. She asked if I would wait for her. She handed me a bottle of drinking water; I smelled it and it seemed void of chemicals: I took a drink and it was OK. I told her to get back as quick as she could as I did not want to go home in the dark. She asked if I had electricity. Now that did make me laugh! She said she would need electricity to charge her computer, cell phone and long distance communication. The first mate asked how long she planned on staying. She told him it depended on what she found there. I had just finished a steamed crab and fed the foxes a couple of steamed clam when I heard the rubber boat approaching. I pulled them ashore and they began unloading things. There was a large suitcase and two smaller ones, plus a small Honda generator and a five gallon can of gas. I was looking at the amount of things they had unloaded and was shaking my head. She asked if there was a problem. I told her if we didn't have help carrying the load it would take four trips for me and her to get the load through the jungle to my place.

I was beginning to be an unhappy camper. Other than situations I encountered in the jungle, my life had been totally uncomplicated. I was about ready to head back to my place and let them figure out what they were going to do. The first mate asked me to wait a minute and called the ship. He asked whoever he was talking to, to hold on; He asked if they helped carry everything, how soon they could get back to the beach. I told him if we left right now we could make it just before nightfall. He asked if they would have to spend the night. I told him either spend the night or hike back through the jungle at night which I did not recommend. I pointed to his side arm and told him there were things here that his side arm wouldn't stop. After another conversation on his phone he told us to load up and let's go. Larry took the generator Hanson took the five gallon of gas and Charzad carried the two smaller suitcases.

I had the big bulky suitcase. By the time we made it my camp the three of them were thirsty; they each had two bottles of water when we started and drank them dry. I still had a couple of drinks left in the bottle they had given me on the beach. I gave them a quick tour; they were astounded. I fixed a vegetable venison dinner topped off with a biscuit with my raisin jelly on it. I had enough bedding for Hanson and Larry to sleep on the floor; Charzad got the bed and I hung my hammock under my house. I treated them to my steam room. Charzad had a swimming suit and it was ok for the guys to go in their underwear. I had a big smile when I gave them all a cup of my two berry tea. I was finishing a piece of jerky when the guys came down the stairs rubbing their eyes. I handed them both a piece of jerky; Larry looked at me and asked "Is this it for breakfast"? I told him no and handed him another piece and he did laugh. The first mate told me he had never slept that well before. I laughed and told him it was the jungle air. My tea was never mentioned. Charzad came down the steps and did the rubbing the eyes thing. It was a very bright sunny morning.

She told us good morning and couldn't believe how well she had slept. Hanson told her they had to get back to the ship; it may be two more days before they got the parts. She said if it was alright with me, she would spend those two days here if I thought she might get a look at the ruins. I told them it was a day over and a day back. She told the first mate that this trip was all about exploration. He asked if I thought they could make it back to the beach alright. I told him they had no choice, unless they had a machete they would have to follow the trail I opened up. I filled their water bottles from the spring and told them if they had any problems getting back to the beach fire a couple of rounds in the air and I would be there. As soon as they disappeared in the jungle I told Charzad to put long pants and boots on if she had them and bring a backpack if she had one. When she was ready to go I told her what I was doing was for her only; I would not allow anyone else to explore my island.

She asked if she could take pictures. I told her no problem. We had to stop twice to give her a breather before we reached the beach.

Two people were the limit in "Me-Too" as we headed for Gigo-Gigo. It was a perfect day for sailing. I anchored Gigo-Gigo and we tied Me-Too up at the stone landing. Charzad took pictures all the way up the steps. She was in total disbelief when she saw the stone structures. She was asking questions just about as fast as I could answer them. I had requested, and they had brought me, thankfully, two dozen flashlight batteries. I took her up to see the upper fortress wall. She was as amazed as I was. She wanted to see an area I hadn't opened up; as I swung my machete I caught something out of the corner of my eye and beheaded a huge boa constrictor as it almost dropped on us. It thrashed about as it died; it scared Charzad and she grabbed me as she screamed. I patted her on her back until she calmed down. As she held me something was going on with me and I gently moved her back. Another minute and I would have been very embarrassed.

    I decided to show her what I thought was the treasury. The boa had unnerved her and she was holding on to me, and I liked it. When she saw the contents of the treasury she was in disbelief. I asked her not to take pictures in the room. She asked why? I told her I had read in my mom's dictionary that gold brought out the dangerous greed in mankind. She looked at me quizzically and agreed. I told her we were going to have to get going and get something to eat. I picked up a gold chain with some kind of bird on it and put it over her head. She asked if it was alright to take it. I told her this is my island and it is OK.

    I told her as we were getting close to the entrance that if there a couple of tigers out there they would probably disappear into the jungle when they saw us. Sure enough! As we stepped out into the sunset there were three tigers about fifty yards away. They were lying down and as soon as they saw us they began pacing. But they turned and disappeared in the jungle. We spent the night on the boat. She was still looking at the pictures she took. I couldn't believe how Sadie and Suzy took to Charzad. What a picture it could be; two foxes sleeping at the foot of the bed with her. I had jerky, biscuit and jam ready when Charzad woke up. I told her it would be a full day by the time we got back to the camp. She asked if we could stay and do some more exploring. I told her no, as I only brought enough food for a couple of days. Not only that but I was going to have to go hunting. She was quiet all the way across the bay. I had just dropped the anchor when she asked if she could stay and if I would help her explore the island. I thought "As long as she doesn't hug me again".

    I kept her busy getting things into Me-Too; I treated her to a steamed crab lunch. She wasn't in shape for hiking trails in the jungle; especially if the trail gradually climbed. She was huffing and puffing by the time we reached the camp. I fixed us dinner and after we finished she asked if she could stay and explore the island for National Geographic. I had lived alone for a long time; she had aroused me when she hugged me. I thought as long as we don't get close to each other and she was willing to help it would be alright. I told her she would need to help pull her own weight. She showed me a bicep muscle where there wasn't a muscle. I looked at her and asked "Has any man ever told you no"? She laughed and asked if I were going to tell her no, I told her she could stay; but how did she plan to get off of the island when she was ready to leave? She said "How about I cross that bridge when I get to it"? I told her OK; but we would have to build another bed and put a partition between our beds. She said "OK". She called someone on the boat and told them she had months of exploring to do and would stay in contact.

    She asked if there was a shower. I told he no but there could be; but it would have to be a cold water shower. She made a face and said "Ouch". I wasn't ready to tell her everything when I put leaves in the water in the steamer. She told me she really liked the smell and I smiled as she drank her two beaner. I was cutting and trimming saplings to make another bed when she appeared in the morning.

She told me she had never slept that good in her life. I showed her how to make pancakes and raisin berry syrup of which we enjoyed for a very late breakfast. By late afternoon we had a new bed and the screen started. I told her tomorrow we needed to go hunting and get a fresh supply of fruit. Plus the garden needed tending to. I didn't mind sleeping in my hammock; but it sure felt good to be sleeping in a bed. We both slept in our clothes and agreed we needed to get the screen finished.

I showed her how to use the machete on the way to go hunting. She had a close call how she was swinging the machete. I told her don't ever swing down again; always swing away from her body. The wind was in our favor and we got close to the animals. I figured it was time she got some learning; so I took a big buck out. I carried it far away from where I shot him to dress him out of which I had her help. She was squeamish at first but did great for a first timer. I was going to have her carry part of it but thought maybe next time. But I filled her backpack with grapes; I filled mine with bananas, coconuts and berries. We lucked out and got three birds on the way back. She was once again huffing and puffing when we got back to camp. She was a trooper though and never complained. I treated us to a steak and vegetable dinner. We were both glad to be in the sweat house that night. I went lighter on the leaves but we did enjoy a two beaner.

The next morning when I woke up I lay there thinking how different it felt to have another human here with me; especially a female; a young good looking female. I got up and said, not so loud to scare her; "reveille, time to go to work". She sat on the edge of her bed and asked if today wasn't Sunday, the day of rest. I'll be darned; she had a calendar in her wallet. I told her God knows survival on my island meant it was a daily challenge of doing what was necessary to live. I told her if she liked we could build a place to worship; and once we were through worshipping we would take care of what needed taking care of. She thought that was a good idea. After breakfast we checked the wood in the smoker and turned the meat. The grapes on the rack were doing fine but the garden needed weeding and a little harvesting. We finished the screen and I looked skyward and said "Thank you Lord". While we were having dinner she asked when we could go back to the ruins. I told her I was going to take her to the north end of the island first.

Chapter Twenty-Six

I took her on a hike to High Hat with me. The National Geographic boat was gone. I asked her if she was ready to spend seventeen years here. She said maybe, Hmmm! I gave four long blasts on my converted flute and she held her ears. She told me the pitch really hurt her ears. I told her that particular sound traveled for a long distance. My family knew it was a sound that I was calling them. I told her when they got here I had another surprise for her. I thought it's a good thing I built the pond as big as I did. When we got back to camp I got one of the two pieces of propeller I brought back and fired up the charcoal in the forge. I told her she was going to need a machete and went to work; now there was a good lady; she brought me a cold drink of water a couple of times. By the time it was dinner time I handed her the machete. I told her I would make a scabbard tomorrow, or at least before she needed it. She made a couple of swings with it and did OK. We were both tired and took a pass on the steamer and tea.

My cloth clothes had gone by the wayside a long time ago. My clothes were either deer or pigskin. I had made a neat pair of deerskin shorts and that is what I wore to bed. Charzad had had very girly pajamas. The screen served the purpose. It was like we had our own bedroom. I woke up to a familiar sound; it woke Charzad up and she was alarmed, I laughed and told her it was OK; our family had arrived. We had five excited gorillas waiting for us. She helped me prepare five biscuits and jelly for them. As I went down the steps I stopped and said "Whoa"; there was six gorillas waiting for us. Charzad was on the ball and quickly prepared another biscuit. The gorilla that was evidently with Guy was about ready to run; we handed the biscuits out and Charzad talked to the new one and held the biscuit out; Guy grunted something that sounded like something stern and she took it. One taste and she about slammed the biscuit down.

    Guy was the first one to make a move. I still had my shorts on; I told Charzad to put her swimming suit on. Buddy was the only one waiting for us; He headed for the pond as we came down the steps. It was evident Charzad didn't know what to think when she saw five gorillas in the pond. Guy's girlfriend was hesitant to get in. Charzad talked to her and as Charzad got in I quickly named the newcomer Molly; Molly very slowly got in. Soon she and Guy were splashing each other.

    I asked Charzad if she would mind if I called her Char. She told me no; that is what her father used to call her. By the time our family was through wiping out the raisins and bananas Molly had pretty well established herself as one of the family. Char had taken a lot of pictures on her cell phone. She told me if she had not seen the gorillas she would never have believed there was a friendly family of six grown gorillas. She asked how often they visited. I told her if I didn't see them every two or three weeks I would call them in. I made the scabbard for Char's machete and she helped me trim and prune the perimeter. I did treat us to a tea and the aromatic leaves in the steamer. We spent the next day getting ready for a long hike. I helped her make her own hammock I was going to take her for a tour of the north end of the island. Our first stop was the ex-Japanese camp which was my home while I erased the Japanese plane. We spent the next day at the first ruins I found, where she took a load of pictures. Our next stop I showed her the alligators and she told me she never wanted to go back there; I told her that was fine with me.

We camped close enough one evening to where the T Rexes lived; we were up early the next morning and lucked out as there was a small herd of deer feeding when all of a sudden the shrill screeches began as four T Rexes came charging out of the jungle. Char grabbed me and hid behind my back; I told her if she were going to take pictures to hurry; they were shredding a young deer. I told her they would be gone in a few minutes; they made ugly screeching noises as the little deer was quickly disappearing. She snapped pictures as fast as she could. The largest one looked our way and I got him sighted in, just in case. I had six large rounds ready just in case. It made some screeching sounds and ran back to where they came out; the other three followed. Char was still leaning on me; whenever she was close things were going on with me that I found could be very embarrassing; I suggested we get a move on; she gave me a strange look and nodded yes.

We enjoyed seafood until it was time to head back into the jungle; she was doing quite well with her machete, although I did stay clear. We shot a hog, got four birds and a load of grapes and a few bananas. We plucked the birds and saved the choice feathers. I got a brainstorm; I told Char we should start watching and if the opportunity came, get some young birds and cage them. I think we may be able to eventually get fresh eggs from them. We had been away a week and she hadn't mentioned the ruins. After we had the smoker going and the raisins harvested and fresh grapes on the screen we gathered the material to build a small cage to retrieve the young ones and carry them to a big cage that took us three days to build; it amounted to a big chicken coup. We split bamboo into half inch strips to build it. All this time Char never mentioned the ruins. I asked her if she would like to take a tour of the ruins. We packed and got ready for an early morning departure.

We were heading down the trail as the sky turned pink; she was tuned in with her machete. I let her row us out to Gigo-Gigo. It was such a nice morning; we sailed all the way around the bay and I had Char take over for about half way. We brought supplies for ten days as we were going to explore as far to the east as we could in that time frame. Char could read things in the hieroglyphics that I had no idea what they were; a civilization built the stone structures about eight hundred years ago. Wars with other islanders, famine, and disease had minimized their civilization; about two hundred years or so ago they became pirates but their population diminished to about sixty people.

They were attacked by a head hunting tribe and their population was captured and wiped out. That was probably where the skulls in the eastern ruins came from. Evidently human heads meant more to their captors than the treasure in the treasure room. I didn't want to alarm Char, but I heard big cats every night; We were taking a break on top of one of the walls when four adult tigers appeared in what seemed to be a big courtyard about a hundred yards away. Sadie and Suzy began to bark and the tigers just slowly disappeared into the jungle. I was very cautious until we were finally walking down the stone stairs to get into Me-Too and head for Gigo-Gigo. A green horn wouldn't last twenty four hours in those ruins. I was sure big cats had kept an eye on us all of the time we were there. There were several times I knew they were close; I kept six wax rounds and twenty four hot rounds in the AK just in case.

We left the ruins early enough to have an early seafood lunch on the beach and still make it home just before sundown. I brought Char the meat and vegetables and she made a fine dinner. What a difference, that was the first meal I had in all of my years on the island that I didn't fix. I thought "I could get used to that". We did enjoy the steamer, less any sleep aid; we both needed a good night's sleep; it was almost like I slept with one eye open at the ruins as

I knew there were big cats prowling. Char kept in contact with people at National Geographic; she told me they would like to plan expedition to the island. I told her there was only one way I would allow people on my island. I was beginning to think I had made a mistake making contact with people on the National Geographic boat; Char had proven to be great company; but maybe I shouldn't have welcomed her to my island.

Chapter Twenty-Seven

She told me a Mr. Ayers, the director of the magazine, wanted to talk with me. I told her there had been no human contact for seventeen years; and those on the National Geographic boat had not even seen the island until I signaled to make contact with them. She told me she had researched trying to find anything about the island; and according to all maritime or scientific research this island does not exist. This is a totally neutral part of the ocean. The records show this island does not exist. I told her "For that reason I claim this unclaimed island". "This is and has been my only home for many years with not one human ever setting foot on it until I allowed you and two people to set foot on my island. If I have to, I will die protecting my island and my friends and family". I told her I will allow Mr. Ayers and one other person to visit until I tell them it is time they left. I will be happy to discuss my island with them. No weapons!

She relayed my message to Mr. Ayers and he agreed to it. We set up a time and would build a fire on High Hat and use a mirror to guide them in. She said they would come in by boat. I told Char they could spend two weeks here while we showed them around. I gave her a list of what they could and should bring. Sure enough; the morning they were to arrive we had a very smoky fire going on Top Hat and the National Geographic boat anchored about a mile off shore. We signaled with a mirror and they signaled back. Char and I went down to greet them. He had an older woman with him. Char and I pulled their rubber boat up on the beach. Char made the introductions. The lady, Mrs. Sorenson, was the head artifact researcher. They both had a large backpack and a small suitcase. We wanted to get them back to camp and told them we had to hustle. Char and I each carried a suitcase. We made it back to camp with daylight to spare. We let them use our beds and we hung our hammocks under my home. By the time we gave them a tour they were astounded. Char fixed a bird, venison- vegetable dinner; Mr. Ayers told us it was "Lip smacking good".

We did the steamer with a light addition of leaves in the water; there was no doubt they enjoyed their two beaner. They were over whelmed the next morning when Char fixed them our version of pancakes, raisin berry syrup and smoked pork sausage. They both agreed they had never slept as soundly as they did last night. Char winked at me. I had gotten up early and called the family in. We forewarned them that we were going to have company. I took Mr. Ayers with me and we picked a bunch of wild bananas. It was early afternoon when Buddy came out of the forest; I think both of our guests were ready to run for the forest; I told Buddy it was OK. I introduced him to our two petrified guests. When he was assured they were OK he called the family in. Mrs. Sorenson got behind Mr. Ayers peeking out.

In a short time we were all enjoying raisins and bananas; I cracked a few coconuts and by the time the last banana was gone we were one big happy family. I motioned with my head to Char; she went upstairs and reappeared in her swimming suit; as per usual Guy was the first one in the pond. Char joined Guy and Molly splashing water on each other. I told our guests how the gorilla family came to be and they just smiled and shook their heads in disbelief. I told them I would be right back and headed for my house. I fixed biscuits and jelly for all of us. When Char got out and headed for the table the gorillas followed her; they knew there was a farewell treat awaiting them. We all enjoyed a sweet biscuit with them. Buddy and Guy and I rubbed foreheads and grunted what only we understood. As they disappeared into the jungle Buddy and guy turned and we waved and grunted goodbye.

Mrs. Sorenson was almost in tears. She had been taking pictures and made a couple of videos on her cell phone. She told us that was the most beautiful thing she had ever seen. I told her we would invite them back before they left. I told them tomorrow we will take you to the ruins on the east side. It would be five days of hiking and we would show them the huge alligators and a surprise. Char took care of fixing dinner; we went in the steamer the same as we did the night before. I told them sleep well as we were getting up early. Char and I both packed extra food just in case. It was still dark when we woke our guests up. I gave them a quick tour of my borrowed camp and headed for the ruins. Our guests took a lot of pictures and made a lot of notes. I told them "let's go, we have to make the beach before dark". We made it to the beach with just enough light to get crabs and clams for dinner. They had the hammocks that were on the list we sent them and we helped hang them.

A hard day's hike had us in good position to see the T Rexes if they showed. A small herd of deer appeared and I pointed out to Char, an older one that was limping. We had forewarned our guests that the T Rexes would look and sound scary. All of a sudden five T Rexes came screaming out of the jungle. The limping deer never stood a chance. In a very short time they had stripped the deer carcass clean; they even ate the bones and went screaming back into the forest. We went out of our way to show them the huge alligators; Mr. Ayers told us they were from the prehistoric times. We made it back to the beach just as the sun was setting; but we did have a seafood dinner. The T Rexes and alligators had pretty well unnerved Mrs. Sorenson. I told Char our guests would probably be sleeping with one eye open. We had biscuit jam and coconut for breakfast. They both commented how adapt Char was with her machete. We made it back to the ruins and decided to spend the night there so our guests could do more exploring. We were about ready to leave the next morning when Mrs. Sorenson let out a blood curdling scream. She had almost stepped on a young boa constrictor; I scared it away; she asked why I didn't kill it. I told her I only kill anything if I think I am endangered.

By the time we made it back to our camp we had two guests ready for bed and the sun was still up. I told them that this exploration trip was just a warm up for the next one. Char told me we had better give them a day of rest and laughed. We let them sleep in and they finally appeared late the next morning. I suggested the steamer after brunch and they both quickly agreed. Char suggested fried bird for dinner; we took them with us and went bird hunting and fruit picking. I shot two birds and we picked grapes, bananas and gathered a few coconuts. Char had frying the birds down to a science; after dinner Mr. Ayers told Char her "chicken" was finger looking good. Mrs. Sorenson agreed as she picked up another piece. Mrs. Sorenson asked if we ever took a day off. Char told her every day here is like we are on vacation. I told them to enjoy a relaxing evening because tomorrow will take you to the big ruins.

I told them once we were there to not wander off. That part of the island was home to a lot of very large tigers. "Just stay in a group and you will be OK". We had a great good smelling time in the steamer; I gave them a one bean tea; after all, they were guests and light weights. We rolled them out just as the sky began to show pink. They were funny to watch as there was no doubt that they were not accustomed to getting up so early. Char and I had some heavy jungle over growth to work over with our machetes and it took longer to get to the beach than I intended. We stopped once for a quick lunch and to give our greenhorns a breather. We got to the beach in time to have a great seafood dinner. As we hung our hammocks Mrs. Sorenson asked if there were tigers on this side. I told her "much farther north yes; this side had lions". She grabbed Mr. Ayers and Char told her I was only joking.

I had to make three trips to Gigo-Gigo in Me-Too; it could only handle two people and their packs at one time. They were totally impressed with Gigo-Gigo. We let Mr. Ayers take the helm for a while and he was thrilled. They were both blown away when they saw the stone landing and steps. As we had requested, they brought extra flashlights and batteries among other things Char had requested; they brought me a thousand rounds for my AK. We decided to explore the east end this time. I told them to be careful where they stepped and keep their eyes open. Char and I had our hands full clearing a path through the over growth. Much of the wall on this end had fallen or was knocked over with jungle growth. I climbed to the top of a solid part of the wall and was barely able to see five tigers lying in the sun between two decaying buildings. I motioned for everyone to be quiet and helped them up. Char had Sadie and Suzy in her backpack so they were quiet. When Mrs. Sorenson saw the tigers she was ready to head back to Gigo-Gigo.

I told everyone we would have dinner and camp here tonight. Mrs. Sorenson told us she would not sleep here and was going back to the boat. I told her OK; but I didn't think she would make it as there were more tigers than the five lying there. I told her we would make a fire and the tigers do not like fire of any kind and we would be safe here. Night jungle sounds were very loud here. I was used to it and Char was getting there but there was no doubt; our guests did not get much sleep. I asked Char if we should show them the treasure room; she said "Why not, it's your island and your treasure". When we got back to the building with the treasure I had our guests reluctantly turn their flashlights off and put their hands on my shoulders and follow me. I blinked my light a few times to find my way. When I had us inside the room I told them to turn their flashlights on. There were a few moments of silence and then Mrs. Sorenson said "Oh my God". I let them each pick out a small statue to take back with them. I had enough exploring and I am sure our guests needed recuperation time.

There were three tigers lounging on the steps when reached them. Mrs. Sorenson almost jumped into Mr. Ayers arms. The tigers were a good fifty yards away. I talked to them and got some low growls in return, but they didn't move. They left me no choice and I hit the biggest one in the rear end with a wax round and they quickly disappeared into the jungle. Mrs. Sorenson said "I thought you didn't shoot anything unless you felt endangered". I showed her a wax bullet and asked why she didn't go down and scare them away for us. It felt so good to be on Gigo-Gigo I took us for a slow cruise around the bay. We had a seafood dinner and hung our hammocks for the night. I was really glad to get back to camp. I kept the leaves in the steamer to a minimum and the tea was a one beaner. The next day Mr. Ayers called and made arrangements to be picked up the next afternoon.

He asked Char if she was packed and ready to go. She told him if he would care to take her off of the payroll, do so; she would not be leaving. She and I hadn't talked about her staying or leaving. I didn't even want to think about it; I figured she would leave with them. She looked at me and asked if she could stay. I told her if she left she would break my heart. She gave me a big hug and that did it; I gave her a hug back and didn't let go. She gave them all of the pictures and pertinent information she had put together on the ruins. We showed them the coins and figures we had brought from the ruins. Mr. Ayers confirmed what I thought; Pirates had operated out of the deserted ruins. He asked if he could come to visit us. We both told him absolutely. The can of gas he had brought would keep Char's generator going a long time. She could keep her electronic end of things going for a long time. He told us to keep him informed of what we may need when he returned.

I told Mrs. Sorenson when Mr. Ayers returned from visiting us I would send a couple of tiger kittens for her. She told me I had better not. I had quickly grown to like Mr. Ayers. I trusted him. We had a nice evening together and stayed in the steamer until almost bed time. As Char and I lay in our hammocks, I thought she was asleep; All of a sudden she said "So you really don't want me to leave?" I told her" no, who would fry the chicken for me?" She told me if that is all I wanted her here for she had better leave. I told her if she tried to leave I would sink the boat. She told me she was not that good of a swimmer. I told her I would sail out in Gigo-Gigo and save her. She asked why I really didn't want her to leave. I told her because I would be lost without her. She said in a very soft voice "OK, I'll stay"! I stayed awake almost all night thinking about Charzad.

We woke our guests up early; they were taking a lot more back than they brought. Char had put together a variety of treats for them to take along. I took two gold chains, with something like a gold bird, out of my pocket and told them they were from me and Charzad and our family. Their big ship was anchored about three quarter mile out and their rubber boat was headed our way. We helped Mrs. Sorenson in and the first mate who we had met began to back up when Mr. Ayers jumped out and waded through the water to give us each a big hug. I got a big lump in my throat as they headed back to their ship. Mr. Ayers was probably in his fifties; He woke up memories of my dad.

Chapter Twenty-Eight

Char and I were quiet all the way back to camp and during dinner I asked her if she was sorry she decided to stay. She told me no and asked if I was sorry she stayed. We held each other and for the first time, we kissed, and we kissed. She did like a fake yawn and headed for the stairs. Things were going on that I didn't quite understand. I was lying in bed when Char came over and snuggled up against me. My life would never be the same from that moment on.

The next morning she told me she had a good idea, I asked her what? She said we could use the divider for another drying rack. That afternoon vegetables were drying on that rack. Being on my island alone since I was six years old left me in the dark about so much that went on in humans and adults lives; I was a confused happy young man. I knew adult humans got married; but how did they get married and what did it mean? I was sharpening our machetes when Char bent over and kissed me. I stood up and told her we needed to talk She took my hand and said we could talk over lunch and led me to the table. I asked her "Because we slept together last night does that mean we are married"? She laughed and told me it could lead to marriage. She told me that marriage meant we would spend our lives together.

I had been alone for so long I couldn't comprehend our living together forever. I was one naïve young man. She asked if I would want to be with her for the rest of my life. I told her the months that she had been here were the happiest days of my life. She told me that she was happier here with me than she had ever been before. I told her I thought people had to get married in a church; she explained about preachers, justice of the peace and priest and a wedding license. I said "so how could we get married on my island"? She told me "we can write our own marriage license and God could wed us". We proceeded to write what we both accepted would be our marriage license. I asked when we would be married. She told me she would think about what would be a good date. She told me for now we were engaged.

We hadn't seen the gorillas for several weeks. We made a hunting trip and brought a deer, three birds and our backpacks filled with fruit. We didn't pick grapes as we had an overabundance of raisins. Char had become a great sidekick. I no longer had to tell her what to do when we were in the jungle; she was a natural outdoors person. I asked her what she thought about a trip across the bay. She was all for it. She had been putting together a portfolio of both of the ruins of which she could not have done without all of her electronic gadgets. She had been attempting to give me lessons on her computer of which I was astounded at what it could do. She put together a five day supply of food and the next day we were sailing around the bay. I told her Mrs. Sorenson would be happy to know there were no tigers waiting to greet us.

We spent the next two days with Char taking pictures and jotting notes for her portfolio. I told her I would like to look around the treasure room. One box contained a wide variety of jewelry no doubt taken from people that were victims of pirates from the island. I told Char to pick out an engagement ring. She asked if I thought that would be the right thing to do as the jewelry had most likely belonged to poor unfortunate souls who were probably killed by their captors. I told her the poor unfortunate souls would be happy to know that their jewelry was finally going to be used for a good cause. She picked out a ring with a little ruby and emerald on each side of a diamond. She handed it to me and said it was time I asked if she would marry me. I asked if she would be my wife. She said "Yes" and hugged and kissed me; she handed the ring to me and told me to put it on her finger, which I did. She told me we were now officially engaged. Just about that time we were both startled as a large tiger was standing at the doorway looking at us. As I raised the AK he just wandered off. I went cautiously to the door and saw three tigers walking slowly towards the forest. Char said "Well, it looks like we had a tiger witness to our engagement". As we walked through the ruins heading for Gigo-Gigo Char kept looking at her ring. All of a sudden she tripped and was lucky I caught her. I told her I should hold the ring until we were on Gigo-Gigo. She told me no way.

We had been back at camp several days when Char told me she had a good idea and wanted my opinion; she thought we should build a guest cottage. I laughed and asked if she was expecting a lot of company. She told me no, but thought if we did have company it would be nice if they had a place to stay for privacy's sake. I let her pick out the spot; that evening she showed me a sketch of what she thought we should build. It was almost double of my old cabin. It had a front porch across the front of it. She thought this could be our home and our cabin could be the guest cabin. She seemed very excited about this project and I thought "Why not, what else have we got to do?" I told her before we start we should go looking for the gorillas; we hadn't seen them for several weeks and I was worried about them. I had no idea where they lived and we could have spent weeks looking for them; so we began gathering material to start the new building.

We were awakened a few mornings later to the familiar sounds of our family; we both quickly got up and went down stairs to a surprise. Not one surprise but two surprises. Guy and Molly were the proud parents of two beautiful baby gorillas. The little guys were afraid of us and clung to their mother. It took some raisins and a piece of biscuit with jam on it to get them loosened up. There was a male and female. I sat on the ground and would give them one raisin at a time. Before long I had two baby gorillas climbing all over me. I told Char we would have to name them. Char suggested Larry and Carrie; I didn't think Larry was a good gorilla name and suggested Charley. She said "OK, how about Charley and Carle?", and Charlie and Carle it was. I told Char we were going to have to teach the gorillas how to make raisins now that we had a family of eight gorillas. Guy grunted and led the family to the pond. It took him and Molly both to get the two screaming little ones into the pond. In just a few minutes they were becoming water bugs. They were taking after their father.

There was no doubt the pond needed to be enlarged; it takes a big pond to accommodate eight gorillas; baby gorillas do grow up to be big gorillas. There was no room for Char and me. I was putting the last vertical in the ground when Char came over all excited and told me Mr. Ayers would be here next month. I told her we would be hard pressed to finish our new home by next month. We had enough smoked meat to maybe last two weeks. We worked out a system where Char cut and hauled the bamboo we needed and I trimmed and installed as fast as I could. We had the walls up in three weeks and almost had the main roof nearing completion when Char got the call our company would be here the day after tomorrow. We decided to gamble and moved our things into our new home. I told Char we had cut it too close and we would need to go hunting after we got Mr. Ayers settled in. We covered our belongings in our new home with palm fronds just in case.

The National Geographic ship was off shore when we got up; we went up on High Hat and built a smoky fire and began signaling with the mirror; we began getting signals back and hurried back to camp to get ready to head for the beach. We wanted to get there before night fall. We made it to the beach in time to get clams and crabs for a seafood dinner. A windy morning rocking our hammocks woke us up; it was a choppy sea. We finished breakfast as a bouncing rubber boat came into sight. Mr. Ayers was the loan passenger, and that suited me just fine. We helped him unload some of the things we had asked him to bring. Char had made getting to the beach a lot faster as she had using her machete down pat. Splitting the things that Mr. Ayers brought made returning to camp a little easier.

He was surprised to get his own cabin. We brought enough crab and clam back to have a seafood dinner. I told them at dinner we had no choice but had we had to go hunting tomorrow. Char told us she had some news; we waited while she came over and sat next to me. She had a big smile on her face when she told us she was pregnant. I almost fell off of my chair. I believe I must have gone into shock; I was speechless and didn't know what to say. Mr. Ayers broke the silence and congratulated us. All I could do was hug Char and try to hide the tears running down my cheeks. I finally told her I loved her so much and I was the happiest person in the world. We asked Mr. Ayers if he would do the honor and marry us. I told them I would call our family in and they needed to be here for our wedding; plus we had a surprise for him. He told us he would be honored.

We went hunting the next day; I shot a large hog and astounded Mr. Ayers when Char helped me dress the big boy out. We split the load up between us thankfully. We got four birds and plenty of grapes, bananas and coconuts. We got back to camp just in time to get the hog and birds in the smoker. The next morning at breakfast Mr. Ayers asked Char when she was expecting; she laughed and said we had about seven months to be nervous. He asked if she wanted to go mainland to have her baby. She told him this was her home and she would have her baby here. Mr. Ayers asked me if I had ever delivered a baby. I told him I had no idea about delivering babies. He asked what we thought about having a mid-wife here; He explained to me what a mid-wife was; I told him I thought it was a great idea. He told Char to keep him up dated and would have a mid-wife here a month and a half before she thought the baby was due.

Mr. Ayers stayed to help us get the roof on our new home. We were within a day of finishing the roof when Mr. Ayers thought I had better call our family in. We prepared a feast for them and the next morning our enlarged family showed up. Mr. Ayers was as excited as we were when he saw Charlie and Carle. It took some sweet enticing but he finally got to hold the twins. He told us they were the most beautiful babies he had ever seen. Char totally shocked me and about blew me away when she came down the steps in a simple beautiful wedding dress. Mr. Ayers said the vows and I got chills of excitement when he told me I could kiss the bride. There was no doubt the gorillas knew there was something special going on as they seemed totally excited as they seemingly jibber jabbered away. Char had made special sweet treats for them and Mr. Ayers was busy tending to Charlie and Carle. I asked him if he would like to be their God Father. Buddy let them know it was time to head home. The twins did not want to go but were no match for mama. Buddy and Guy waved as they disappeared into the jungle.

Mr. Ayers and Char had taken a boat load of pictures; the best one was two baby gorillas sitting in Mr. Ayers lap as he fed them raisins. Char and I both were sad to see Mr. Ayers heading for his ship. He had been a lot of help and had become a very dear friend. The next months seemed to fly by. Char was definitely showing her pregnancy; She told me maybe we should tell Mr. Ayers it was getting close to time to have a mid-wife here just in case. We had no idea if it were a boy or girl; she gave Mr. Ayers a list of baby things to bring when he brought the mid wife. Two weeks later the National Geographic ship dropped anchor and we exchanged signals. I helped pull the rubber boat in the next morning. We thought it best if Char waited at the camp for us. She was really showing her pregnancy.

Chapter Twenty-Nine

Mr. Ayers introduced me to a middle aged Miss Lila Clark the midwife. I was surprised when Lila put a large backpack on; Mr. Ayers had a backpack and a large suitcase. I loaded up my backpack and carried two one gallon cans of gasoline. We had to stop a couple of times to give Lila a breather. We had about an hour of sunlight left when we reached camp. After introductions Mr. Ayers asked if we would call him Ron; He said his name was Ronald, but preferred to be called Ron. Lila wanted to examine Char so Ron and I brought each other up to date on anything of importance. The ladies both appeared with smiles. Lila told us within three weeks and there were two babies waiting to be delivered. I had made a neat rocking crib and Char laughed and told me two for the price of one; we needed one more crib. Ron called the ship and told them to weigh anchor and would call for their return. I told him we had a project before the sun went down.

I took him over to help me get the screen that was made for our room divider; he told me it was OK, they didn't need a screen. About all I could say to that one was "OH"! Char had a light dinner ready; Lila asked if we had electricity. I told her no; we had oil lamps and flashlights. Ron told us he had brought two rechargeable LED lamps. Lila asked about hot water. I told her I would have it ready for her. Char asked if we had put the screen in the guest cabin. I told her Ron said they didn't need it. She gave me a quizzical look and I had to laugh when she said "Oh"! We hadn't been going in the steamer as I wasn't sure it would be good for Char. Ron asked if we were going in the steamer tonight; I told him we hadn't been going in as I wasn't sure it would be good for Char. Lila told us it would probably be good for her.

We all enjoyed the sweet smell of a few leaves in the water and a one bean tea. We were all tired; it had been a long day. Ron and I spent the next day making another crib. He asked if I preferred boys or girls; I told him all I cared about was that Char was OK and the babies were healthy. He asked about Charlie and Carle. I told him they were two very rambunctious babies; in fact, they weren't teeny babies any more. I told him I would call them in. I showed Ron the pond and showed him how it needed to be enlarged. He said "Let's do it". He hauled the stone and I put it together; the ladies came down to check on us and to tell us lunch was ready. I really didn't want to stop but Ron was looking like he needed a break. One of the lamps Ron brought was enough to more than light our immediate area. Ron was stiff and sore the next morning. I told him he would feel great once he began hauling stone. He gave me a dubious look. By late morning I had to stop and laugh; I had Ron mixing the clay and grass for the mortar and plastering; He looked like a big walking mud pie. By late afternoon the pond was filling.

I didn't want to tell Ron; but I was one sore young man as we stood back and admired our work. We both enjoyed the much needed steamer that night. The next morning Lila gave us an update; she told us two weeks and I would be singing lullabies. Ron and I checked the pond; it was full near capacity. I took him up on High Hat with me to call the gorillas in. He held his ears when I blew the high notes for them. I told him those high notes traveled a great distance. We spent the rest of the day enlarging the smoker. I asked Lila if it would be safe for us to be gone five days. She laughed and said "Of course, just hurry". I told Ron he and I were going hunting the morning after the gorillas left. Just like clockwork we had a gorilla family calling us in the morning. Charlie and Carle recognized Ron and came running to him. We had forewarned Lila and showed her pictures of Ron's God children; she was hesitant at first; but she soon had two little gorillas sitting on her lap as she fed them raisins. Guy headed for the pond and Ron and I got in with them. Charlie and Carle had a blast splashing each other.

Lila said she would go in the next time. It was obvious who the boss of that family was when Buddy got out and grunted loudly. Ron carried one baby, and I carried the other one, to the edge of our camp and their mother sent them skedaddling for the jungle. Buddy and Guy grunted and waved goodbye; I grunted goodbye to them and they disappeared into the jungle. Lila told us never in her life would she have believed what she was seeing if someone just told her. Ron and I left to go deer hunting early the next morning. We were in good position just before sundown on the second day. We left Sadie and Suzy with the ladies and it was a good thing. We woke up to some growling the next morning. A large tiger and her cub were working on a young deer when four T Rexes came screaming out of the jungle; the mother turned to take the T Rex on and her cub came running in our direction. I hit three of the T Rexes and the four of them ran for the jungle. It was obvious the mother tiger was hurt but managed to get to the north side of the jungle.

I saw and heard the cub and found it about hundred and fifty feet away. It was a frightened little guy. I picked it up and sat down and gave it little bits of jerky, it was hungry. I thought" now what?" What if the mother came looking for it? But if she didn't it was too young to make it on its own. I cracked a coconut and dipped my finger in the milk and it would suck the milk off of my finger. I told Ron to feed it the coconut milk; I still had to get a deer, two if possible. I carried "Tommy"; that is what I named him. We spotted a herd of deer about two hundred yards away. I told Ron to stay there with Tommy. If he heard shots get over there with me; we had deer to dress out and get the heck out of here. I hit two medium sized bucks and the herd scattered northward. Ron came down and I cut teeny bits of tongue and Tommy knew what to do with it.

Ron didn't know how to dress a deer; but he was a great help and we soon each had a deer across our shoulders heading south. Tommy was snuggled in my arms fast asleep. How many people have slept in a hammock with a baby male tiger curled up against them? We had a cold early breakfast the next morning because I wanted to make our camp before dark. Ron was a real trooper but I still stopped twice to give him a breather. I knew he must be about ready to drop when we reached the edge of our camp. The ladies were beside themselves when they saw Tommy. Char asked if we were going to keep him; I told her we would do some research to see if it was feasible. I told everyone" I am not sure how much a grown tiger eats; but I'm sure it is more than I can keep up with". Sadie and Suzy wanted *nothing* to do with Tommy.

Ron asked what I thought about building another guest house; I told him we weren't expecting guests. He told me he would like to explore the ruins on the west side. I told him that would be very dangerous; the roofs had long ago rotted and caved in. I had barely gone ten feet into them and backed out when two of the largest boa constrictors I had ever seen were there to greet me, and I haven't gone back. He told me with my permission he would like to bring Dr. Barbara Collins to assist him. She had explored some of the most dangerous ruins in the world. I told him I wasn't for it; but if he took full responsibility I would talk with Char about it. She told me Ron had done a lot for us; Make it a onetime deal, and give them six weeks. We would not be involved in anyway. They would have to use the rubber boat to get there and bring supplies to last those six weeks. Let Ron help build another structure first. We talked it over with Ron and he totally agreed.

Having an extra hand made all of the difference in the world and ten days of hard work, we finished a large bare bone cabin. I was so thankful for Lila; Char had begun to get morning sickness; I felt helpless but Lila told me that was normal many times just before child birth. I built a cage for Tommy and he slept under our cabin. I decided to leave the cage open one night and Tommy was gone the next morning; I almost fell over as that evening he came wandering in and went straight to his cage. Evidently he could handle going into the wild on his own. Our family paid us a visit. The two babies were definitely not little babies any longer; they kept their mother busy. Once again they had to be dragged out of the pond; they actually acted like two spoiled brats. They were a bit much and I was finally glad when Buddy and Guy waved goodbye.

Ron was becoming quite adept at jungle living; He had begun to make bamboo furniture for the new cabin. Char woke me up before sunrise and told me I had better get Lila. I turned the LED lamp on and ran to get Lila. She told me she needed hot water. Ron helped me as I was one nervous guy; we sat outside and drank coffee. Ron was a coffee drinker and had brought his supply of coffee grounds. The sun was beginning to come up when we heard a baby cry. A few minutes' later two babies were crying a duet. Lila came to the door and waved for us to come in. I stepped inside and could not believe my eyes. Char was lying there smiling with a red faced baby lying in her arms. She looked at the baby in her right arm and said "Cody, meet your father"; She smiled and looked at the baby in her left arm and said "Jodi, meet your father". Ron laughed and said "We had better get busy and build a stroller".

Between Ron and me we built probably the only stroller with wooden wheels. We built springs out of bamboo and it rolled with very little jiggling or bouncing. Tommy continued to come and go.

I liked to rough house with him but had to give that up; his claws were growing with him. He did follow me around when he was there; and he didn't turn a meal down. Sadie and Suzy were staying away for long periods of time. I figured they had pups out there someplace. Lila had Char bring the babies outside on their fifth day in the world. I had to laugh at the way they blinked their eyes. Lila picked Jodi up and handed her to me and showed me how to cradle a baby in my arms. Jodi began to cry and Lila traded and gave me Cody. I could not believe I was holding my son and daughter. I wanted to go where no one could see me and cry I was so happy; Tears ran down my cheeks anyway. Char asked if I was Ok. I was too choked up to answer and nodded yes.

By the end of the babies first week I was getting used to falling asleep rocking two cradles. I was a six year old boy when I was washed up on the shore of my island; seventeen years alone and now I am married and the father of two beautiful babies I have a family of eight gorillas, two foxes and a baby tiger. Ron had become a close friend and I thanked God for Lila. I have been gifted after spending the early years of my life totally alone. Ron told us they would have to leave in two weeks. I told him I would like to get one more hunting trip in before they left; He had been working in the garden and looked funny in his big homemade straw hat. We left to go hog hunting the next day; Tommy followed us part way and disappeared. I told Ron that he went hunting on his own. He was over three times the size he was when we brought him home. We had a good trip; we returned with a large hog, four birds and our packs loaded with grapes and bananas plus the sack I brought along loaded with coconuts. Lila used small amounts of coconut milk mixed with the baby's formulas. We had the family visit before Ron and Lila had to depart.

Charlie and Carle were totally blown away with Cody and Jodi. They would cautiously come up and touch the babies and run back to their mom jibber jabbing ninety miles an hour. They soon lost interest in the babies and were splashing in the pond waiting for the rest of the family. As per usual, their mom had to drag them out of the pond when Buddy let them know it was time to go. Ron surprised me and waved goodbye as Buddy and Guy disappeared into the jungle; He told me he felt sad every time they left. I laughed and told him join the crowd. Thanks to Lila I had become well accustomed to fixing formulas and washing diapers. I wasn't so afraid to hold the babies anymore. I hated to see Ron and Lila leave; I don't know what I would have done without their help and the baby supplies they brought. Char had taken motherhood in stride. She told me I handled the babies like I was afraid I would break them. Living in and off of the jungle with a wife and two babies left very little spare time! I loved spending as much time as I could with the babies; as little as they were I had a blast with them. Char and I had very little alone time; I made sure she was number one and the babies a close second.

I always hated to leave Char alone with the babies when I went hunting; I was very happy when I came in from a hunting trip and Char told me Ron and associate would be here in two weeks. Ron wouldn't believe how the babies had progressed; they both smiled a lot and would laugh when I would tickle them. I told Char I thought they would be singers as they both had a powerful set of lungs; when they cried they let you know it, normally a pacifier would satisfy them. It was a good thing Ron and I built their buggy as big as we did; when we put them in it the first time I told Ron we built it big enough for eight babies; Now they were close to filling it. I probably said it before; Char was a natural mom. She did everything with the babies like she had been taking care of babies all of her life. She was just a natural mom.

I was on the beach when Ron and his associate Barbara Collins ran the rubber boat up onto the beach. He introduced me to Barbara;

she was middle aged and looked to be in very good shape. As per usual I carried the two gallon gas cans; I told Ron we had enough gas to last another year. The three of us had fully packed backpacks; Ron had a large suitcase and Barbara had two smaller suitcases. We stopped about half way and Barbara hadn't even begun to sweat; there was no doubt she could handle the jungle. We made good time and Char was outside with the babies. Ron and Barb each got to hold one; Char had made a mouthwatering stew and there were no leftovers. Tommy came wandering in limping; Barb about jumped into Ron's lap. Tommy was getting to be a big boy. I checked and he had a thorn in his right front paw; I gave him a big piece of jerky and had the thorn out before he finished the jerky. He went over and lay down under our cabin. Ron asked if I would call the family in before they began exploring the north ruins.

Two mornings later we had a yard full of gorillas grunting and waking us up. Get this- Char had made them biscuits and jam for breakfast. Charlie got brave and made the mistake of going over to check Tommy out; Tommy never even got up; He let out a snarl and Charlie ran back to his mother. They had a blast in the pond; Charlie never seemed to let well enough alone; He splashed Molly once too often and she gave him a good swat. I told everyone he looked just like his father when he went to the corner of the pond and pouted. Barbara had been taking pictures ever since she arrived in camp. The gorillas were cleaning up the raisins and bananas when Tommy came carefully strolling up; I gave him a piece of jerky and he lay down beside my chair. Buddy gathered up his family and he and Guy waved goodbye.

Ron and Barbara left the next morning. They would take their boat out to the ship and get the supplies for their exploration of the north ruins. I spent about an hour talking with Barbara about what to expect; there was no doubt she was not a greenhorn. Her rifle was like a cannon; it was a three hundred magnum Winchester. I had loaded twelve rounds with large wax projectiles. She told me she had previously used bird shot. She was a wildlife activist so I didn't worry about her killing animals just to kill. She had an encounter with boa constrictors before and knew what to watch out for. I told her if she had to use the wax bullets and got down to four have Ron call Char and I would come over and replenish her ammo, but don't stay with just four rounds. She left me a dozen live rounds to reload if necessary. I lived all alone for many years and it seemed like the last two years I was always saying goodbye. Ron told us they would return for a couple of days before they departed.

    Six weeks went by and we never had one call from Ron; we began to worry; Char asked if I thought I should go check on them; she had tried to call Ron but got no response. We waited three more days and I began to prepare to go across the bay and find out what was going on. That evening they showed up. Ron apologized; He had dropped his phone in the water when they were unloading; Barbara had used six wax rounds on tigers; they had several close encounters with Boa's; she had to kill one. She said wait until you see this; she showed us a picture of a large pile of skulls all missing the top of the skulls; Ron estimated between six and seven hundred. There was another area with a very large pile of bones and Barb showed us pictures where all of the bones had marks made with a sharp instrument. The inhabitants had been head hunting cannibals. Barbara said she was bringing enough out to help her analyze and get an idea of the time frame and population; she asked if it was necessary could she come back. We told her yes.

Chapter Thirty

It was almost six months before Ron called again; He said Barbara would like to make one more trip to the north ruins; I told him we thought it was a good idea and would look forward to seeing them. I had enlarged our garden; Char asked if I had ever considered being a vegetarian; I told her I was and always would be a meat and potato man. Tommy still stopped by; He was one big boy. He was a beautiful animal but still a wild animal; there was no doubt he was my buddy; but I always made sure the twins were carefully watched. Speaking of twins, I had to make a door screen for our place; Char caught Cody just as he was about to crawl out the door. Yes, our twins were crawling all over the place. Sadie and Suzy showed up with two pups; they hung around long enough to indulge in some jerky treat; I lay on the ground playing with them and then they trotted off to the jungle. Our gorilla family showed up about once a month; thankfully they didn't have any new babies.

Ron called and told us they would be on the beach the day after tomorrow. Char made us an apparatus so we could each carry a baby on our chest; yes we were going to take the babies to the beach with us. Barb and Ron about cracked up when we showed up with the twins. It had been a little tricky using the machetes but our kids didn't seem to mind at how hard we worked. There was plenty for each of us to carry. Lila had picked out clothing for our growing twins thankfully. When we got back to camp Ron told us he had some great news. He took a map out of his pocket; there on the map was a new discovery; a private island called "Scott's Island". I just shook my head and smiled in disbelief; I asked him if we had to pay taxes? He told us no, we were in international water. Char outdid herself and we had fried bird for dinner.

Barb told us they would definitely stay in contact with her own phone radio. I gave her the twelve wax rounds I had prepared for them. They called us twice; once to tell us all was well and the second time to tell us they were coming back. They had some great stories to tell us, and had a load of good pictures. Barb said she had enough now so that she could write all about how the ruins began and what happened to the population. I took Ron and Barbara so Barbara could take pictures of the alligators that were definitely evolved from, we thought, the huge T Rexes. Then she got pictures of the small T Rexes as they tore a crippled deer I shot. We went around to the north part of the island and I took two deer out. Ron carried one and I carried the other. We enjoyed seafood on the way back. We made it back to camp early enough to enjoy venison steak for dinner; Tommy must have known we were back as he showed up and I gave him a deer heart I brought back just for him. I smoked the other one for another time.

Barbara asked if we would ever consider letting others live here. I told her probably not. I told her I respected her and Ron as they respected what we offered on our island and they would be welcome, but not close by. I told them "For myself, I have gotten very used to privacy". There is enough game to support one family and not deplete the wildlife. We are content to live with what we have; we don't need all that it takes to live in the modern world. She asked if we would ever consider leaving the island; I looked at Char and she shook her head no. I told them the day may come when we visit the mainland for a week or so. She asked about our children's education. I told them my sister and I had been home schooled; Char had all of the electronic skills and our children would be well educated. Ron asked "what if they want to go to college, or just leave the island?" I told them when our children reach college age they can make their own decisions. Ron and Barb used the steamer; I spent the night with my family.

Like always, we hated to see them go. Lila had sent a fine collection of clothes for the kids. Char asked what I thought of Barbara's questions; I told her I could understand her curiosity as long as it didn't reach too far into our private lives. About five months had passed since Ron and Barbara left. I was cutting wood for the smoker when Char called me to get there quick. I was afraid something had happened by the urgency in her voice; I dashed up the stairs to see Jodi take three steps before she plopped down on her butt. I was going to help her up and Char told me" wait." Judi finally got it figured out and stood up; she was a bit wobbly but got four steps in before she plopped down on her butt again. Char laughed and said "Chalk one up for the females". I laughed and told her now you had really be watching; next thing you know she will be wandering off into the jungle.

It took Cody a week and I got the come quick call from Char. Jodi was walking more now than crawling; still kind of wobbly but covering more ground without falling down. Cody would get two or three steps in and fall down. About the fourth time he fell on his butt he just sat there; Jodi walked over and began jibber jabbing and I'll be darn, Cody got up; He took about four steps and bumped into Jodi and they both sat down and started crying. I looked at Char and raised my eyebrows; she raised her eyebrows and started laughing. I picked Jodi up and she picked up Cody. Jodi wanted down; I sat her down and she walked over to Char and held her arms out to be picked up. Char handed me Cody and I stood him on his feet. He took several steps before he sat down. I told Char they would really need watching now. A few weeks later Ron called; they had been busy putting a special together on the "Lost Civilization" with no reference as to where it was at.

We updated each other; I told him both kids were walking now; He laughed and it wouldn't be long and they would want a car or something. He told me he thought the bay might hold some interesting things; I told him no doubt; I had seen sharks in there. He asked me how I would like to do some scuba exploration. I told him no thanks; I have two kids to raise. He told me we would be in a diving cage and be perfectly safe. I told him I would talk it over with Char. That night I mentioned my conversation with Ron; she told me she had done underwater exploration and no matter how you look at it, it is dangerous. Ron called the next day and I told him I would take a pass. I had enough to keep me busy here. He told me to ask Char what she thought of Rhonda Jacques; I told him hold on; I asked Char what she thought of Rhonda and she told me that all Rhonda did was under water exploration. I told Ron it was OK, bring her. He told me he would bring their special dive boat into the bay and let us know when they would arrive.

A week later Ron called and said their ship would be dropping anchor in two days. I climbed High Hat early and the National Geographic was already anchored. I gave the mirrored signal and got mirror flashed back. I told Char I would head for the bay and meet them; she wanted to go and I told her I am not taking the kids out on the bay in Me-Too. She said "Let's see what I can do". She called Ron and he told her they could pull the dive boat right up on the shore. I told her I would go for that. Our trail needed a lot of trimming; Char held the kids back while I reopened the trail. The dive boat was a beauty. I had told Ron to make sure it was towing his rubber boat. We handed the kids up to Ron and we climbed aboard; He introduced me to Rhonda Jacques; She and Charzad had worked together on a couple of projects and knew each other well. We had harnesses on our kids with enough lead as to where there was no way they could fall overboard.

They dropped anchor about two thirds of the way across the bay. It was too late to do a dive but I helped them get their gear ready for in the morning; Ron told me the extra suit was for me if I decided to dive. The dive boat was first class everything; and the food was gourmet all of the way; the ships bell woke us up in the morning and scared both of our kids. Pancakes with strawberries for them quickly quieted them. Ron and Rhonda were secured in the cage which was swung over the water and lowered. The bay was exceptionally deep and dark. The cage was equipped with all kinds of lighting. Ron had radio contact with the ship's pilot and directed him to move slowly southward; all of a sudden Ron told him stop. The cameras picked up what looked like the beginning of a graveyard of burned sunken wooden vessels. Ron could control some of the cages movement and Rhonda manned the cameras; When Ron asked to be brought up he sounded excited. I watched the monitor in amazement. It was a continuous graveyard of burned ships.

Once he and Rhonda were out of the cage they both agreed; there was a great documentary lying on the bottom of the bay. Our kids had all of the adventure they wanted; it was too late to go ashore so we spent the night aboard. They took us to shore the next morning; Ron said they would be doing about a week of filming and come up to our camp when they were finished. Once again I had to clear our trail that led up to our place. By the time we got home our kids were cranky and I was getting that way. Once the kids were in their cribs sleeping we latched the door so they couldn't get out and Char and I did the steamer with a few extra leaves and a one bean tea. She asked me what I thought about the documentary. I was sure other than some old cannons there was nothing salvageable so it was OK.

She told me she thought Ron felt a little bad because I didn't want to dive. I told her I have a loving wife and two young children that depended on me; I was more interested in my family than those burned out ships lying on the bottom of the bay. Sorting through those burned out ships would be a diver's nightmare; First of all we had what was taken off of those ships. Secondly, it was a death trap for any diver as there was nothing stable down there. I have no interest in the documentary and I was more than content playing in our pond. Ron called the fourth day and said they were coming in; He had an accident and broke his arm. He and Rhonda showed up at camp two days later. Ron had a cast on his arm and had a slight limp. He told us there was one wreck in particular he wanted to take a look at. He left the cage and when he stepped on the side of the wreck it gave way. Rhonda had to exit the cage and find him through the black cloud he had stirred up when he fell through the caved in ship. She had just got him back in the cage when a very large shark slammed into the cage. They had a one person submersible submarine of which Rhonda spent two days in and got all of the pictures they would need for the documentary. She said she saw several sharks and not one small one.

They stayed long enough for Rhonda to meet our family and Tommy. She wanted to see the T Rexes but Ron needed to get some professional medical help. I carried his things for him and felt better because his arm did not look good and he would be on his way to get it taken care of. I hated to see them go but it was important for Ron to get medical help as soon as possible. When I got back to camp Char asked me what I thought. I told her he had a compound fracture and probably should have called a helicopter in to get the medical help he needed. About a week later Ron called and said he had a close call. They told him another day without medical help and he would have lost his arm; they had to pin it and he wouldn't be using that arm for quite a while. He gave Rhonda credit for saving his life and getting everything they needed for the documentary. He told us we might be getting a visit from a cripple; we told him we would be waiting for him.

Char and I took the kids in the pond almost every day and they loved it; after about two weeks they could actually swim from one side to the other. They couldn't understand why the gorillas got to go in and they couldn't. We were sure the Gorillas would never intentionally hurt them; but the kids were so small in comparison to Charlie and Carle; Plus Charlie could get very over active until his mother gave him a good whack. I hung two swings from a tree beside our cabin. If we had let them, the kids would have worn both of us out pushing them. I told Char I had an idea to where they could keep each other occupied; I built them a teeter totter; they loved it and spent a lot of time on it. Ron called and sounded excited; he asked if we would like some company. He said he had completed the therapy and his arm was almost like new. National Geographic told him to finish out the year and he could retire on full salary. We told him we would be waiting for him.

Char had a green thumb and had transplanted grape vines on the entire perimeter; she had me build a rock garden type thing complete with a neat little waterfall. She transplanted a variety of the beautiful wild flowers that were in abundance on the island. She turned our clearing into a beautiful piece of landscape. She even had the kids helping her; this way it kept them busy and she could keep an eye on them. They found out that throwing mud at each other could be a lot of fun until Char taught them that covering each other with mud was not a lot of fun. I almost rolled laughing as I watched our two kids sit and pout. Char was a great mother and our kids would be the best for it.

Chapter Thirty-One

Ron called and said they would be there in about two weeks; He didn't say who "they" were so Char and I figured he would be bringing one of his lady friends. I made two hunting trips; we had a deer, a pig and four birds in the smoker. Our little smoker had grown to meet the need. I got five more birds; Char spoiled me and we had fried bird for dinner. She made a batch of her famous raisin berry jam and syrup. I asked if she thought a whole boat load of people were coming ashore to visit us. She pointed to our twins and said they ate more as they were growing fast. She told me Ron was bringing a fresh load of clothes for them. I had to laugh as their pants were up past their ankles and I had to rework their shoes to fit them. Our garden made us both proud; Ron had brought seeds the time before when he was here and we had a blue ribbon garden. He also brought me a hand crank meat grinder and spices we had asked for. We were not lacking for food. I asked him to bring us a dozen baby chickens of which we would build a good sized chicken coop for.

Bamboo was plentiful and easy to weave; it still took us three days of finger blister work to build one fine looking chicken coop. We planned on having up to eighteen chickens at a time; hopefully there was a rooster or two in the dozen chickens Ron was bringing. We expanded our corn crop; we had husked enough corn from two crops to get a half bushel of corn of which I broke up into chicken feed. We had tried using wild bird eggs; they didn't seem to be right for human consumption. We hadn't heard from Ron and he wasn't answering his phone. Two weeks had passed since we heard from him. About the time Char decided she would call National Geographic headquarters Ron called; He had misplaced his phone and just found it. He said he felt foolish, but could not locate our island. I asked his coordinates. He was way off base; I gave him coordinates and estimated they would arrive tomorrow morning. I told him I would build a smoky fire on High Hat. We got up early the next morning; after breakfast. I climbed High Hat and soon had a very smoky fire going. I waited about an hour before I saw a ship approaching from the northwest. When it was close enough I began signaling with the mirror. After several minutes we exchanged signals and I headed home.

    I was working in the garden with my two helpers, I had Cody and Jodi helping me pull weeds. I had put them in a little area that didn't have vegetables as they had begun to pull the baby vegetable plants up. I heard Char holler we had company; I told the kids "Let's go, someone is here to see you". As we came around the buildings there were several people talking to Ron. I began to get upset as he knew I did not want a lot of people visiting our island. As I got closer I stopped; the near bald guy looked like my dad. They hadn't seen us yet; the older white haired woman looked like my mom. As I walked up to them the woman said "Oh my God" and hugged me; next the guy and younger lady were hugging me. It was my mom and dad and sister! My mom and sister were crying buckets of tears. My eyes weren't exactly dry.

    I introduced Char who suggested we all sit down at our picnic table and benches and she brought a pitcher of her berry drink and gourd cups for everyone. They thought I was a goner for sure; Dad had gotten mom and Stacey into the survival raft, but I was gone. They were adrift at sea for almost two weeks when they were rescued by a freighter. I told them I had washed ashore on a section of roof from our boat; I wasn't sure if I was unconscious or asleep from exhaustion; but I woke up on the beach. I thanked my dad for teaching me what he had or I wouldn't have made it. Jodi was sitting on moms lap and Cody was sitting on dads lap. Ron suggested unloading and putting things away they had brought. My kids and I took the baby chicks over to their new home and they went to work on the ground corn.

Char had put a great pork roast, brown gravy and plenty of vegetables on the table; my family kept complimenting her about her cooking. We were just about finished with dinner when Tommy showed up; I calmed everyone down and gave Tommy the fatty trimmings from the roast. My mom and Stacey had no desire to pet my Puddy cat. Dad laughed and said he may pet Tommy tomorrow. Dad asked about our gorilla family. I told them I would call them in tomorrow. We had time to show them around before the sun set. Stacey asked what we did for entertainment; I told her Char and I had each other and our kids kept us busy. Ron asked no one in general if they should show us now. He and dad went to the jungle at the edge of our property and came back with two tricycles; a pink one and a red one. Mom and Stacey helped the kids get started. I fired up the yard lantern to let the kids learn how to ride their trikes. It finally came time for them to go to bed. There was no way we could pry them loose from their trikes. Mom and Char carried them upstairs and after a lot of persuasion got them to lie down with their trikes parked besides their beds. Yes beds! The cribs were for babies and our two kids were no longer babies.

My mom tripped out the next morning when Char put pancakes with her syrup and jam on the table along with the sausage patties. I took dad up on High Hat with me when I called the gorillas. He wanted to try the flute and got some good high pitched notes out of it. When we got back to camp my mom took my dad to show him the crude but efficient kitchen Char had. We took my family around and showed them various things that made up our living area. That evening Char put a venison stew on the table that would get a blue ribbon at any cooking contest. I cracked up when my mom and Stacey asked Char to give them the recipes of the various things she prepared. Our kids had pretty well mastered the art of riding a tricycle. They proved to be our entertainment center for the evening. We treated everyone to the steamer with a few leaves and a one bean tea. They all commented how relaxing the steamer was and were ready for bed. I winked at Char and she smiled.

True to form my island family woke us up; I had forewarned my parents and Stacey not to panic; the gorillas were our island family. As we ate breakfast Char had a platter of biscuits and jam for our island family; I was very proud of my gang; that was my nickname for the eight gorillas; my gang! As I expected, Guy was the first one to head for the pond; I went up and put my swim trunks on; Ron told everyone "Now the show begins". I climbed into the pond and Charlie and I immediately got into a splashing each other; He and Carle weren't too far from being full grown. My dad asked if he could go in with just his underwear. Next thing we knew, he and Charlie were having a blast splashing each other. I had enough and got out. Dad started to get out and Charlie pulled him back in the water; my dad got a snoot full of water and I hollered at Charlie; wouldn't you know it? He went over in the corner and pouted. I got back in the water and after talking to him we rubbed foreheads and he grunted happily back into the pond. Char and Ron were laughing; my family was in shock and astounded to see their son so close to so many gorillas.

It was Char's idea; she had made a plate for each of them; I couldn't believe what she did; they not only had their raisins, she had dipped their bananas in her jam. When they had cleaned their plates she sat a jam covered biscuit on their plate. I sat on the ground with them while they had their treats; when the last one finished

I stood up; Buddy and guy stood up; we bumped foreheads and Buddy took his family to the jungle He and Guy turned around and grunted goodbye and waved.

My parents and sister were in total disbelief. I told my dad I would take him hunting tomorrow. Char brought the kids out with a new outfit on. I thought our kids are growing too fast. I decided to take Cody hunting with us tomorrow. He could walk the beach and dad and I would take turns in carting him in our backpacks in the jungle. We left early the next morning. As we got ready to head out I held the AK up and asked dad if he recognized it. I told him about our boat being washed up on the rocks and how I salvaged what I could before it sank in the ocean. We were just about to the mud bog when I looked over and Cody was sound asleep in dads backpack. I could hear the hogs; the wind was right and we got within about seventy five yards of them. I woke Cody up and motioned for him to be quiet. It took a bit and I picked out a good sized one that was out of the bog. I knocked him down but he got back up; He didn't get up when I put the second round in him. We dragged him to an open area and dressed him out; I asked dad to watch Cody while I dressed it out. Dad took Cody and I carried our pork chops. I treated dad and Cody to a seafood dinner; Cody was hesitant at first but a bite of the crab and he did like seafood.

I was very happy to get back to camp; this hog was heavier than any I had shot before. By the time I had porky in the smoker dinner was ready. Mom and Stacey had helped Char fix dinner and they put quite a spread on the table, complete with flowers. After dinner we kicked back and enjoyed our conversations with each other. Ron asked what I thought of their new ship. National Geographic was on the market for a new ship. They had asked him to give this vessel a forty five day trial. He liked it and was sure that they would buy it. I asked what a ship like that would cost. He said equipped the way they wanted, about twelve million dollars. My dad asked if I was thinking of buying one and laughed. I told him no, we had a sailing ship. They all wanted to see it. I told them we would take them to it tomorrow. My mom said "So when do you and Charzad plan on bringing your children home?" I looked at Char and winked. I told mom "we are home, this is our home and we love it. We may come for a visit, but this is our home". She said "Do you mean you plan on spending your entire lives here?" I told her that was our plan.

    I asked dad why they didn't buy a boat like the one Ron brought them here in. He laughed and said "Oh sure" as he rubbed his fingers together in a money gesture. I told them to roll their hammocks up to take with us tomorrow. Mom asked if we were going to sleep outside. I told her that was the plan. Char and I packed our backpacks to take care of all of us for four days. I figured it would be a three day adventure with extra supplies just in case. We had a quick breakfast and headed for the trail, which needed a lot of trimming; Dad and I did the machete work; Ron and mom and Char took care of the twins. Char and mom thought it best if they stayed on shore and dad, Stacey and Ron sailed over with me. I didn't want the twins on the water yet.

    True to form there were three tigers lying on the steps near the top. As we approached the landing they meandered off into the jungle. I showed my dad the bullets with the wax loads; he asked what if that didn't stop them. I told him I only shot what we could eat, but would shoot to kill if I had to. We went carefully to shore; Me-Too could handle three people but that was pushing it. My dad was good with a machete and we made it to the east ruins by late morning. I lost no time as we worked our way to the treasure room. We all had flashlights and the treasure room sparkled. There was a box about ten inches square and eight inches deep that I had looked at previously that I picked up to take back. I had dad pick out whatever he wanted for mom and Stacey.

Chapter Thirty-Two

We sailed back in time to get hammocks hung and get ready to camp out for the evening. I had to laugh as the three ladies prepared dinner. The kids had worn themselves out playing on the beach and were ready for some sleep time after dinner. Dad patted his pocket and asked if it were OK; He had picked out a beautiful diamond emerald ring for mom and a gold cross necklace for Stacey, inlaid with diamonds, rubies and emeralds. They about came unglued. In the civilized world those two pieces of jewelry would be worth thousands. Jungle sounds woke us up early which was good; going back was uphill all of the way. We all took turns carrying the twins. Dad was still a good chugger and had no problem; we took a couple of breaks for Ron and mom and Stacey. We were all glad to get back to camp. I asked Char to bring her laptop down after dinner; I had something I wanted to show everyone. Char fired it up and I pulled a boat up on the screen; it was an ocean going yacht. It was a big one at ninety feet long. Dad asked what that was on the aft of the ship.

I told him it was called a survival pod. It had supplies on boards to last six people forty five days at sea. The ballast was set up that it would always remain upright no matter how rough the sea. It had a rudder and could be propelled forward with a pedal system similar to pedaling a bicycle. One inch thick glass windows were unbreakable. The ship could sleep eight people comfortably. It had a dining area and living room. It was a made to live aboard ship. I looked around and asked in general "so what do you think?" Mom looked at me and asked if I were going to buy it. I asked her and dad how they would like to own it. Dad said he would buy it in a heartbeat if they had a couple of money trees. I looked at Ron and said "You once told me that you knew people who were always on the market for good antique jewelry and precious stones". I opened the box I had brought back with me so everyone could take a look. Char didn't even know I had this treasure. It was full of diamonds, rubies and emeralds. Ron just shook his head.

I said" I am not an appraiser; but from what I have researched, there are many millions of dollars of stones in this box". Ron agreed with me. I asked if he thought it feasible to bring one of his top buyers here with his head appraiser. Ron laughed and said if who he had in mind knew of that box of precious stones he would swim here if he had to. I asked mom and dad if they would like to own that boat. Dad chuckled and said "Oh yeah". Mom just smiled and shook her head yes. I told them it was a done deal. I would give them the information to go and see this ship; I told them the final living features were on hold until they could see it and get it finished the way they want; and Ron," let us know when you can have a buyer here". It had gotten dark and I said "How about a little steaming tonight?" A few extra leaves and a one bean drink and we were all ready for bed.

Ron and my family were leaving tomorrow; I took Ron and my dad to my old borrowed campsite. I took them to my cave and opened it up; I thought they were both going to pass out. I told them the best I could come up with was about twenty four million dollars. I asked Ron if they had to go through any customs. He told me no. I put three ingots and thirty four coins in my backpack. I put the cover on and pulled the vegetation back over the cave. When we got back I gave my parents, Shelley and Ron one of my gold coins. I laid the contents from my pack on the table. I told them" there is in excess of a half million dollars there"; "Ron said he would line you up with a legitimate gold buyer". "Take the money to the boat manufacturer; that is your earnest money". I think everyone was in shock as we enjoyed the "leafed up" steamer.

My dad asked why I was buying the boat for them. I told him I wasn't so sure I ever wanted to see the outside world again; but with a ship like you will have, it should be no problem for you, mom and Stacey to visit us every so often. That night mom asked what we would do if the twins wanted to go stateside to go to college. I told her "the kids will be home schooled; when they become of age they will go where they want when they want. Char and I will back their every decision." She asked what if Char wanted to see her family. "Char's mom died when she was very young, she was an only child". "Her father was a renowned attorney that wanted Char to be an attorney. She told him she wanted to be an archeologists and he disowned her." "She worked her way through college." "What you have seen here is her family". I told my mom I would probably bring my family less the gorillas for a stateside visit. I told my mom I could understand how difficult it must be for her to understand how we preferred to live on our island.

It was a tremendous hurt to watch my family head for the ship anchored out at sea. Jodi and Cody waved and kept saying "Bye- bye grandpa and grandma' until they were out of sight. It seemed the walk home took forever. I was really in the dumps. It was going to take a while for me to feel like my normal self. It was two weeks to the day when Ron called. He said he had shown the pictures of the precious stones to Mr. Levine and they could be here in three weeks. They would helicopter in; He asked where would be the best place to land. I told him the widest stretch of beach was in front of where they beached the rubber boat. He told me he would call the day before they would be here and would I have a smoky fire on High Hat. I told him yes and asked if he still had the coordinates that I gave to him. He assured me he did. He told me my parents as well as him fell in love with their ship. They had to negotiate, but got the price that you suggested for the gold. The ship was two months away from completion.

Our chickens were doing great in their cage. There were two roosters and the little rascals were funny when they tried to crow in the morning. It sounded more like they were croaking. I told Char I could taste fried chicken every time I looked at them. The kids enjoyed feeding them. Suzy and Sadie showed up late one afternoon; they had two pups with them. When we got up the next morning two hungry pups were crying; but Sadie and Suzy were gone. I cut up bits of venison and they knew what to do with it. It was obvious they were weaned. One seemed to be a leader and one a follower. We called the leader Shiloh and the follower Pokey. Training a fox was very different than training a dog. I would keep Pokey with me and repeatedly call his name. Char did the same thing with Shiloh. It was a blast to see the twins riding around on their trikes and the foxes running after them.

We got the call from Ron that they would be here in four days in the late morning. The trail was in fair shape but I trimmed it anyway. Char asked me what I thought the stones were worth. I had spread them out to get a good idea of what we had. I even researched it on the web. Thankfully Char taught me the raw basics on her laptop. I told her at the very least ten million. I showed her one diamond that had to be ten carat. There was a matching emerald and ruby that had to be priceless. There were ten perfectly matched black pearls. I guess we'll find out when they get here. I beat the roosters gargled crowing and had the fire ready to light by the time the sun was up. There was one particular leaf that was the smoker and I began to add them to the fire. About an hour later I heard the helicopter approaching. There was no doubt Ron directed them where to land. I didn't think it necessary to be on the beach to greet them. Ron knew how to get to our place; Follow the trail; Duh!

It took them longer to get to our place than I thought it should; when they finally appeared two men in suits were puffing and panting; Ron introduced Mr. Levine, the buyer, and Mr. Goldman, the appraiser. The foxes were inquisitive and came to check our guests out; Mr. Levine asked if those were wild fox; I told him with a grin "No, those are tame fox". I didn't like Goldman right off of the bat; they hadn't even sat down yet and he said "Could we take care of business". I had to do it and I said "You got a date waiting for you?" Well, we were on even terms; it was evident he didn't care for me either. About then Tommy came meandering in out of the jungle and it took Ron and I both to calm both men down. Char had put a white table cloth on the table; I slowly dumped the boxes contents on the table and watched their expressions. I could almost see an intense hunger on their faces. They both just sat there staring at the stones. They finally began separating and made four piles. Just for the heck of it I picked the big diamond up and said "Hey Ron" and pitched it to him. Both men looked at me incredulously and Goldman said "Are you crazy?" I laughed and held my hands up and Ron pitched it back to me.

I told Ron to take over and got a big piece of grizzled pork and took it over to Tommy. Next I checked on the chickens; then I pushed the twins on the swings. The twins and I went over to the garden and pulled some weeds. I stalled around doing odd things when Ron called me over; Mr. Levine said they were ready to make an offer; I told him all right; what is your offer. I almost had to laugh; both of them were no doubt nervous. Mr. Levine said he was willing to offer three million dollars. I said "Wow, really?" I began putting the stones back in the box and stopped. Char had come out and was listening. I told them "Evidently you either think that is a generous offer or you thing I am one stupid guy". I finished putting all of the gems back in the box and closed the lid. I did all of this very slowly. Mr. Goldman told me very nervously that was just their first offer. I told them if they wanted that box I would take ten million for it. They both started talking at once. I handed the box over to Char and asked her to put it back in the house.

Mr. Levine stood up and said "just a minute!" and Char kept walking; He turned and told Char "Just a moment please lady". He looked at me and barely nodded his head yes and asked how I would like to be paid. I told him the ten million would be deposited in a Swiss account made out to my trust;" I'll furnish you the trust information." "When Ron verifies to me from Switzerland that the money has been deposited, you can come back and pick the box up." He asked for the information; I handed him a printout with everything needed. I asked if they would like to spend the night, free of charge. Ron walked away as he was about to start laughing. Levine said they would like to leave; I asked Char to put the box away and get a flashlight for Ron.

Ron told us he would call tomorrow. It was going to be dark in about three hours; it would take them at least seven hours to get back to the beach. I slapped Ron on the back and told him to be careful. As they disappeared in to the jungle Char told me thought both of them were glad to get out of here. I laughed and asked if she thought ten million was enough to get the twins through college. She laughed and said "No kidding huh". I was hungry and my darling warmed up the last of the stew. She and the boys had eaten earlier. As we enjoyed a few extra leaves and a two beaner in the steamer I asked her if she felt like a millionaire. She laughed and said now she did. I barely remember going to bed. I felt more drained from the wheeling and dealing then I did if I had spent the day swinging my machete.

Chapter Thirty-Three

Ron called a couple of days later and told us Mr. Levine was interested in buying more gems. I told Char I should go get the box of rings we looked at; She said 'The box of necklaces too." I told her I would go over tomorrow; she didn't want me going by myself; I told her Cody was too little and Jodi was afraid of bugs. I told her I would make it a one day deal and be very careful. As I sailed across the bay I thought this is the first time I had been on Gigo-Gigo by myself in a long Time. Char really did not want me to go alone; I reminded her again that Cody was too little to go and Jodi was afraid of bugs. I asked if she had any other ideas. She thought I should wait until Ron got here; I thought about it and here I was, sailing alone.

There were no tigers visible as I neared the landing. I dropped anchor and rowed Me-Too and tied up at the landing. I looked around and all was quiet until I neared the top of the steps; one very large tiger appeared; I hit that big boy four times before he snarled and disappeared into the jungle. As I walked cautiously towards the treasure room I thought I may be overly cautious. I picked up both boxes and put them in my backpack. Just as I turned to go a large boa constrictor knocked me down and immediately began to wrap around me. I couldn't get to my machete and barely got my fingers on my sheath knife; It had wrapped around me once and I thought I felt my ribs crack. I was able to get my knife out and able to stab the monster; it loosened its grip on me just enough that I was able to cut its belly and it loosened up some; I was able to get my machete and cut that big monster into pieces. I was having a difficult time breathing but I was alive. I had to take tiny breathes of air as it hurt terrible to breathe.

I thought I better get out of here as this would be the end if I passed out here. I checked and I still had both boxes in my pack. I hurt with every step I took going down the steps. I almost screamed rowing Me-Too out to Gigo-Gigo. There was a gentle breeze that moved Gigo-Gigo quickly to the other side. I was able to pull Me-Too high up on the bank; I had to stop and lean against a tree quite a few times. I didn't want Char to see me hurting but I had no choice; once I made it to our clearing, I almost cried, dang I hurt. I didn't think I could make it up our stairs and hollered for Char once; I wouldn't holler again as a pain shot through me and I almost passed out. She opened the door and I whispered "don't panic, I have broken ribs." I was able to make it inside with her help. I couldn't lie down as the pain was overcoming and I couldn't breathe. I sat in a chair and she researched broken ribs on her lap top. She told me they don't wrap broken ribs any more. I asked her to make me a four beaner. She told me it normally takes up to six weeks for broken ribs to heal.

I slept in a chair for about a week and a half; I was living on four beaners. Ron called twice and I told Char to tell him I had the goods but was too sore to do business. Char rationed out the meat and we had plenty of vegetables. I was feeling a lot better in four weeks. I took it very easy and was still careful if I sneezed or coughed. By the fifth week I was beginning to feel like myself again. Char and I went through the jewelry I brought back. She picked out a couple unique pieces. I told her don't be bashful and take what she wanted. I had to go to the bathroom; when I came back her fingers were covered with rings and she had at least a dozen necklaces on. She asked what I thought; I told her she was beautiful and looked like a million dollars. She held her hands up and looked at them and said "Is that all?" She asked what I thought the worth was. I told her no less than ten million. She asked how I was feeling. I told her carefully better. I told her" Go ahead and call Ron, I'm ready". She got a recording but Ron called a couple of hours later. They could be here in five days. I told Char I had to trim the trail.

    I swung my machete very carefully; I unconsciously found myself swinging with a little more authority in a short time. I was still sore; but not the kind of pain where I would almost pass out. I thought back how I almost insanely chopped the boa into a lot of pieces. That was a close call. I was almost to the beach when I heard the helicopter approaching. People were unloading when I cleared my way to the beach. Ron was the first one off of the chopper followed by Mr. Levine and my buddy Mr. Goldman. Greetings and handshakes and we headed up the trail. Char had spread the jewelry out on the table and had cold drinks ready when we got to camp. There was no doubt Mr. Levine was very interested as they closely examined each piece. Finally Mr. Levine leaned back and said "Scott, you evidently have an idea what the value is" and pointed to the jewelry; I told him "To save time, the selling price is fifteen million". He sat thinking about it and looked at Mr. Goldman; they sat looking at each other and Mr. Goldman nodded his head yes. Mr. Levine asked how I would like to be paid. I told him give Ron nine and a half million and put the balance in our trust account.

    I got Ron aside and told him to take eight and a half million to the boat manufacturer and pay my parents boat off; the balance is eight and a half million; Give my parents a half million and you keep a half million for all of your help. The balance goes in the Swiss account. He told me I didn't have to pay him. I told him that wasn't pay; it was thank you!" Let me know when the entire transaction has taken place." We would do like we did before; when the money deal was done Ron would release the jewelry to them. I told him to hurry back and spend some time with us. I gave him a flashlight as it would probably be getting dark by the time they made it back to the chopper. I hated to see Ron leave but I wouldn't miss the other two. I could read greed in both of their eyes. Char said "I thought you said ten million?" I laughed and told her "Ten or fifteen mil; they bit and I set the hook".

Ron called in two weeks and told us the money was a done deal; my parents were getting their things aboard their "Southwind"; they had already taken a short shakedown cruise and were within three weeks of heading for Scott Island, and he was coming with them. My rib injury was healed but tender if I bumped them. I told Char it would be about three months before they arrived. The biggest news for the next two months was; we had a major tropical storm, Cody and Jodi seemed to have doubled in size and thankfully, there were no additions to any of our animal friends and family. The storm took down most of our garden fence. We were able to salvage most of it. To live as comfortable as we did meant there seemed to always be something that needed tending to or taken care of. Char was always ready to help and our twins were willing to do their share. Char had begun to give the twins their first taste of home schooling. Jodi loved it and Cody would rather be with me doing whatever I was doing. I made a deal with him; Go to school five days a week and whenever I went hunting he could go with me. It worked.

Ron called and let us know they had departed; He put my mom and dad on and it sounded like they had found heaven. The next time Ron called he told us they had gone through a terrible storm that last three days; the Southwind came through with no damage but it was a wild ride. He told us as much time that he spent on the ocean he should have joined the navy. We didn't hear from them again until Ron called and told us to build a fire on High Hat, they were getting close. I got a good smoky fire going and several hours later the Southwind came into view; Wow" She was a beauty. Ron called and said they would stay on board until morning. I told Char and she said "let's spend the night on the beach". It didn't take long and the four Scott islanders were hurrying off to the beach. It was dark by time we hung our hammocks.

Chapter Twenty-Two

I was very proud of the twins; they were without question true islanders. They were quick learners and were generally able to take care of themselves. I had made Cody a bow and I didn't have to tell him to practice. Jodi liked being outdoors with me; But with a smile I can say she was a mamas girl. I was the first one up and had steamed crab ready when my troops got up. Cody let out a yell and was the first to see the rubber boat coming in. We beached the boat and there was a whole lot of hugging going on. Ron kind of surprised us and Lila was with him. He told us they were now a Mr. and Mrs., and this was their honeymoon. They had a load of things in the boat to unload. Mom told us it was mostly things for the twins, like clothes and books. Dad and I, with Cody's help of course, dragged the boat up and secured it to a tree. We split the load between us; I told everyone in general if they had brought one more thing we would be making two trips. We were all huffing and a puffing by the time we made it to our clearing.

There was still enough light that we got everyone's things in their cabin and the four ladies, that included Jodi, put a fine dinner on the table. I said Grace and instead of saying amen, I looked skyward and with a lot of emotion said "Thank you God". As we ate I looked around the table and thought "Please don't let wake up and this was all just a dream". It was just too good to be true; my wife and twins, my parents and Ron, our dear friend, and his newly married wife. I was awakened the next morning by a familiar sound; Buddy and family were paying a timely visit. Cody, Jodi and I went down to greet them; the kids loved their big friends and their friends no doubt loved them. By now everyone was up and the ladies were fixing breakfast for all of us.

Cody and Jodi went over and collected the eggs. Yes, we had all of the chicken eggs that we needed and then some. The kids and I had built the coop bigger as we had two dozen chickens. We did have fried chicken quite often. The ladies and Ron sat at the table and had pancakes, eggs and sausage as did we guys sitting on the ground having breakfast with the gorillas. They had pancakes dripping with syrup and jam. The twins and I went in the pond with our gorillas; Chad and Guy had a water fight; Cody had some growing to do before he stood a chance with Guy. Mom and dad stayed busy taking pictures. The gorillas had wiped out their raisins and biscuits with jam when Buddy stood up and we bumped foreheads; Guy got up, bent over and bumped heads with Cody. We all walked with them to the edge of the forest; Buddy and Guy grunted and waved goodbye. We loved those gorillas.

Chapter Thirty-Four

Dad wanted to go hunting and Ron wanted to go to the south ruins. When he said south ruins I couldn't help but mention the bad experience I had. Dad, Cody and I did a five day hunting trip. I let dad take out two deer I picked out. I had to smile as we dressed out the two deer; here I was with my dad who taught me what we were teaching Cody. We had gone to the far north herd and took a pass on the T Rexes. Dad and I both had a deer on our back; Cody wanted to carry something and I let him carry the AK. We took a pass on the birds as the chickens were all that we needed; we didn't need grapes, as thanks to Char, our place was surrounded with grapes. We were glad to be walking across our clearing. It did make for a faster easier trip not having to hunt birds and pick grapes. We took a day of rest but got ready to go exploring the next day. Mom and Char decided to stay home and grandma's girl Jodi wanted to stay and "help" grandma. Ron, Lila, Dad Cody and I spent the night on the beach; I went out in Me-Too and threw a line ashore; Dad pulled Gigo-Gigo into the shore and everyone loaded up. Dad shoved us out and the sails caught the wind and we were soon tying up at the stone dock less any tigers.

    I told everyone just walk slow and keep your eyes open. Dad had purchased another AK and it was full automatic. I told him we never shoot anything unless our lives are endangered or we are going to eat it. Other than the usual jungle sounds all was quiet. We had plenty of flashlights and lit the treasure room up good. Once we were sure it was safe I had Ron and Lila go through the boxes and pick out a wedding present. Lila finally picked out a bracelet and ring that almost matched. I took dad and Cody up on the wall to show dad how the place was once defended. We could see most of the bay from the highest point. I told dad that, that is where he ought to park the Southwind; He laughed and said he was thinking of the same thing. Just as we were nearing the steps three tigers that were lying on the steps disappeared into the jungle. Dad had reacted and I held my hand up no. Lila had seen them; she didn't scream, but her eyes were as big as saucers. Cody told us he liked Tommy better.

I sailed around the bay to give dad a better picture of the bay. He asked what I thought about going out to the Southwind with him and bringing it into the bay. I told him I thought it was a good idea. We spent the night on the beach and everyone was treated to steamed crab and fried oysters. It was a hot muggy day when we started up the trail. By the time we made it to our clearing we were drenched in perspiration and ready for a late dip in the pond; there was room for everyone without the gorillas. The gals had made a chicken stew and there were no leftovers. Dad surprised us all when he said he thought it would be a good idea to park the Southwind in the bay and live on it there until they decided what they wanted to do next. Mom was hesitant and only agreed if they moved on if she had enough.

Cody and I went with dad; we spent the night on the Southwind; it was absolutely beautiful and seemed to lack nothing. I could feel the power when dad fired the engine up. It had an automatic anchor hoist; After seeing the anchor once it was up I could well understand why it was raised automatically; Dad said it weighed a half ton. He told me to take the helm and take it out to sea. I let Cody stand on the seat and take the helm for a few minutes. I brought it around and headed back for the bay; the opening seemed to have shrunk; or maybe it was that the ship was so big. I asked dad to take the helm and he told me I was doing just fine. The water was calm enough; but as big as the ship was, I could still feel the riptide. I took it about and went a ways out to sea. I told dad to watch how to get it in the bay; I headed back for the bay I took it off center to the north; as we got close I increased the speed and went through the opening with room to spare. We dropped anchor and headed for shore in the rubber boat.

We got home in plenty of time for dinner. While we were in the steamer Ron asked if Char and I would like to visit the mainland for a few days. I looked at Char and she shrugged her shoulders. Mom and dad both thought we should take Ron up on his offer; Char had told me a lot about mainland civilization and showed me a lot of pictures. I vaguely remembered things about city life; I had a feeling it was important for Char to make the visit; Mom and dad said they would watch things while we were gone. Char said the first day we were there we would go clothes shopping; Dad told me that was a ladies thing. I told everyone my island was basically the only life I had ever known. Yes I had known some not so pleasant times. I was doing fine and since Char and I found each other my life had been wonderful." It seems everyone here thinks I ought to make a mainland visit". "Do I feel I need to go for myself?"" No! But I will go! ""You told me it is a two day travel to and from". " I will go mainland for five days". The next day Ron told us he made arrangements for a helicopter to pick us up next week. We told the twins; Cody asked in front of everyone why we had to go. What is wrong with our home here? I could have kissed him.

Ron said there was something he wanted to talk to me about; We got a glass of tea and sat at the patio table; He told me every time they were in the area of the island the compass's all went haywire and would spin uncontrollably; the island was never visible unless I signaled them in. He asked if that didn't seem strange to me. I told him I had never thought about it; there were reasons for everything. Maybe this was God's way of protecting all those that lived on the island. I told him" maybe the island is an optical illusion; or maybe this is all just a dream; or accept it for what it is". "Maybe call it the mysterious island, or lost island or just accept it for what it is." "From the looks of the ruins and the jewelry, mankind was overcome by greed even then. It looks like the island rejected mankind once." "The only thing I can tell you is, I am going to the mainland to satisfy everyone else; I love this island and all within"." I would do everything in my power to protect this island from mankind". "I will visit your mainland and be respectful; but my heart will not leave this island". Ron smiled and shook my hand.

Chapter Thirty-Five

The twins were both excited and afraid as we boarded the helicopter. Char and I were both taking ten of our, or my coins. This going to the city was all new to me; I figured as long as we were there, do everything and get everything that we wanted. Shortly after takeoff on the plane I began to feel like I suffocating; it was getting to my nerves and getting worse; Mom had given Char some pills in case this happened to any of us; I chewed two of the terrible tasting pills and almost immediately began to feel better. Ice water seemed to help although I could taste the chemicals in the water. I had to take the pills one more time during the flight. We had to change planes about three times; we held tightly to our twins. By the time we finally landed in San Diego, California I told Char I had all of the flying I ever wanted to do again. She said "Oh are we going to stay here?" Good for Cody when he said loud and clear "No Way!"

    We waited outside the terminal until Ron's limo showed up. I, Char and the twins were choking from the terrible smelling air. We boarded Ron's limo when it arrived; Char explained the AC and answered all of my and the twins questions on the way to Ron's place. Ron and Lila had a large private home of which I was thankful for. Everything was so different from home. Turn a handle and there was both hot and cold running water. Turn a handle and the toilet flushed. Flip switches and lights went on and off. The twins wanted to take a television home. We spent the first two days sightseeing and shopping. The third day was the twins delight; we spent the day at Disneyland. We got back to Ron's late that night and all of us were worn out. The fourth day we visited the museum and the zoo; my family and I felt sorry for the animals; Cody told us he would like to turn them all loose; I agreed with him. SeaWorld was about all we could do the fifth day besides get ready for our trip home.

I told Ron if it didn't take so long, I preferred going home on a ship. Char handled the entire deal a lot better than me; I tried to keep a happy face; but I didn't see one thing that would encourage me to live in this kind of a smelly loud dangerous place. I did buy an antique handle pump. I had an idea and was anxious to try it. I thought I might be able to pump water into our home. Ron suggested another hand pump and dashed me to a hardware store and I purchased one; I was going to purchase a new hand saw and extra blades but Ron told me I couldn't take it on the plane. I asked why? He explained terrorist and the danger they were. I told him I wasn't a terrorist; He told me no one was allowed to bring anything on a plane that could be used as a weapon. Ron took us and saw us depart from the airport. Char gave me two pills as we took off. I took four more on the flights home.

As I departed the helicopter and set foot on the beach my parents were there to greet us. My mom hugged me and said "well?" I told her I was tired and very glad to be home. She asked Char how it went. Charzad told her it was a good experience but she was no longer a mainlander; this was home and she was glad to be home. I felt revitalized as we entered our clearing. We were all very tired and the twins headed straight for their beds; I needed to drink some clean water and we decided we would talk in the morning. The next morning Char told me I almost broke our bed I fell in it so hard. Char fixed us all breakfast; the twins told my parents that everything there was loud and dirty, but they had fun. Char had a plaque made that got a frown from my mom and a laugh from my dad; it said; "You can take us out of the jungle, but you can't take the jungle out of us". Dad told us mom was ready for a cruise; she wanted to do a Mediterranean cruise. Ron had hooked them up with a direct line to Char's phone. It was a limited use line; but at least they could keep us informed.

I and my family did not want to see my parents go; my dad could have made it on the island but not my mom. Jodi came back from the visit wanting to be a marine biologist; Cody wanted to work for the betterment of zoo animals; I looked at Char who was smiling and said "Wow". She nodded her head yes. Cody told us the first thing he wanted to do when he was of age was get a pilot's license. He always wanted the island to be his home; but if he had a pilot's license he could come whenever he wanted for mom's fried chicken. Jodi said and yes, she could fly home with Cody and make sure we were taking care of ourselves. I sat there wondering where had the years had gone. Evolution! Ron and Lila continued to visit until Ron showed up one time without Lila. He told us she made her trip to heaven a year ago. He told us we either had to get an escalator up from the beach or he wouldn't be able to make it again.

Cody had to go to Greece and get mom and the boat. Dad wanted to be buried at sea near our island. Mom wanted to go back to San Diego; she had a younger sister she was going to stay with. Cody was capable of handling the Southwind; we agreed to sell it when he got to San Diego and put the money in the bank for mom. Several months passed and we heard a helicopter and we were sure we knew who it was as it circled us a couple of times. Char and I weren't as young as we used to be but we could still swing a machete; we didn't set any records but made it to the beach with plenty of sunlight left. We couldn't believe our eyes; Cody was the pilot! Jodi came running to us and Ron stood and waited for us.

I believe we all had tears. Ron told us he told Cody to put a parachute on him and boot him out over our place. It was slow going and well after dark when we got back to our place. Over breakfast the next morning Ron told us he had to make it back one more time. Jodi was using some of her vacation time. Cody told us he had something going if it was alright with us. He was working with an animal activist company; there were several animals near extinction; could he set up an area on the island and bring these animals long enough that they reproduced and take them back to a safe environment. He decided not to sell the Southwind. Mom was doing fine financially; He and Jodi both thought the ship would be beneficial in her marine biology work. Char and I both agreed that no carnivorous animals could be brought to the island. Cody told us that was part of his plan. He knew there was an abundance of plant eating animals that needed help.

It was tough to watch them leave but Ron still worked with the National Geographic and they agreed to bring the supplies to the island that Cody would need to set up a rehabilitation center for distressed animals. Jodi would be working with the National Geographic in the south pacific doing research on coral and deep sea turtles. The National Geographic was refurbishing the Southwind for underwater exploration and it would be ready to go when Jodi returned to the mainland. We thought it was really great how our twins had done whatever they had to do to stay close to us. Both of our kids had been married on the mainland and had families and were basically following in our footsteps; Cody's wife Kelly was a nurse; they're son Ted and daughter Shawna were finishing college. Ted had majored in animal husbandry and would be working with his dad on Scott's Island. Shawna would be working at a medical facility in Australia.

Jodi's daughters, Meghan and Michelle were intelligent beautiful young ladies already successful in marketing and investing. All of our grandchildren had spent time on the island with us. I reminded Char that it wouldn't be long and we were sure to be great grandparents; Char laughed and said "How can that be, I just arrived here". We knew we were two of the luckiest people on earth. We were proud of our twin's accomplishments. We were lucky to know and have known so many wonderful people. Our health was still good and we loved our home; Cody had helped me make sure that we had running water and a toilet that flushed. He made a trip to the mainland once a month and kept us supplied with all of our needs. Jodi swung a deal and was studying the underwater ecology surrounding our island and the nearest islands to us.

Our animal family never ceased to amaze us; somehow they continued to be a family of eight. Guy was the oldest of the family; he took after his dad and gave us a new Little Buddy who was no longer a little Buddy. Tommy left and never came back; there were several foxes that would visit for a few days and head back into the jungle. Jody anchored in the bay every so often and even brought our granddaughters to visit every few months. Ron even made a couple of trips on the Southwind; He was moving slow and used a cane, but he was still moving.

Char and I were woke up one morning to the louder than normal familiar grunting of our gorilla family; we went downstairs and were greeted with a tiny baby gorilla; It only took Char a few minutes and several raisins and she had him sitting in her lap. I hand fed his mother Becka a few hands full of raisins to let her know our new Little Guy was in good hands. Char handed Little Guy to me and came back with biscuits and jam for the entire family; she knew the way to Becka's heart. We were very surprised when the family went to the pond and left Little Guy with Char. I thought why not and went over and got in the pond with our family. When we got out and they came back to where Char was sitting to clean the raisins up I was overcome with emotions; Little Guy was snuggled up against Char sound asleep.

Char continued rocking and patting Little Guys back; Becka

came over and got a still sleeping Little Guy. Chard had a big smile when she took my hand and said there was something that she never told me; and she told me that she knew she loved me when I helped her off of the rubber boat. I had to laugh when I told her I knew when I looked at you and helped you off of that boat something was going on, like I was very lost or confused; I knew what love was and I knew at that moment, I loved you.

She snuggled a little closer and said "we aren't old, were just getting older"; she asked if I thought our meeting was destiny or good luck? I told her "good luck". She told me to hold my forefinger up; I did and she put the tip of her forefinger on mine and said; "when I count to three immediately say what is on your mind out loud. Char has beautiful eyes; we were looking into each other's eyes and she was melting me. She counted one, two, three and we both said "I love you". Then she said "Do you know what else? " There is no place on earth as perfect as our home"!

Good luck and Goodnight

About the Author

My name is Roy Paul Shields. Although I am writer, mostly I am a dreamer and a storyteller with a big imagination

I have worn many hats in my life's journey. I have done everything I set out to do in life; from gold mining to driving race cars and everything in between. In *Bad Luck Good Luck* I gave Scott the benefit of my Marine survival training and experiences in other adventures in my life.

CPSIA information can be obtained
at www.ICGtesting.com
Printed in the USA
LVOW08*0300220218
567416LV00010BA/124/P

9 781480 854826